Also by Jenna Hartley

Love in LA Series
Inevitable
Unexpected
Irresistible
Undeniable
Unpredictable
Irreplaceable

Alondra Valley Series
Feels Like Love
Love Like No Other
A Love Like That

Tempt Series
Temptation
Reputation (coming 2024)

For the most current list of Jenna's titles, please visit her website www.authorjennahartley.com.

Or scan the QR code on the following page to be taken to her author page on Amazon.com

Temptation

usa today bestselling author
jenna hartley

Copyright © 2023 by Jenna Hartley.
All rights reserved.

No part of this publication may be reproduced, distributed, or transmitted in any form or by any electronic or mechanical means, including information storage and retrieval systems, without written permission from the author, except for the use of brief quotations embodied in a book review and certain other noncommercial uses permitted by copyright law.

This is a work of fiction. Names, characters, businesses, places, events, and incidents are either the products of the author's imagination or used in a fictitious manner. Any resemblance to actual persons, living or dead, or actual events is purely coincidental

ISBN: 9798386459765

Editing: Lisa A. Hollett
Cover: Qamber Designs

For the good girls who always secretly wanted to break the rules...

jenna hartley

Content Warnings

This story contains explicit sexual content, profanity, and topics that may be sensitive to some readers.

For more detailed information, visit the QR code below.

CHAPTER ONE

Kendall

Hayley peeked her head behind the curtain, her black scrubs covered in little cartoon turkeys in honor of Thanksgiving approaching. "Can I get you anything?"

Mom barely stirred. "Thanks, but we're good."

Hayley nodded and checked my mom's vital signs while she dozed in the oversized leather chair. She looked so small, so shrunken beneath the plush blanket. Her skin was pale, but her bright lipstick matched the colorful scarf wrapped around her head.

"Why don't you grab some lunch?" Hayley said. "I can text you when she wakes up."

I kept my attention on my computer screen, intent on finishing my lesson plans for next week. "I'm okay. Thanks."

"I'll check back in a little bit. Come find me if you need anything."

I nodded, finally glancing up at her to smile. "Thank you, Hayley. I appreciate it."

She lingered a moment then said, "It's nice of you to keep her company. Having a support system has been shown to improve patients' recovery."

I'd seen that in my research, but even if I hadn't, I'd still be here. "I wouldn't want to be anywhere else."

Hayley pumped the hand sanitizer unit on the wall and rubbed her hands together. "A few of us are going out tomorrow night. We'd love for you to join us."

"Thanks, but, um—" I tucked my hair behind my ear. "I can't."

"Okay. Well, text me if you change your mind." She winked before disappearing once more.

A moment later, my phone vibrated in my pocket. I pressed the button to connect the call, careful to keep my voice low so as not to disturb my mom or the other patients. "Hello?"

"Kendall?"

"Yes?"

"This is Staci from the Hartwell Agency. Do you have a minute?"

"Yes. Of course." I switched my phone to my other ear and slung my purse over my shoulder. The strap was fraying, the leather worn from overuse. When my mom opened her eyes slowly and focused on me, I mouthed, "Be right back," and stepped out of the room.

"Give me just a second," I said to Staci as I wound through the hallways until I was stepping through the sliding doors to the parking lot, leaving stale air and the scent of antiseptic behind for a beautiful, sunny Southern California day.

For the first time in hours, I felt as if I could breathe fully again. The treatment center wasn't as bad as a hospital, but it wasn't much better either.

"Hey. Okay." I inhaled deeply, calming myself. "I can talk now."

"I'm calling because we may have a placement for you."

"Oh." I straightened, perking up at the prospect. "That's great news."

I'd signed up with the Hartwell Agency a month ago, and I'd been waiting for a placement ever since. They were a bespoke recruitment service that placed nannies, jet crew, and other household staff with wealthy clients around the world. My best friend, Emerson, was a nanny for the agency, and she'd suggested I apply.

"Now, I know you were hoping for translator or tutoring positions. But as I mentioned previously, they're pretty rare."

My heart sank. I'd really been hoping for something that would allow me to use my degrees and practice my French or Spanish. I got to do that for my online tutoring gig, but I was hoping for more of a challenge. Even so, I wasn't terribly surprised. The Hartwell Agency had told me as much when I'd interviewed.

"That said," Staci continued, "I found something else I think would be a good fit."

"I'd love to hear about it," I said, trying to infuse my voice with enthusiasm I didn't feel. Between grad school loans and my mom's medical bills, I didn't have the luxury of being picky. My online tutoring gig helped pay the bills, but only just barely. What little savings we'd had had long since been depleted. I was barely making ends meet, let alone making a dent in our debt.

"One of our clients is looking for a house sitter."

"House sitter?" I frowned.

I wasn't entirely sure what that involved or how well it would or wouldn't pay, but I'd specified no live-in positions. That was a big reason why it had taken so long to find me a placement. Most of the Hartwell Agency's clients wanted someone full time for their yacht crew or a live-in nanny. And I couldn't commit to something like that. Not when Mom was still undergoing treatment and needed me.

Even if I were available, I wasn't interested in being a nanny. Emerson loved it. She adored kids. She wanted to be a mom someday. But me...well, I was just trying to survive. And if being a parent was anything like shouldering the responsibility of taking care of my mom since her diagnosis, I wasn't sure I wanted to sign up for something like that.

Especially not if it meant being a single mom like mine. I saw what my dad leaving had cost her. I didn't have many memories of him, but I remembered the effect of his absence —both on my mom and me. At least it had taught me a valuable life lesson—the only person I could rely on was myself.

"Between you and me," Staci said, lowering her voice. "It's one of the sweetest gigs we have. Placements like this are usually snatched up immediately."

Yet she was presenting it to me. The fact that this one was available at all seemed like a pretty big red flag.

"You rarely interact with the client," she continued, oblivious to my internal debate. "You get paid to live in a beautiful home, and the duties are typically pretty light."

I frowned as more warning bells blared in my head. "What's the catch?"

"No catch," she said in a light tone. "The main rule is that parties aren't permitted under any circumstances. And some clients can be very particular about how the house is kept, but that's understandable, considering the cost of the homes and furnishings."

I nodded, thinking that wasn't unreasonable.

"It sounds promising," I finally admitted. "But—" I glanced back at the treatment center, my thoughts on my mom.

"Look," Staci said in a firm but professional tone. "I know you're not interested in live-in positions, but since there's no childcare involved, you'd have a lot of flexibility. Plus, it's in Holmby Hills. And it doesn't start for another month or so."

My jaw dropped, my mind still stuck on the location.

Wow. Holmby Hills was *the* neighborhood of celebrities

and legends. Walt Disney had once had a home there, as had Frank Sinatra. It was... I couldn't even imagine who I might run into. Let alone how incredible the house would be. And I'd get to live there? It was definitely a step up from an air mattress in the corner of my mom's living room.

"What would be expected of me?" I asked, mostly out of a perverse sense of curiosity. I couldn't actually take the position, could I?

But my mind was already calculating ways to make this work. How far it would be to Mom's condo, where I'd been living the past six months. The logistics of getting her to and from her appointments.

The more I thought about it, the more I realized Holmby Hills wasn't out of the realm of possibility. And Staci *had* said it was flexible.

"I can email you the details for this client's specifications. The house is currently undergoing renovations, so you'd help supervise those."

"But I don't have construction experience."

"You don't need to. The designer will handle all that, but you'd let in the contractors who need to work. Plus, you'd help manage the cleaning crew and grounds team, coordinate pool maintenance and deliveries. But generally, you'd have the place to yourself."

Pool maintenance? That meant there was a pool. I'd always dreamed of living in a house with a pool.

That was a big selling point. Not to mention the fact that it would bring in some more cash. And the rest of the requirements didn't sound so bad.

"Can I think about it?"

"I need an answer by the end of the day, or I'll have to call the next person on my list."

I nodded. "Okay. Thank you. I'll call you back as soon as I can."

We ended the call, and I gazed up at the sky. I closed my eyes and allowed the warmth of the sun to permeate my skin. I imagined what it would be like to lounge by the pool at a celebrity's mansion in Holmby Hills. I pictured how nice it would be to pretend that was my life, even if only for a moment.

A life filled with staff who took care of everything. Where I wasn't constantly on the go. Where I wasn't exhausted with worry. Where...

My phone vibrated in my pocket. I frowned and opened my eyes, the fantasy fading instantly. A calendar reminder popped up on the screen, telling me to schedule a refill for one of my mom's prescriptions. I sighed and headed back inside, my shoulders hunching the moment the sterile air hit my face.

When I returned to Mom's side, she opened her eyes and peered at me briefly before shutting them again. "Everything okay?"

I nodded, crossing my legs. "It was the Hartwell Agency."

She opened her eyes again, hope replacing fatigue. "They found you a placement?"

"Sort of."

She furrowed her brow. "What does that mean?"

I lifted a shoulder. "It's not a translator position."

"Is it local?"

I bit my lip, fighting the buzz of excitement. "Yes, but—"

"Kendall, take it!" She was enthusiastic. Well, as enthusiastic as she could be when her body was in this state. And that made my heart lift.

"You haven't even heard what it is," I said.

"I don't need to. It's a job, and you were smiling when you walked back in."

I frowned. "How did you know that? Your eyes were closed."

"I'm your mother. I sensed it."

I rolled my eyes. "You're so full of it."

"Tell me more about this position."

My phone vibrated, an alert for a new email appearing on the screen. I opened my inbox and read the message from Staci. "Here." I handed the phone to my mom.

"Holy—" She shook her head, her attention focused on the screen. "You'd get paid that much to live in some celeb's mansion for a few months?"

I nodded. "I know."

It might be a few months. It could be even longer, depending on how long the renovations took.

"What are you waiting for?" she asked, and the machine that dispersed her medicine beeped. "Tell her yes."

"I can't." I slouched in the chair, all thoughts of sleeping in luxury and lounging by the pool vanishing in an instant.

"Why not?" She skimmed the email again before handing back my phone. "It's flexible. You could still do your online tutoring. And you'd have a real bed. In a real room."

"Yeah, but…"

She frowned, placing her hand over mine. "Kendall, sweetheart, we've talked about this."

I glared at her. "Mom."

"What?" She lifted her hand, the one with the IV attached. "You heard Dr. Johansen. I'm showing progress."

And for that, I was incredibly grateful. It had been a long six months, filled with constant concern for my mom. Diagnosis. Surgeries. Treatments. Watching her lose her hair. Seeing her health fade.

"Yes, but you never know how the treatment will affect you. What if you need help?" I asked, thinking of how unpredictable the side effects could be.

Sometimes, she'd start off fine. But then a few days after treatment, the nausea and exhaustion would set in. There had been times when she could barely move, let alone function without substantial help. And while she was getting stronger, her health was still fragile.

And then there was the money...

She raised a brow. "You're not the only person who can help me."

"Hey!" I chided.

"I appreciate you and everything you do. You know that. But it doesn't all have to fall on your shoulders. I'm not your responsibility."

It wasn't the first time she'd told me that, but as an only child, I felt responsible. Not out of a sense of duty, but out of desire. She was my mom, and she'd done everything for me, especially after Dad had left. This was the least I could do for her.

I loved her, and I wanted her to be okay. She *had* to be okay.

"Sweetheart—" She patted my hand. "We've talked about this."

I stared at the floor, counting the tiles as her heartbeat played a steady cadence on the monitor.

"Kendall," she said in a gentle tone. "You can't keep putting your life on hold for me."

"I'm not—"

"Yes." She nodded. "You are. Turning down Hayley's invite."

I opened my mouth to protest, but then I realized she'd been awake the entire time. She'd heard everything. I narrowed my eyes at her, but she wasn't deterred.

"It's not just that, Kendall. As soon as you found out about my diagnosis, you turned down your dream job. Canceled your move to New York."

And I would do it all again. I might have given up the

chance at my dream job, and I knew it wouldn't be offered again. But I could never give up on my mom.

"You never go swimming anymore. You never go out with friends."

"I do yoga. And I hang out with Emerson," I protested.

She continued on, despite the mention of my best friend. "And what about Jude?"

"Jude?" I jerked my head back at the mention of my ex. "What about him?"

"Does he even know you stayed?"

I waved a hand through the air. At this point, our relationship had been over for almost as long as we'd dated. "It doesn't matter."

We'd been together for six months before I'd told him I was moving to New York to take a job as a translator at the United Nations. He hadn't wanted to leave LA. I wasn't willing to give up my dreams for a man. And neither of us was interested in a long-distance relationship.

"I bet if he knew you were still in LA, he'd want another chance."

The problem was, I wasn't sure I did. Jude was a nice guy, but the longer we'd been apart, the more I'd realized I didn't love him. Wasn't sure I ever had.

Cancer had a funny way of showing you what was important. And my relationship with Jude had always seemed so... surface level. Maybe it was because he was almost two years younger than me. Maybe age had nothing to do with it.

"It wasn't just about the distance," I said. "He was always such a flirt."

It was something I'd hated. Something he'd tried to play off as no big deal, but to me, it was.

Mom lifted a shoulder. "Some men are just like that. Especially men like Jude—young, handsome, rich."

That was the problem. I wasn't sure he'd ever grow out of

it. And neither his looks nor the balance in his bank account somehow magically made it okay. At least, not to me.

Time apart had shown me how right I'd been to end things.

"That's not the type of relationship I want."

"What do you want?" she asked.

"Someone who's completely devoted to me. Who only sees—only wants—me. And makes sure everyone else knows it." I didn't even realize that was what I wanted until I'd said the words aloud. "Someone who makes me their priority."

She clicked her tongue. "Mm. That's a hard thing to find, especially in a town like Hollywood."

I leaned back in the chair and crossed my arms over my chest. "Well, it's not like I'm looking for it anyway."

"You sure?" Her hazel eyes scanned my face. Her body was waging a war, but she was as sharp as ever. "Because it sounds like you've given it a lot of thought."

"I'm sure," I said, wanting to put an end to the matter. "Now, can we please talk about something else?"

Mom grinned. "Like the placement?"

I groaned and stared at the ceiling. She was tenacious. Always had been.

"You're not going to let this go, are you?"

"Nope. Not until you accept the job."

"Are you sure?" I asked. "Is this what you really want?"

"It's not just what I want. It's what I need—what both of us need."

"What?" I jerked my head back. "Are you trying to tell me you're sick of me?" I teased.

"I could never be sick of you. But if this experience has taught me anything, it's that you should seize opportunities. I don't want us to miss out on any more of life than we already have."

"I'm not missing out," I said, hating the defensive tone to

my voice. When she tilted her head, eyes narrowed, I added, "I'm *not*. Spending time with you is more important than anything."

"I know." She smiled, placing her hand over mine. "And I'm grateful for all the time we've had together. But, honey, you need to start living again."

"I am."

"No." She shook her head slowly. "And that binder—" She eyed my trusty blue binder warily. It was where I kept all her schedules, prescription details, doctor contact information. "Says otherwise."

"Hey! That binder keeps us organized."

"It does. And taking care of me has been a full-time job. Now it's time to take care of you."

I wasn't even sure I knew how to do that anymore.

"Call Hartwell," she said. "Tell them you'll take the position."

"Are you sure you're okay with it?" I asked once more, needing confirmation.

"More than okay. I want this for you. For us. And don't worry, I plan to visit."

"Oh." I straightened, an idea occurring to me. "Maybe you could live with me."

She shook her head, patting my hand. "A little space will be good for both of us."

"Are you trying to get rid of me so you can spend more time with Joe?"

"Joe?" She laughed, but I didn't miss the way her cheeks blushed at the mention of him. "From my support group?"

"I see the way you two look at each other."

"That's the way Jude used to look at you," she said, clearly trying to sidestep the issue. "You should give him a call."

I shook my head. I wasn't interested in calling Jude, and my mom needed to realize it was over. "That ship has sailed."

"Fine. But will you at least go out with friends? Consider going on a date? Hell, have a fling."

"Mom!" I shot a furtive glance around the space, grateful the other patients seemed absorbed in their tasks.

"What? When I was your age…"

"Okay. Okay." I held up a hand, not wanting to hear about her exploits. My mom had traveled the world modeling. She'd partied with royalty and rock stars alike. She'd posed almost nude for covers. She'd skydived and snorkeled and done so many incredible things.

But that was what *she'd* wanted. That wasn't what I wanted.

"How I had such a serious child is beyond me," she teased. "You've always been so sensible, and I was wild."

"I know, Mom. But I'm not you."

"Maybe not, but there's got to be some of that wild child in there. Just waiting to come out." She smirked.

"I'm twenty-seven. If it hasn't come out yet, I don't think it's going to."

"You never know," she said with a knowing grin. "It might just be waiting for the right person."

"Mm-hmm." I crossed my arms. "Sure."

"I'm serious. Sometimes it takes the right person to bring us out of our shell. To help us release our inhibitions. Someone like Maxwell…"

"Stop." I squeezed my eyes shut. "Please just stop."

I really did *not* want to hear the story of her fling with the British duke again.

She laughed, and I was glad to see her smile, even if it was at my own expense. But then she winced, and my heart sank.

"Are you okay?" I asked.

She took a few deep breaths, clutching my hand. Finally, she said, "I will be. But I need you to promise me something."

She loosened her grip, and I leaned closer. "Anything."

"Seize opportunities. Have fun. Live!"

"And if I do that, will you promise to take care of yourself? And you'll call me if you need *anything*."

"I promise. Now promise me that you'll let loose."

I rolled my eyes but smiled as I muttered, "I'll do my best."

CHAPTER TWO

Knox

I poured myself another glass of whiskey then braced my hands on the suite's wet bar as I took a deep breath and replayed the evening. The loss. The disappointment.

And then I counted to ten and straightened. No use dwelling on it. I couldn't change the outcome; I could only learn from it.

There was a knock at the door, and I frowned at my reflection in the mirror behind the glass shelves. My tie hung loose around my neck, my hair askew from tugging on it. The culmination of a year of hard work, gone in a moment.

"I know you're in there, Knox," Jasper called from the other side of the door.

I rolled my eyes. I should've known.

I strode over to the door, the patterned rug soft beneath my feet. I peered through the peephole to verify it was, in fact, my cousin and then swung open the door.

"Oh good," Jasper said, brushing past me, bottle of Louis XIII Cognac in hand. "You already started."

"Started what?" I asked.

"Drinking." He flashed me a mischievous grin. "I like a good pregame."

"Pregame?" I shook my head. "This is the postgame." Both literally and figuratively.

"We're going out," he said as the door opened again. My younger brother, Nate, entered, followed by our other cousin Graham. Though, the four of us had always been more like brothers than cousins.

I was the eldest, then Graham, Nate, and finally Jasper, who was six years younger than me. Sloan, my only female cousin, was the baby. She was four years younger than her brother Jasper. But she lived in London, while the rest of us were in LA.

I dragged a hand down my face, my beard smooth beneath my palm. "Seriously? How many times have I told you guys that you can't just barge in like this?"

I would've reported them to security, but seeing as Graham ran the damn place, I knew nothing would change. I got the feeling Graham secretly relished annoying me, if only because he wanted the suite back. And even if Graham had been willing to do something, Jasper would charm any number of hotel employees to give him access—and not just to my room.

"Oh please." Jasper rolled his eyes, grabbing four glasses from the bar and setting them on the dining table. "You love it."

I growled. It wasn't that I didn't love my family, but I liked my personal space. Especially coming off the loss we'd just suffered. It had been brutal.

"I'd *love* some peace and quiet." I gnashed my teeth. "Why I ever decided that moving in to the presidential suite was a good idea is beyond me."

"You're welcome to leave anytime," Graham said.

As the CEO of Huxley Hotels, he was more focused on

the bottom line. I might be a paying customer, but I got the room at a significant discount.

"I'm giving you guaranteed occupancy and revenue."

"This room is almost always occupied," Graham said. "If anything, you're costing me money. And not just because of the discounted rate. But because some of our favorite clients only want this suite."

"Yeah, but at the holidays?" I asked.

"Especially at the holidays," he said.

I didn't get it. I'd much rather be at home, surrounded by family, for the holidays. I could remember Christmases as a kid and how wild and wonderful it had been to spend them with my brother and cousins. One big, loud, happy family.

That's what I'd always envisioned having myself. A loving wife. Lots of children. Laughter and presents and chaos. But life had turned out differently; I was divorced and only had one son.

"You could stay at one of the extended-stay properties like Hux House Suites," Nate teased, referring to the more budget-friendly line of hotels our family owned. They were nice, but they couldn't compare to a hotel like the LA Huxley Grand.

The Huxley Grands were the jewels in the Huxley Hotel crown. The high-end properties competed with other luxury hotels such as the Four Seasons, the Ritz, and the Waldorf Astoria.

"Only if I thought you fuckers would actually give me the peace and quiet I crave."

"Doubtful." Jasper winked.

I slumped into a chair. "I thought I'd be in the house by the holidays."

I couldn't wait to move. Not because of the lack of privacy from my family—they were right; I did love it. Them. I'd always loved being part of a big family.

But my dream of having a big family of my own was dead, and I needed to feel settled. I needed a home, though I wasn't sure my new house would fill that void. It might be smaller than my previous one, but I suspected it would feel just as lonely.

"How much longer do you think your house is going to take?" Nate asked. Graham seemed just as interested in my answer.

"Weeks? Months?" I shrugged. "Fuck. At this point, your guess is as good as mine."

"Don't forget," Graham said, "you have to be out of the suite for the weekend of—"

"I know. I know," I sighed. He'd only told me about a thousand times.

"Do you want to talk about the game?" Nate asked.

I downed the rest of my drink then placed the empty glass in the sink. "No."

"What do you think?" Jasper looked to the others. "In or out?"

"Fuck no," I said in a firm tone. "We're not going out."

"Agreed," Graham said. "In." His tone was firm when he cast his vote. But he almost always voted "in."

"Out," Jasper said, ever the extrovert to Graham's introvert. "Definitely out."

I sighed and stood, starting to pace. My team had lost the game in the final seconds, and the only place I wanted to be was *in* bed. Asleep. Preferably after another glass of whiskey and a long, hot shower.

Nate tapped a finger to his lips. "You know..." He circled me, evaluating. These guys were getting on my last fucking nerve. I'd already told them I wasn't going out, yet they persisted with this game. "I'm going to go with 'out.'"

Jasper fist-pumped the air. "We have a majority."

Graham glowered at the floor, and I let out a heavy sigh,

dragging my hand through my hair for the thousandth time that night. It wasn't that I minded going out, but I wasn't in the mood.

"It's tied," I said.

Jasper waved a hand through the air. "You know the rules."

If one of us was having a bad night, the others chose whether we'd go out or stay in. But whoever was struggling didn't get to cast a vote. In this case—me. Thus preventing a tie.

I pinched the bridge of my nose. We'd been playing this game since we'd been old enough to sneak into clubs. A lot had changed in the years since, but we'd always been close, especially after our parents' plane crash.

That was the night that everything had changed. That...

"Come on," Jasper said, patting me on the shoulder. "Put on some jeans and a shirt, and then we'll go."

"But I already took off my shoes."

"Good. One step taken care of," Nate said, using the same tone he would with his eleven-year-old daughter, Brooklyn.

"I'm really not in the mood. Can't we just..." I surveyed the room, searching for another idea. Something that might mollify them without forcing me to leave the comfort of my suite. "Play poker and drink here?"

"Sounds good to me," Graham said, pulling out a chair and taking a seat.

"No," Nate said, tugging me toward the bedroom.

"What about the bottle you brought?" I asked Jasper in a last-ditch attempt to persuade them to stay in.

Jasper shrugged. "It'll keep. Unless..." He smirked at Nate, mischievousness painted across his features. "You'd rather have a party here." He pulled his phone out of his pocket as if searching through his contacts for *all* the people he wanted to invite.

"No. Absolutely not." Graham practically leaped out of his chair. "Get dressed, Knox."

"Guys." I massaged my temples. "Seriously?"

Nate and Jasper huddled together, not even trying to keep their voices down. "We could invite Samantha and Trish."

"Absolutely. Oh and—"

Graham's scowl deepened the longer they schemed.

"Is that what you would prefer?" Jasper asked, glancing up from his phone. "We can send out a text blast right now." He looked at the screen again. "Got it ready to go. Just need to push—" his finger hovered over the phone, taunting us "—send."

"Don't you dare," Graham said, snatching the device out of Jasper's hand.

While Jasper struggled to get it back, Graham said to me, "You know these fuckers won't relent. It's better to just get on with it so we can all go to bed at a semi-reasonable hour."

Nate chuckled. "Who said anything about reasonable? Brooklyn's spending the night at her friend Sophia's."

"This better not be a repeat of the last time we went out together," I said, giving Jasper and Nate a pointed look.

"What?" Nate lifted a shoulder. "It's not my fault the paparazzi swarmed us."

"Can you blame them?" Jasper asked. "You left the club with Cece Golden." Rising Hollywood star. Young. Blond.

"Talk about a mistake." He scoffed. "Had I known..." He groaned. "It doesn't matter."

She'd tried to get close to Nate so he'd give her a part in his latest film. And when he'd tried to tell her it wasn't the right fit, well, she'd gone nuclear. The paparazzi had had a field day, and part of me suspected it had been staged by Cece.

Either way, it was a fucking disaster. Flashbulbs everywhere. People shouting his name as we'd left the club. I didn't know how he dealt with it.

"Stop stalling and get changed," Jasper said.

"Fine," I huffed. "Fine."

After I'd washed my face and changed, I headed back out to the dining room. Jasper spotted me first and gave me a wolf whistle.

"Not bad for an old man." He smirked.

"I'm not old."

"You're forty-seven," he deadpanned.

"Exactly. Forty-seven isn't old," I said, giving his shoulder a playful shove.

At forty-one, Jasper was the baby of the group, at least if you didn't include Sloan. But we didn't see her as much since she'd moved to London to manage the international Huxley locations. As Graham's driver ferried us across town, I wondered if I shouldn't join Sloan in London. Maybe then I'd get some rest.

When we arrived at the club, we were immediately escorted to a VIP section. It was quieter but still afforded us a good view of the dance floor, which was packed. Bodies writhing and shaking. Music thumping.

"Mm." Jasper hummed, surveying a group of women who passed by. "This club is hot."

"Who are you going for tonight?" Nate asked. "The blonde?"

Nate and Jasper sounded like my son and his friends, despite the fact that they were over ten years older. I worried that this would be my son's future too. I worried that my divorcing his mom had soured his view of long-term relationships, even if my ex and I remained good friends.

"She's gorgeous," Jasper said. "But did you see the redhead? She's got some killer curves."

After they'd decided on their approach, Jasper and Nate

stood and headed for their respective targets. I shook my head and turned my attention to Graham. He stuck out like a sore thumb in his three-piece suit. And unlike everyone else, he was sitting in the corner, quietly sipping his whiskey as he took it all in.

"How's the new resort in Ixtapa coming along?" I asked. Graham was reserved, but he'd always talk about the Huxley empire. It was his passion.

When our grandfather had first announced his decision to have Graham take his place as CEO, it had stung. Since I was the eldest of his grandchildren, everyone had assumed he'd pass the mantle to me. It hadn't taken me long to realize he'd had chosen the right person to lead the Huxley Hotels brand.

If Pops had selected me, I would've taken on the responsibility. But it would've been done out of duty. Not passion.

I didn't have the inborn knack for it that Graham did. I could've run it—sure. And I could've made it a success, but I would've been unhappy.

I'd realized that after working in the family business for a few years. It had been good training, but then I'd left to pursue my own entrepreneurial interests. The more time that passed, the more I'd realized how right Pops had been. How perceptive he'd been—and not just about me and my career path. But about all of us.

Nate had become an actor and executive producer, leaving my cousins to run the family business. Sloan, Jasper, and Graham excelled at honoring the legacy and traditions of the Huxley Hotel past while firmly rooting it in the modern era.

"The numbers are looking good," Graham said.

"But...?" I asked, sensing he was holding something back. Something was concerning him.

He rubbed a hand over his jaw. "You know that blogger I told you about?"

"Golden Goose Travel?" I joked, mostly because I couldn't remember the real name of the site.

He snorted. "Gilded Lily Travel."

"Yeah." I pointed at him, the alcohol making my body hum pleasantly. "That's who I was talking about." Though the actual name wasn't much better.

"I obtained a preview of her post—"

I arched an eyebrow. "Obtained?"

He wore a dark expression. "Don't ask."

I held up a hand. "Okay. I won't. But what did the review say? Judging from your expression, it wasn't glowing."

"Fuck no." He leaned against the leather banquette, draping his arm over the back. "It never is. It's like she has a personal vendetta against me or something."

"I'm sure it's nothing personal," I said. Graham rarely got worked up. He was passionate about the brand, but still... "She's one blogger. One of many."

"You don't get it." He took a big swig of his drink. "She's not just *one* blogger, she's *the* blogger. Her site is synonymous with luxury travel. Everyone looks to Lily for recommendations, and she can make or break a business."

"Surely that's a bit—"

"No." He leaned forward, resting his elbows on his thighs. "It's not."

"Okay, so..." I took another swig, putting my back to Jasper and Nate. They each had their arms draped around two women. "You said the review hasn't been posted yet, right?"

"Right."

"Which means there's still time to change her mind."

He frowned, little lines forming between his brows. "She posts anonymously. No one knows who she is."

"Yet you 'obtained,'" I said, using air quotes, "a preview of an unpublished post."

"Yes, but…"

"Surely with all the money and resources at your disposal, you can discover this woman's identity."

"I don't know," he hedged. "It feels like I'd be breaking some unspoken code."

I couldn't help it; I laughed. "I think it's a little too late for that, don't you?"

"Is it too late to leave?" he asked, eyeing Jasper and Nate and their new friends warily as they approached.

"Probably," I said. "You know what's going to happen next, right?"

He glowered. We both knew what was coming. I counted down from three on my fingers. And just as I curled the final digit into my palm, one of the girls said, "Oh my god. This is my song. I'm dying to dance."

Graham went back to sulking, burying his head in his phone.

"Knox," Nate said, clapping a hand on my shoulder. "You heard the lady."

When I didn't move to get up, he tightened his grip on my shoulder. He leaned down and spoke low into my ear. "Come on. She's practically begging you to fuck her."

I rolled my eyes. I was too old for this shit. And I didn't get why my brother and cousin felt it necessary to try to be my wingmen.

I wasn't interested in a night of meaningless sex. And even if I had been, I sure as hell didn't need a wingman.

I thought back on the last few women I'd dated… We hadn't clicked. They'd struggled to understand the demands on my time. They'd wanted more than I could give.

"Come on," Jasper said. "It's just a dance."

With a heavy sigh, I stood, not wanting to be rude.

Graham remained where he was, unwilling to budge. I downed the rest of my drink and set my glass on the table before allowing one of the women to lead me to the dance floor. She was gorgeous, but I wasn't interested.

There was only one woman I wanted, but I couldn't have her. And even if I could, she'd never be interested in me.

CHAPTER THREE

Kendall

"Holy shit. This place is insane!" Emerson said as I guided her through the front door.

She'd been skiing with her family for the holidays, so I hadn't seen her since before Christmas. But now that she was back in town, she'd come over after our weekly yoga class to hang out and watch our new favorite show. And—after a quick stop at the guard shack to introduce her to Vincent—I'd been giving her a tour of my temporary new home.

"Right?" I laughed, the alarm chiming twice as I closed the door. I was still getting used to living in such a luxurious mansion myself.

The house was massive. A grand entrance with a fountain and gated drive. And when you stepped through the front door, a curved staircase drew the eye up to a chandelier that glittered overhead. But it wasn't just the chandelier that sparkled, the entire house was a gem.

A gem that would be coveted by many. Which was why they'd hired me. Part of the appeal of house sitters was that they acted as a deterrent for would-be burglars. If the house was occupied, someone was less likely to break in.

"Come on." I looped my arm through hers. "I'll show you around."

She paused. Frowned. "Where's all the furniture? Or is this like a modern design thing?"

I laughed. "No. The owner is still moving in. That's part of why I'm here—to sign for deliveries from his designer."

"Who's the designer?" Emerson asked.

"Lauren Clarke."

"Ooh. I love her and her work."

"You know her?" I asked.

"She decorated my dads' cabin in Aspen."

"Oh cool," I said, continuing the tour. "How was Aspen?"

"Gorgeous," she said with a dreamy sigh. "I wish you could've gone."

"Me too," I said, thinking of holidays I'd spent with Emmy and her family in Aspen in the past. "But we had a good time."

"How's your mom doing?"

"Pretty good," I said. "All things considered."

"Good." Emmy peeked inside one of the boxes and arched her brow.

Every day, more items arrived for the home. So far, most of the deliveries had been fitness equipment for the home gym or signed sports memorabilia. I couldn't wait to see it all put together.

"And you still have no idea who owns it?" Emerson asked.

"Nope," I said, letting the "p" pop.

From what Staci had told me, the owner had only recently purchased the house. Not that I knew who the true owner was. According to the client dossier from the Hartwell Agency, the home was owned by a limited liability corporation.

It could've been Lady Gaga for all I knew. Except I didn't

peg Gaga as a huge sports fan. That was one of the few clues I had about the owner.

That, and the fact that he liked designer clothes. Though, that wasn't surprising. Someone who owned a home of this size would have the best in everything.

"Wait till you see the closet," I said.

She ran a hand through her hair. "This is the sweetest gig ever. Maybe I should switch from nannying to house-sitting if all the placements are like this."

I laughed. "I lucked out."

Though the house was definitely more appealing during the day. At night, it seemed huge and cavernous. As if anything could be lurking in the shadows, despite the top-of-the-line security system.

The alarm was so fancy, it had several different chimes based on the situation. When someone was admitted at the guard shack, there was a sequence of three beeps. But if a door was opened or closed, a double chime would sound.

"No joke," Emerson said. "You hit the jackpot."

"Apparently, house-sitting placements are fairly rare. But you could join a yacht crew if you're sick of nannying."

Her expression softened. "I can't imagine doing anything else, even when it's hard. I love working with the families, but not when there's so much tension. It's been awful. Dan and Judy waited until the holidays were over, but then they finally told the kids they're getting divorced."

I winced. "That's hard. How are the kids taking it?"

She lifted a shoulder. "Not well, but I try to be there for them."

"I'm sure you are. I'm sure you're helping them a lot just by being a constant presence."

She frowned, and I could tell the situation was wearing on her. "I love those kids, but everything's about to change. Pretty sure I'll be looking for a new placement soon."

I gave her hand a squeeze. I knew how invested Emmy got in the families, especially the kids. It made it even harder to say goodbye when the placements inevitably ended.

"Enough about that," she said, shifting. "Let's talk about something more fun. Go on any hot dates lately?"

I barked out a laugh. "You're joking, right?" When she shook her head, I asked, "When would I even meet someone?"

"Surely you've come across some hot doctors lately." She bumped my hip with hers.

"Hot and douchey."

She pursed her lips. "That's disappointing."

"Meh." I lifted a shoulder. I wasn't sure I had the time or energy to date at the moment. This job was certainly going to help with some of the stress from the bills, but it was a Band-Aid, not a long-term solution. Mom and I had barely celebrated Christmas this year—mostly sticking to smaller gifts that were handmade. Too bad I couldn't give her the one thing we both really wanted—a clean bill of health.

"Speaking of dating…" Emmy leaned into me. "Supposedly, Jude's got a new girlfriend."

"Good for him."

"Doesn't bother you?" she asked, studying me.

"What? That he moved on?" I frowned. "No. Why would it?"

"Well, because…" She huffed. "I don't know. I always like to be the first to move on."

I would've laughed, but I knew she wasn't joking.

"I did move on. He thinks I'm in New York, remember?"

"You know what I mean." She rolled her eyes. "You aren't upset?"

"It's not like you're trying to tell me that you're dating him, right?" I asked, knowing she'd never be interested in Jude. Still…she was acting weird. Cagey or something.

"No." She shook her head quickly. "Definitely not. He's too short. And too young for me."

"Em—" I rolled my eyes. "He's practically your age."

I didn't even bother arguing with her on the height thing. Jude was six feet tall, which made him four inches taller than her. But that wasn't enough of a height difference in Emmy's opinion.

"Exactly," she deadpanned. "No, I prefer someone older. Someone like—"

"His uncle?" I teased.

"Mm-hmm." She got this dreamy look in her eyes. "That man is fine. Though, your dating Jude certainly had its perks. Free tickets to the Leatherbacks games." She ticked off a finger. "Staying at luxury hotels on vacation." She ticked off another. "Hanging out on the yacht…"

"Yes. Those were all incredible," I said. "But none of them was reason enough to stay with him."

"Not to mention how competitive he can be." She dragged a hand through her long blond hair. It was always so shiny. "God, was that annoying. Tell me the truth." She leaned in. "Did he have a small dick?"

I nearly choked on my own spit. "Emerson!"

"What? It's a valid question."

I shook my head. "No." It wasn't. "I'm not going there."

"I mean, it's not like you're dating him anymore. I won't tell anyone. He did, didn't he?"

I ignored her request, leading her through the primary bathroom. She stopped and stared at the enormous freestanding tub, and I had to hold her back when she tried to climb in.

"Holy shit. This bathroom…" She was peering up at the chandelier as she said it.

"I know, right? And it's one of thirteen. Though it's the most spectacular."

"Thirteen?" she choked out. When I nodded, she said, "Damn. How many bedrooms?"

"Seven."

"Oh, only seven. Psh."

We laughed and headed for the closet. When we stepped through the doors, the lights immediately switched on. Emmy's eyes widened.

"Okay, forget Jude and his perks. I want to marry whoever owns this house."

I laughed, though I knew how she felt. After living here for only a few weeks, I was already in love. I was scared to meet the man who owned it for fear of falling for him as well.

"This is... Wow. This closet is bigger than my last apartment," she said.

"I know." And it had more custom built-ins than the Container Store. It even had a freaking couch.

Emmy plucked a hanger from the rack and held up one of the shirts. I'd wondered what the man who owned them looked like. Judging from the cut of his shirts and pants, he had a good body.

I told myself he was probably a jerk. Or married. Or a serial cheater.

"Stop that!" I chided, trying to take the shirt from her. But she was fast. Too fast.

"Why? It's not like he's going to know." She perused the rest of them. "It's not like you were trying it on or wearing it out."

Judging from the mischievous look on her face, she was imagining doing just that. "No," I said in a stern tone. "Put the shirt down and step away."

"But it's Prada," she whined, admiring her reflection in the mirror. "And the sleeves look like they'd actually be long enough."

"I don't care," I said in a stern tone. "I need this job."

She pouted when I held out my hand expectantly for the shirt. "But you already have another job. Besides, who's going to ever know?"

"Emmy," I whispered. "This house has a security that could rival the Louvre. And the Hartwell Agency warned me that owners can be crazy particular. As in, some of them are so anal, they get pissed if you disturb the vacuum lines from the cleaning crew."

She shook her head but returned the shirt. "Always such a rule-follower. Don't you ever get tired of doing the right thing?"

"Maybe I would if I had a choice."

"Mm." She crossed her arms over her chest and leaned her hip against one of the built-in dressers.

"What?" I asked, sensing she had something more to say. Something that was bigger than trying on designer shirts or breaking the rules.

"That's almost the same thing you told me when you gave up your dream job to stay home with your mom."

"Seriously?" We'd talked about this. "She has cancer. Who else was going to take care of her? Huh?"

"But she's getting better now, right?"

I nodded. Mom was doing better, but she was still undergoing treatment. There were still risks—generally and that she might backslide in her recovery.

"Don't you think it's time you finally stopped living in limbo?"

I jerked my head back. "What?"

"House-sitting? Tutoring?" she asked.

"What's wrong with my jobs?"

"Nothing. Except for the fact that they're not your dream."

"And nannying is yours?" I asked, even knowing the answer.

Before Emmy had started nannying, she had been a two-time Olympic gold medalist. But ever since she'd torn her plantar fascia and had to miss the qualifiers, she'd been floundering. At first, she'd been intent on returning to training as soon as she was healed enough.

But that had been nearly a year ago. And while she'd rehabbed her body, her mind wasn't in the right place to compete. Not at the level she was used to. She claimed she needed to live life, enjoy having some freedom after training so hard for so many years. But I sensed there was more to it than that.

"I love working with kids. And nannying allows me to be picky about my future job."

"Are you being picky, or are you procrastinating?" I asked, knowing that she kept putting off any decisions about competing. But by not choosing, she was effectively deciding.

"Pot meet kettle," she said, hand on her hip.

"It's not the same, and you know it."

"At least I still have dreams," she shot back. I couldn't believe she was pushing me on this.

"Yeah, well, that's what happens when someone you love has cancer." I turned my back to her and angrily swiped away a tear.

She crossed the room and hugged me. "I'm sorry, okay? I wasn't trying to be insensitive. I just don't want to see you give up on your goals."

I nodded. "I know. But my brain is so full of all the stuff for my mom and my tutoring classes and now this house. I can't make space for much more, let alone my dreams." And even if I could, it was too painful.

I'd landed my dream job. I wouldn't get it again. It didn't matter now.

"Can we please just go watch TV?" I all but begged. The last thing I wanted to do was argue with my best friend.

She was quiet a moment then finally, mercifully, nodded. "Sure."

We spent the next few hours marathoning our show. Usually, it was a good escape from reality, but my mind kept going back to our earlier conversation. Was I really living in limbo? Had I given up?

We didn't speak of it again. And after Emmy left, I set the house alarm and tidied up. Then I logged on to my computer and put in a few hours of tutoring. By the time I'd finished with my students, I still wasn't ready for bed, but it was getting late.

I didn't know how long I stared at the ceiling, watching the way the light of the moon reflected off the waves of the pool, dancing on the space above me. It was mesmerizing.

When I heard a noise, I jumped. But everything seemed fine. I was probably just keyed up from staying up late. Besides, I got a boost of energy from teaching my classes, and it often took me a while to wind down.

But, deep down, it was more than that.

I was worried about my mom.

I pulled the covers closer, missing her and the sense of home she provided. Worried about the future—a potential future without her.

I swiped away my tears. I couldn't think that way. I had to stay positive.

After all, I'd been worried about moving out. And so far, my concern seemed unnecessary. She was doing well, all things considered.

Despite all the thoughts swirling in my head, I must have drifted off at some point. But when I awoke, it was with a start. I squeezed my eyes shut and strained for any sound, wondering if I'd imagined the chime of the house alarm.

I blinked a few times and pushed my hair away from my face. But then I heard it, the double chime signaling that a door had been opened or—more likely—closed.

I grabbed my phone and checked the security app, my heart racing all the while. The security app confirmed my fears—someone was in the house. My mind spun with possibilities.

They hadn't triggered the alarm, but that didn't mean they'd been given the code. A sophisticated alarm system like this would attract experienced burglars. Ones who might know how to disable it.

With shaky hands, I pressed the button to alert the alarm company. They would inform the police. *Oh god, Vincent.*

I wondered how the intruder had made it past the security guard. What if they'd hurt him? I wasn't safe.

I crept toward the stairs before backtracking to the media room, where a new shipment of sports memorabilia had arrived. I grabbed the first thing I saw—a hockey stick autographed by the goalie for the Hollywood Hawks—and tiptoed down the stairs as quietly as I could.

I'd intended to slip out the front door. Maybe hide in the garden or the pool house until the police came. But when a light turned on, I froze, momentarily unsure what to do next.

Perhaps acting on instinct, I lifted the hockey stick and spun to face the intruder, only to stop short. "Knox?"

I hesitated, stick poised in midair, my brain still processing.

Knox Crawford.

Owner of the Leatherbacks, LA's pro soccer team.

A billionaire.

And my ex's dad.

Standing in the foyer staring at me.

He set down his bag. "Kendall?"

"I..." I furrowed my brow. "Yeah. Um." I shook my head as if to clear it. "I can't believe you're here."

He muttered something that sounded a lot like the same in reverse.

And then I remembered why I was here, and that I was supposed to be doing a job. "I hate to ask this, but does the owner know you're here?"

He chuckled, dragging a hand through his dark brown hair. Silver flecks lined his temples and beard, and creases formed at the corners of his blue eyes when he smiled. "I *am* the owner."

"Oh." I lowered the hockey stick and cringed. "Sorry."

He tilted his head to the side. "What are you doing here? And why are you wearing..." He cleared his throat. *"That."* His eyes lingered on my skin, burning a trail so hot it had me wishing I could strip away what little remained.

But then I peered down at myself and cringed. I was wearing a silky tank top with black-lace trim and matching boy shorts. *If only the earth would open up and swallow me whole.*

My ex's dad was my new boss. And he'd just seen me in my underwear. While brandishing an autographed hockey stick that was probably worth more than the contents of my suitcase.

Before I could die of embarrassment, the doorbell rang.

Through the glass panes, I could see the red and blue lights of a police car. An officer pounded on the door, and I shot a desperate glance at Knox. "I'm so sorry. The Hartwell Agency said..."

He leaned his head back, understanding dawning on his face. "Ah. So, you're the house sitter."

I nodded. "Yes. I thought you were an intruder. I thought..."

"Hey." He placed his hand on my shoulder, his tone

soothing even though his touch was electrifying. "It's not a big deal. Are you okay?"

I hesitated a moment, distracted by the way he stroked his thumb back and forth over my skin. But when the officer pounded on the door again, I jumped.

Knox frowned, gently taking the hockey stick from me and leaning it against the wall. "Give me just a sec, and then we'll get you settled."

Get me *settled?* I wanted to laugh. This was *his* house. I was here to do a job—for him.

Knox spent a few minutes talking with Vincent and the police. He was as calm and charismatic as I'd remembered. He explained the situation, and then they talked soccer. I grabbed a blanket to cover myself. And when the officers left, I could hear the smiles in their voices.

"You okay?" Knox asked, returning to me.

I nodded, though I felt like a Coke bottle that had been shaken up.

"Come on," he said, steering me toward the kitchen. "You look like you could use a drink."

I clutched the blanket to my chest, feeling exposed. Adrenaline was still flooding my system, and my heart was racing.

The intruder had turned out to be the homeowner, and someone I knew. But as the prospect of danger faded, my quick pulse didn't. And I realized that perhaps it had more to do with being near Knox than anything else.

CHAPTER FOUR

Knox

I couldn't believe it.

Kendall was seated on one of the barstools—one of *my* barstools—her legs crossed. She had a blanket wrapped around her, but it had slipped from one of her shoulders, tantalizing me with that small bit of bare skin. Her hair was mussed and her face devoid of makeup. She was stunning.

She always had been.

My mind went back, as it often did, to the first time I saw Kendall. She'd walked across the deck of my yacht like she owned it. Like she belonged there.

She'd been wearing a neon-green bikini that left little to the imagination. A thin string connecting two small triangles that scarcely covered her tanned skin. The strings wrapped around her waist, forming an X, as if to mark the spot. The bottoms had barely covered her ass. And what an ass it was.

But it wasn't solely her physical appearance that captivated me. She was knowledgeable and passionate about soccer. And that had been just as much of a turn-on.

At the time, she hadn't been dating Jude. And if I could travel back in time, I would've done things differently. I wouldn't have hesitated to make her mine. But despite all my money, I couldn't buy a time machine. I couldn't change the past.

I also couldn't stop staring at her. Part of me was afraid she'd vanish if I looked away.

She'd always had a quiet confidence. A...strength and resilience that I both respected and admired. Probably because it reminded me a lot of myself.

It was what had first drawn me to her. Her eyes had been focused on the horizon while everyone else partied around her. She didn't seek anyone's attention, though she certainly attracted it. She undoubtedly commanded mine—not just that night, but ever since.

"I feel awful about scaring you," I said, still trying to wrap my head around the fact that she was here. That it was really her.

Kendall waved a hand through the air. "I'm just glad it was you."

I tried not to read too much into that. Just because I'd always felt a connection to her didn't mean she felt the same. She'd dated my son, for chrissakes.

"Are you sure you're okay?" I asked, loosening my tie and dropping it on the counter before undoing the top two buttons of my shirt.

She watched me, rapt. For a moment, I allowed myself to imagine that she was attracted to me. That she wanted me. But then I realized she was probably still stunned from the entire ordeal.

While I was impressed with how she'd handled the situation, I felt terrible for ever putting her in that position. For doing anything to make her feel unsafe, especially around me.

If anything, I'd always gone out of my way to make sure she was comfortable. Even when Jude should've been the one to notice that she was cold or not enjoying an activity.

Kendall nodded. "Yeah. I'm okay. Thanks."

Even though she spoke in a calm tone, her shoulders remained tight. I ached to massage them, to soothe away her concern. I wanted nothing more than to wrap my arms around her, even as impossible as that seemed. To make her feel safe once more.

Who knew if she'd even want that. I sure as hell *shouldn't* want that.

Yet I'd always felt a connection to her. And now she was here. In my kitchen. Something that had also seemed impossible even an hour ago.

Impossible…just like everything was when it came to Kendall. And so, I forced myself—like always—to shove my attraction down. To push it away.

"I didn't realize you bought a new house," she said.

I straightened, trying to ignore the way my body reacted to her. Her coconut scent perfumed the air. And my blanket was touching her bare skin. And…

I am a dirty old man.

"Knox?"

"It was time to downsize," I said, clearly delirious from a long day of travel.

She choked on a laugh. "Right. *Downsize.*"

"What?" I asked, resting my hip against the counter.

"Not sure a seven-bedroom, thirteen-bathroom home qualifies as 'downsizing.'" She used air quotes.

"I would, considering it has 10,000 fewer square feet than my last one."

She laughed, the sound rippling through my house. Breathing life into the space. Into me. "I guess that's true."

"Though I'm not sure I can call it home yet. I haven't spent much time here."

"Well, the renovations did seem to stretch on," she said. "It's nice to have them complete."

"Yes." I nodded. "Thank you for being here to keep an eye on everything."

"My pleasure," she said. "I really enjoyed getting to know the contractors. Especially this one guy—Santos. He was so funny. And they were all very skilled."

I laughed.

"What?" she asked.

"Only you…" I rubbed a hand over my mouth. Of course, Kendall would enjoy socializing with the contractors. Especially if it allowed her to converse in other languages.

Perhaps sensing the need for a change of subject, Kendall said, "Did you have a nice Christmas?"

Was she fishing for info about Jude?

"It was nice, if a bit hectic. I think I was still trying to recover from the end of the season."

"I'll bet." She shook her head. "The finals—I mean, that was intense. Especially when Esposito evaded four of the other team's players and scored." She continued gushing about the plays made and the effort of the Leatherbacks, regardless of the fact that we'd lost. But then she suddenly stopped talking and closed her mouth. "Um. Sorry."

"Why are you sorry?" I frowned, disappointed. I'd always loved how passionate she was about soccer.

Kendall was well versed in the plays. Not only did she appreciate the game, she could see it strategically in a way most couldn't. Like a pool shark plotting out their winning shots. And her memory for facts and figures was remarkable.

"I just…you probably don't want to talk about work when you're at home. With an employee." Was that a reminder for herself or for me? Perhaps both?

"Kendall," I said as she stood and pushed in her barstool.

"You, of all people, know how obsessed I am with soccer. Besides, I don't consider you an employee."

"But that's what I am." She smiled and placed her empty glass in the sink. "And I should probably, um—" She hooked her thumb toward the stairs. "Let you get to bed. Or do whatever you were going to do."

"I'd rather talk with you," I said. "I've always enjoyed talking with you."

She smiled, but then the blanket slipped, revealing more of her torso. I tried to keep my eyes on her face. Tried and failed. She rushed to grab it and cover herself. "Sorry. I, um, wasn't expecting anyone."

I chuckled. "I've seen you in far less."

And I'd imagined her in absolutely nothing.

Her cheeks pinkened, and she dipped her head. *Shit.* She might be my son's ex-girlfriend and the star of my fantasies, but she was now my employee. And I was making her uncomfortable.

I pressed my palms to the marble countertop, the cool, hard surface setting a clear boundary. Drawing a line that I should not—could not—cross.

Boss. Employee.

Older man. Younger Woman.

My son's ex.

The fact that she'd dated my son was the biggest line I shouldn't cross. Much as I might want her. Had *always* wanted her.

And yet here we were. Completely alone. Sipping whiskey in my kitchen. Her in her sexy fucking pj's.

I should've said goodnight. I should've let her go. But instead, I found myself trying to make her stay.

"Did you see the game live?" I asked.

She shook her head. "Tickets were crazy expensive. But Emmy and I watched it on TV."

I made a mental note to get her tickets to the next Leatherbacks home game. And any other game she wanted to attend. Hell, I'd fly Kendall there personally on my private jet if it meant she'd smile again like she had earlier.

"Really?"

"Yeah. Why?" She frowned.

"I didn't realize Emerson was a big soccer fan."

She laughed. "She's not. Not really. But she can appreciate the athleticism that goes into it. And she's a fan of parties and watching hot men run around the field." Kendall held up her hand. "Her words, not mine."

"Now that sounds more like the Emerson I remember. Most of the women my son hangs out with are more interested in the players than the game."

She scoffed. "Right. Of course."

"I'm sorry." I held up my hands, wondering if it had been a mistake to mention Jude. But I'd been curious how she'd respond. "I didn't mean to offend you."

"I'm not offended. I'm also not surprised," she said. She didn't seem bitter, but I couldn't get a read on her thoughts where Jude was concerned.

"Trust me. I don't include you in that group," I said. "You were always…different."

She arched one eyebrow but didn't push me on it. "Since you're here, does that mean you plan to move in sooner? If so, I'll need to let the Hartwell Agency know so they can start looking for another placement for me."

"No," I said quickly, too quickly. "No need for that. I assume it will still be a while before the house is completely finished."

The only reason I wasn't staying at the presidential suite tonight was because it had been reserved—for the actual president. Of the United States. Graham had offered me another room at the Huxley Grand, but I hadn't wanted to deal with all the extra security precautions. Especially not after just flying back from the SuperDraft.

"Oh. Okay."

Was she disappointed? Surprised? I wasn't sure what she was thinking.

And I found myself saying, "It would be nice to have you here. Living in my house." I shouldn't like the sound of that so much.

"Right. Of course. Well, that's why I'm here." She straightened. Brightened. "You have a beautiful home."

"Not sure it's much of a 'home' at the moment," I said, glancing around at all the blank walls and stacks of boxes.

I wasn't sure anywhere felt like home anymore.

"It will be," she said with confidence. And somehow, I believed her.

"Speaking of…why are you here? What are you doing in *my* house?"

"In all fairness, I didn't know it was *your* house. I had no idea you'd moved. Besides, everything was addressed to an LLC."

I nodded. "That was my lawyer's idea. Asset protection."

She was quiet a moment, and I waited for her to answer my question. But she didn't.

"So…?" I prodded.

"The Hartwell Agency placed me," she said.

I narrowed my eyes at her. We both knew she was dodging the question. I wanted to know why.

The last thing I remembered Jude telling me was that Kendall was moving across the country. As my mind raced through possible scenarios for why she hadn't, my expression softened as concern took precedence.

"Are you okay? I know you and Jude aren't together anymore, but I always liked you, Kendall."

"Thank you." She dipped her head. "And, yes. I'm okay."

"I—Jude—thought you were moving."

"I was." She lifted her shoulder, her expression both wistful and somehow pained.

My memories of Kendall couldn't compete with reality. They dulled in comparison to how beautiful and vibrant she was in person. Her light brown hair flowing down her back and over her shoulders. Those soulful hazel eyes that both saw too much and said too little.

"Does he know you stayed?"

"No." She shook her head, clutching the blanket to her. "And I'd appreciate it if you didn't tell him. Just…for now," she tacked on, though the words were said with some reluctance.

I considered it a moment, not sure what to make of her request. I didn't think things had ended badly between the two of them. But the fact that she hadn't told Jude she'd stayed, well, I didn't know how to interpret that.

I wondered how Jude would react to the news. He was dating someone new—Christine or Chrishell or something. He hadn't introduced us yet, so I didn't get the impression it was that serious. But it had been with Kendall; Kendall had been important to him.

"I shouldn't—" she started. Stopped. Then swallowed hard. "I'm sorry. I shouldn't have asked you for that. Besides, I'm sure he'll come over at some point."

I shook my head. "He knows I have a house sitter, so he doesn't have any reason to stop by." Even so, I didn't like lying to my son, especially without good reason. "Can I ask why it's so important to you? Not telling him."

"I just—" She blew out a breath, her lips forming a perfect "o." "My life is complicated at the moment."

I briefly wondered if the move to New York had been a ruse or an excuse. I didn't realize I'd said as much until she barked out a laugh and said, "I wish."

"What, then?" I asked, concern churning my gut.

I told myself I was being protective because she was younger than me. Because she'd once been attached to Jude. And as a father—as his father—I felt somehow responsible for her. But I knew my feelings toward Kendall had nothing to do with Jude.

When she said nothing, I added, "Come on. If I'm going to keep your secret, at least give me something." I was teasing, sort of.

Selfishly, I wanted to know what was going on. I *needed* to know she was okay.

"My mom has cancer," she blurted.

I stilled but quickly recovered. "I'm sorry, Kendall."

If I remembered correctly, Kendall was an only child. Her father wasn't in the picture, hadn't been for a long time. I hated to think of the stress she had been under since learning of her mom's diagnosis.

"I can't even fathom how difficult that's been for both of you," I said, knowing she'd always been close to her mom. "How are you doing?"

She lifted her chin toward the ceiling, her eyes watery. "You know—" She let out a shaky breath. "You're the first person who's asked me that. Everyone else tries to encourage me to live my own life. But how can I when she's the only family I have?"

I placed my hand over hers, wanting to comfort her. Wishing I could do more. "Tell me how I can help."

She shook her head, a sad smile crossing her lips. "You just did."

"I'm serious, Kendall."

"This job helps. And the fact that you offered means..." She let out a shaky breath. "Well, more than you could ever know."

"Of course," I said, though I was determined to do more.

We fell silent for a minute, and I was honored that she'd trusted me with her secret. That she'd let me in. Part of me wondered why she'd chosen to confide in me about this when she hadn't even told Jude.

"Can I ask you something?" She finally broke the silence.

"Anything," I said, and I meant it. Kendall had no idea how captivated I was by her, and I needed to keep it that way.

"What are *you* doing here?" she asked. "I mean, I know it's your house, but it's also the middle of the night."

I chuckled, rubbing a hand over my face. "That's a long story."

She cocked her head to the side. "I've got time."

I considered it a moment then poured us both another drink. "I just returned from the SuperDraft."

"Holy..." Her eyes widened. "I didn't even realize." She shook her head. "That's right. How'd it go?"

"Pretty well. We had a good time, and I got a few players I really wanted."

"That's awesome."

"It was." I nodded, taking a sip of my whiskey. "I mean, apart from a few tedious meetings about newly proposed rules for the league."

The new rules ranged from nonfraternization to an expansion of the player buyout policy. But most people wouldn't care about them. I doubted even someone as invested in the team as Kendall would, despite her interest in the sport.

"I always wondered...why soccer?" she asked. "Apart from the fact that you played in college. Because you could've bought any pro team, yet you purchased a failing component of a relatively unpopular franchise. I mean, compared to buying a football team like the Hollywood Heatwaves."

"Because I saw an opportunity to build something. And I like a challenge."

She smiled. "Why does that not surprise me?"

"It was more than that, though. The passion people have for soccer is like no other. And the fans... I spent a year in London, working at the Huxley Grand." I lifted a shoulder. "When I went to the games, I fell in love."

She smiled wistfully. "I get that. One of the few memories I have of my dad is him taking me to a soccer match. It was...exhilarating."

"Exactly."

"Did you ever get to see Beckham play while you were in England?" she asked.

"Yeah." I chuckled. "Why? Did you have a crush on him?"

"Doesn't everyone?" Before I could respond, she added, "He's one of the greatest players of all time."

"He is. He's achieved a level most can only dream of."

"Did you ever want to go pro?" she asked.

"That's the dream, isn't it?" I asked. "But I was never talented enough to play at the professional level. Owning a team is something I can do, regardless of my age or physical ability. Because my body certainly can't perform at the same level it used to."

"Maybe not on the field, but I'm sure it's more than capable," she said, and I wondered if I'd imagined the way she'd looked at me. With lust and heat and a question in her eyes.

I was probably wishing for something that wasn't there. It was late, and she was my employee. Not to mention, over twenty years younger than me. And my son's ex. I couldn't think of someone more off-limits.

CHAPTER FIVE

Kendall

"So did you meet the homeowner yet?" Emmy asked. We'd just finished yoga and were headed to our favorite juice bar.

"Yep," I said as we rounded the corner.

"And..."

"I thought he was a burglar."

Her eyes went wide. "You're kidding."

I shook my head. "Nope. Called the police and everything."

"Holy shit. Did you get fired?"

I laughed. "No. It gets even crazier."

"Crazier how?" she asked, gracefully dodging a French bulldog as we walked down the sidewalk.

"You're never going to believe who owns the house," I said. I was still trying to wrap my head around it myself, and I'd had a week to get used to the idea of Knox being the owner.

"Let me guess." She tapped a finger to her lips. "Taylor Swift?"

"No, but that would be amazing."

"Right? Ugh." Her shoulders slumped. "I guess I should've known that wasn't the answer, considering all the men's clothes in the closet."

"Mm-hmm." I pressed my lips together to keep myself from blurting the truth.

"Ryan Reynolds."

I laughed. "Wrong again. Ryan has a wife and kids."

"Oh yeah. So...the owner is single?"

I considered it a moment. "I think so."

"Hot?"

Yes. But I couldn't admit that, so instead, I said, "He's my boss, remember?"

"The two don't have to be mutually exclusive."

"Trust me. In this case, they do."

She arched an eyebrow. "So, who is he? Someone famous? I'm dying here."

I was tempted to draw it out even more just to mess with her, but I couldn't wait to see Emmy's expression when I told her. "Knox Crawford."

"Knox Crawford?" She said his name slowly, emphasizing every single syllable as her eyes widened. "Owner of the LA Leatherbacks. One of the heirs to the Huxley Hotel fortune. Philanthropist. A man who somehow manages to get hotter every year."

"And let's not forget—" I held up a finger to stop her because she'd left out the most important part, at least where it concerned me "—Jude's dad."

I'd said it mostly to remind myself. Because the more time I spent with Knox, the more difficult it was to remember the fact that he was off-limits.

"Hello, Zaddy." She licked her lips.

I rolled my eyes, though I didn't disagree. "Don't you think he's a little old for you?"

Knox was in his late forties, and the man had aged like a

fine wine. No. Wine wasn't right. Knox was more like fine whiskey. Smooth and complex. Dignified and rich. Intoxicating. Delicious.

"No. And don't call him old." She acted as if she was personally outraged on his behalf. I would've laughed if she weren't so serious. "He's distinguished. Experienced." She gave me a meaningful look. "Total DILF. I'd do him."

I inhaled deeply and let it out slowly. Her comment about him being a dad she'd like to fuck made me angry, irrationally so, considering he was my boss and my ex's dad.

"You wouldn't?" she asked, tilting her head as she appraised me.

"No," I answered firmly and quickly. Perhaps too quickly, judging from the amused look on her face.

"Interesting." She quirked a brow.

"What's interesting?" I asked, trying to seem completely *disinterested*, despite the fact that my heart was charging ahead like a soccer player racing across the field, intent on making the winning goal.

"Are you harboring a secret crush on your boss?"

"What?" I jerked my head back. "No. That would be completely inappropriate."

"Yet totally understandable, considering who he is."

I crossed my arms over my chest. "I do *not* have a crush on Knox." At least, that's what I kept telling myself. Maybe if I repeated it often enough, I'd believe it was true.

Emmy held the door to the juice bar open for me. "Didn't you ever look at Knox and imagine that was what Jude would look like in twenty years?"

"I honestly didn't look that far ahead," I admitted as we joined the line.

"Because you always expect the relationship to fail." She elbowed me.

"I don't expect it to fail. I-I..." I searched for the best way to describe it as I pretended to concentrate on the chalkboard menu hanging over the cash register. "I set reasonable expectations."

"Mm-hmm." She crossed her arms over her chest, and I could feel her disapproving stare on my face. We placed our orders then found a seat outside.

"What?" I threw up my hands.

"You never let anyone close. You never let them in."

"I let you in," I said.

"Men," she said, exasperation bleeding into her tone. "You never let *men* get that close to you. Just because your dad left doesn't mean every man will."

"Easy for you to say," I muttered. Emerson's dads adored her. Doted on her and her twin. They'd always been wanted. Loved. Emmy had never had to struggle like my mom and I had.

"Just…" She sighed. "Never mind."

She changed the topic, and while part of me was grateful, another part hated the idea that she might be disappointed in me. Or worse, right.

I'D CHANGED INTO MY SWIMSUIT AND HEADED DOWNSTAIRS. I found a note on the counter in Knox's scrawl, the keys to his Range Rover resting on top.

K,

CAN YOU PLEASE PICK UP THESE THINGS FROM THE STORE AFTER YOUR SWIM?

> **Almond milk**
> **That chocolate you like**
> **My protein powder**
> **Pineapple**
>
> **Take the Range Rover. The tank is full.**
>
> **Thanks,**
> **Knox**

I smiled to myself, reading his note again. I loved these little notes he left for me. I loved that he wanted me to get my favorite chocolate. That he'd made sure the gas tank was full. I was taking care of him, but it felt as if he was taking care of me.

I wandered outside and slipped into the pool, swimming laps until my heart was pounding and the ache between my legs had faded.

I closed my eyes and rested my arms on the side of the pool. Though the day was still cool, the heater kept the water warm. I was trying to take advantage of the pool, swimming laps daily because I knew this wouldn't last much longer.

Over the past few weeks, Knox had been spending more and more time at the house. He'd been setting up his office, interviewing personal chefs. I got the impression he was trying to drag it out as long as possible. Part of me wondered if he was just being kind. If he felt bad for me since I'd confessed the truth about my mom and her cancer, and he was trying to keep me employed.

Not that he'd ever said anything to that effect.

In fact, the more time he spent at the house, the better I

got to know him. The more I liked him. And that was dangerous.

He still hadn't moved in, at least not fully. He stayed at the Huxley Grand every night, but he stopped by almost daily to work or use the pool. His designer, Lauren, was putting the finishing touches on the house.

I knew the placement would have to end soon. And while I told myself I was staying for the money, it was more than that.

I climbed out of the pool and dried off, wrapping the towel around myself before heading inside. When I passed through the kitchen, Knox was standing at the fridge. He was shirtless, the muscles of his back flexing as he lifted a bottle of Ultim8 Hydr8 water—one of the team's sponsors—to his mouth. My own mouth went dry at the sight, and I couldn't stop staring.

He turned, his gaze finding mine. I looked away quickly and hurried forward, desperate to pretend I hadn't been ogling my boss. But I was going too fast. The tile was too slick. And the next thing I knew, my feet slid out from under me.

I windmilled my arms, trying to regain my balance. But all it did was loosen my towel. And I finally landed on the floor with an "oomph."

Knox rushed around the island. My cheeks were on fire, and I scrambled to grab my towel and escape.

"Are you okay?" he asked, crouching down beside me.

My pride was wounded, and I was pretty sure I was going to have a massive bruise on my ass. "I'm...yeah."

"You sure?" he asked, his eyes scanning me, lingering on my lips, my breasts, my legs.

The temperature seemed to rise by a thousand degrees. Maybe it was all in my imagination, but I got the impression he liked what he saw. Or maybe I'd hit my head in the fall without realizing it.

Knox offered me his hand, sending a jolt of electricity through me. He helped me stand, his palm lingering on my forearm even as he remained on the floor.

He stared up at me, his gaze full of longing that resonated deep within me. His jaw tightened, his nostrils flaring. And I wondered if he could smell my growing arousal. I wondered if he was struggling to fight this too.

When I wobbled, he placed his hands on my hips as if to steady me. I swallowed hard, loving the sight of his large fingers splayed over my tanned skin.

At least until the alarm chimed three times, breaking the spell.

I drew in a sharp breath, and Knox shook his head as if to clear it. He stood and handed me the towel. "Can I get you some ice? Or maybe I should call the team doctor?"

"No. No." I shook my head. "I'm fine. *Really.*" His concern was touching, but if I didn't get out of here soon, I was going to combust.

Between the way he was looking at me, the lack of clothing between us, and the thoughts that had been playing in my head way too often lately, I needed…out.

Out of this room. Maybe even out of this house and this job. I figured this placement would be ending soon anyway. Considering my body's reaction to Knox, I wasn't sure that was such a bad thing.

"Thanks for your help," I said, holding the towel in front of me as if to enforce the barrier between us. "I should see who's here. Are you expecting someone?"

Knox shook his head. "It's probably another delivery or Lauren stopping by to check on the progress."

I nodded, still trying to regain my composure after… whatever the hell had just happened. "Okay. I'll handle it."

TEMPTATION

The front door opened, and the house alarm chimed twice.

"Thanks," Knox said, heading for his office and tossing a shirt over his shoulder. "Come get me if you need anything."

As I watched him go, my mind conjured up all sorts of ideas about what "anything" might entail. But I told myself I was being ridiculous. Even if Knox was interested in me, there were a million reasons why we couldn't be together.

"Hello?" I called, wrapping the towel tighter around myself as I headed toward the front door. "Lauren? Is that you?"

I'd gotten to know Knox's designer over the past few months, and I really liked her. She was brazen and unapologetic yet professional and savvy. I enjoyed hanging out with her, and every time she asked for Knox's opinion, he asked for mine. I didn't know why he cared so much what I thought—it was his house. But it was empowering and flattering all the same.

I stopped short when I spotted Jude standing in the entryway in his tracksuit and designer sunglasses. I wondered if it was too late to hide.

Jude smiled at me then did a double take. "Kendall?"

I didn't know why I'd avoided him for so long. I'd assumed our paths would cross at some point. It was inevitable since I was working for his dad and living in the guest room. But we'd gone this long. Maybe part of me naïvely hoped the placement would end before I'd have to face him.

"Hey." I gave him a little wave. "Hey, Jude."

He stepped closer, his eyes scanning me from head to toe. Dust motes swirled in the air, and I felt as if I'd stepped back in time. He was just as I'd remembered, yet different somehow.

The longer we stood there, the more I realized I didn't

feel anything toward Jude—not even an inkling of desire. Certainly not anything like what I felt anytime Knox was near.

Shit.

"What are you doing here?" Jude finally asked.

"I, uh—" The words caught in my throat, my mind spinning as I realized that maybe I'd been attracted to his dad all along.

What the hell is wrong with me?

"Kendall?" Knox called.

His footsteps preceded him, but when he entered the foyer, he stopped short. He was now wearing a shirt, but I was positive we both looked guilty as fuck. Knox glanced between Jude and me, and I tried to get a read on his expression.

"Oh. Hey, Jude," Knox said, his casual tone completely at odds with my unease.

Jude furrowed his brow. "Dad?"

Knox went over to his son and shook his hand before pulling him into a hug. "I didn't realize you were coming by today."

"I wanted to see the new house since you said it's getting close. But..." He focused on me again. "I don't understand. Why's Kendall here?"

Knox turned his attention to me, his blue eyes searching. Seeking. Asking if I was okay. When I nodded, he said, "Kendall works for me."

Jude gave my bare shoulders a pointed look. "Doing what?"

"She's been house-sitting," Knox said.

"Oh." Jude nodded. Then he said, "Ohh. Are you with the Hard—" He cleared his throat. "Hartwell Agency?"

I nodded, still feeling caught between two worlds. Between two men. Past and present. Son and father.

Jude furrowed his brow. "But I thought you moved to New York."

"I...was going to," I said, dipping my head. "But my circumstances changed."

"Why don't you come in?" Knox said to Jude, and I was grateful for the interruption. "I'll give you a tour."

"So, you..." Jude frowned, massaging his temple, his feet rooted to the spot. "Wait just a second." He lifted his hand, completely ignoring Knox. "You never left LA?"

I shook my head. "Just before I was going to move, my mom was diagnosed with breast cancer."

Jude's expression morphed into something more sympathetic. "I'm sorry, Ken." He stepped closer, taking my hands in his. "Is she okay?"

I lifted a shoulder. "We're taking it one day at a time. She's had a double mastectomy, reconstructive surgery, and chemo."

"Shit." He swiped a hand down his face. "Why didn't you call me? I would've been there for you."

Would he?

Jude was a nice guy, but I didn't see him as a caregiver. Deep down, I'd always known that. But Emmy's words came floating back to me, and I wondered if I'd been wrong. I wondered if I hadn't even given Jude the chance to be there for me for fear of being disappointed.

Because if I didn't let someone in, it didn't hurt as much when they inevitably let me down.

"Everything happened so fast," I said, clutching the towel to me. "My entire world was turned upside down, and we'd broken up. I figured I was the last person you'd want to hear from. And honestly, my focus was on my mom."

He nodded. "That's understandable. And I wasn't trying to make this about me." He blew out a breath. "I wish I'd known, that's all. All this time…" He rubbed a hand over his chin.

I lifted a shoulder, the bridge of my nose stinging as I fought off unwanted tears. Talking about my mom and her diagnosis made me emotional. She was the one person I could always count on. The one person who had always been there for me, apart from Emmy.

"Come on," Knox said, taking my shoulder and steering me toward the stairs. I shivered from his touch, but he said, "Why don't you go change, Kendall, while I give Jude a tour. You can join us when you're ready."

I nodded, grateful for the out.

"Can I get you anything to drink, Jude?" Knox asked his son.

"I'm fine. Thanks." But there was an edge to his tone that hadn't been there before.

Was it because Knox had touched me? Had my expression betrayed how much I liked it?

I jogged up the stairs, mindful not to slip once more. I changed quickly and twisted my hair into a bun. I debated hiding in my room for the rest of the day, but I knew I had to face Jude sooner or later.

I forced myself to return to the kitchen, knowing I couldn't put it off any longer. Knox pulled out a chair for me, and I took a seat at the counter. Jude sat beside me, angling his body toward mine.

"I still can't believe you're here." He smiled and lifted his hand as if to touch me but then stopped himself.

"Neither can I," I said, shifting my gaze to Knox, then quickly back again.

"How long have you been working for my dad?" He turned to Knox before I could answer. "Why didn't you ever mention this to me?"

"I—" I cleared my throat, hoping to get ahead of the situation. "I asked him not to."

"What?" Jude looked stricken. "Why?"

I stared at my hands, hating myself for the mess I'd caused. My actions were hurting Jude and driving a wedge between him and his father. And for what?

"My life is complicated. I don't know where I'll be in six weeks, let alone six months. And I worried if you knew I'd stayed, well, you'd be upset."

"Because you stayed for your mom?"

And not you.

I nodded. Jude and I had broken up because I'd gotten my dream job. Because I was moving.

He leaned closer and placed his hand over mine. "I understand why you stayed. Of course I do." He gave my hand a squeeze before letting go. "I wish you would've let me be there for you. I still hope you will."

Out of the corner of my eye, I felt Knox watching us. When I finally chanced a glimpse at him, his jaw was clenched. His hands balled into fists on the counter. But then he turned away, and I wondered if I'd imagined it.

"I need to make some calls," Knox said. "I'll leave you two to catch up."

I opened my mouth as if to stop him, as if to say something, but then closed it. There was already enough tension between Jude and Knox because of me. I didn't need to make it worse.

CHAPTER SIX

Knox

"I still can't believe you're here," Jude said, a note of awe in his voice as it carried down the hall from the kitchen.

I wished I could see Kendall's expression. I wished I knew what she was thinking. Was she happy to see him? And why did I care so much?

You know why.

I dropped my head to my chest.

I needed to shut that shit down real quick. Kendall was off-limits. And my little crush was embarrassing. Not to mention inappropriate and dangerous.

God, if Jude knew how I felt about her…how I'd always felt about her. I pinched the bridge of my nose.

At least he didn't seem upset with me. I wouldn't be surprised if he were. For the moment, though, he seemed so happy to see Kendall that nothing else mattered.

I should go. Leave.

And yet I lingered in the shadows, Jude's and Kendall's voices carrying back to me.

It was a shitty thing to do—eavesdrop on their conversation. But I'd been doing a lot of shitty things lately where my son was concerned. Hiding the fact that Kendall was working for me, living at my house. But that wasn't even the worst of it.

The worst part. The most shameful, disgusting part was that I'd been lusting after Kendall. And not just lately. Always.

Since the moment I'd locked eyes with her on my yacht, and every time since, I'd noticed Kendall. It didn't matter how many times I'd told myself she was with him. I'd seen her first. And I couldn't help but be drawn to her.

Now that she was living in my home, now that I'd gotten to spend more time alone with her, my attraction had only grown stronger.

It wasn't just about her beauty—though she was definitely gorgeous. Long brown hair streaked with gold. Soulful hazel eyes that harbored wisdom. Sun-kissed skin that begged for me to caress every curve, explore every dip.

When I'd placed my hands on her hips earlier, it was as if she'd been made for me. She intrigued me. Relaxed me.

And I found myself making up all sorts of excuses to spend time with her. I'd even asked her to tutor me in Spanish to improve my fluency, though she refused to let me pay her. She said *I* was doing *her* a favor by letting her practice with someone.

And then there was her personality. She was smart and hardworking and selfless. And she really cared about others—her mom, me, even Jude, despite the fact that they'd broken up.

But that was just it. *My son* had *dated* her.

And even though he was now dating someone else, I had no right to think the things I did about his ex. To feel the way I felt about Kendall.

She might be single, but she would never be mine. And

the sooner I got that into my head, and her out of my house, the better.

I STUDIED THE FIELD A FEW DAYS LATER, WATCHING THE TEAM run its drills. "Looking good, Esposito," I called.

Number forty-four held up his hand and waved at me.

All the players were looking good. Strong. We'd had a stellar preseason so far, and if we kept it up, the Leatherbacks would have another shot at the League Cup.

"This might be the year," Jude said from beside me, echoing my thoughts.

My son and I had always been close. We'd always had an uncanny ability to read each other well enough to guess what the other was thinking.

It was part of why I'd been so thrilled when he'd decided to work with the Leatherbacks and me. I'd never wanted Jude to feel pushed into a career path, but I was grateful he'd decided to follow in my footsteps. And while I didn't plan to step down anytime soon, I hoped that one day I could leave the team in Jude's hands.

It was my job as his father to prepare him for the world. To prepare him to take over this team one day or to forge his own path. Just as my grandfather had prepared us to take over the family's hotel dynasty or build our own empires.

I might have inherited a fifth of the Huxley Hotel fortune, but I'd tripled it, thanks to my investments. And I'd always tried to encourage Jude to do what was right for him— whether it was the Leatherbacks or something else.

"I know." I clapped a hand on his shoulder. "We came so close last year. The team is hungry for it."

He nodded. "I can see that drive, that determination, even in practices."

"Yes," I said. "It's all coming together."

We fell silent a moment, watching the players as they ran drills. The maintenance team was working on the digital signs, where the Ultim8 Hydr8 logo was currently displayed. The company was focused on distilled water with electrolytes, and they were one of the Leatherbacks' biggest sponsors.

"So, were you ever going to tell me about Kendall?" Jude asked.

I'd been expecting—and dreading—this conversation. I was only surprised it had taken him this long to bring it up.

"I wanted to," I said. "I really did."

"I get it." He laughed, seeming far too at ease, considering the subject matter. "She can be very persuasive."

I fantasized about all the ways Kendall might be *persuasive*. Then I remembered that my son had firsthand knowledge and cringed.

"Still—" I gripped the railing.

He clapped a hand on my shoulder. "Dad, it's fine."

If he only knew...

"Really?" I asked, still trying to wrap my head around the fact that Jude had accepted this so easily. That he wasn't mad.

"Yeah." He crossed his arms on the fence, his gaze following the team as they progressed across the field. "It was really nice to see Kendall again."

I frowned. Did that mean he still had feelings for her? And what about his new girlfriend, Chrissy?

I was too chickenshit to ask. It was better to believe that he'd moved on. He *had* moved on.

And, again, nothing was going to happen between Kendall and me.

No matter how much I might want it to.

No matter how many times I'd dreamed about it. Jacking off to the image of her in that damn neon-green bikini. Imagining how she'd feel wrapped around me. The sounds she'd make. The...

"How much longer are you going to pretend you need a house sitter?" His question caught me off guard.

"What do you mean?"

"Oh, come on, Dad. You could've moved in a week ago—maybe more. Yet you didn't."

"Lauren's still working on the finishing touches," I said, which was true. But it wasn't the whole truth.

He pushed back from the fence and crossed his arms over his chest. "Mm-hmm."

"What?"

"We both know that's not the real reason why you haven't moved in."

"We do?" I asked, grateful my sunglasses hid the arch of my brow.

"Yes." He shook his head. "And I think it's nice that you're trying to keep Kendall employed, but there has to be another position you can offer her. One that doesn't require you to continue living in a hotel."

If it was that obvious to Jude, did Kendall know too?

And if Jude could see through me on this, could he so easily read my feelings for her as well?

"Don't look so surprised." He chuckled.

"I, well, yeah. I've thought about keeping her." I cleared my throat. "I mean, keeping her around. We work well together."

In the short time she'd been helping me with my Spanish, I'd noticed a huge improvement. I now spoke the language with more confidence, and I could more quickly pick up on conversations. It was going to be a huge asset with some of our players and even other teams.

"Exactly," he said, apparently not noticing or caring about my slip.

"And you'd be okay with that?"

"Why not?" He shrugged. "She clearly needs a job. At least I know you'll be good to her."

Oh, the things I wanted to do to her. The ways I wanted to spoil her.

"Right?" Jude asked, turning to me.

"Right." I shook my head as if to clear it. "Did you have a specific role in mind?"

"You keep whining about finding someone to manage all the stuff with the children's charities."

"Whining?" I stared at him, aghast. "Me?"

He laughed and rolled his eyes. "Yes, you. I know they're important, and I think we need some help."

"And you think Kendall's the right person for the job," I said, already knowing that was the case. I couldn't believe I hadn't thought of it before.

"I think she'd be a good fit. You already know she's responsible. You said yourself that you work well together."

I nodded, afraid to say more. Afraid to reveal my true thoughts where Kendall was concerned.

"Plus, she's got a big heart. This would be right up her alley."

"You're right," I said. "But I'm guessing she might have other plans."

He shrugged. "It's worth a shot. I think she'd be perfect for the job."

I think she'd be perfect for me.

Which was exactly why I *shouldn't* offer her a job.

I'd barely survived the past few weeks. And that was only because I'd been able to avoid the house. Anytime I was near her, our connection became even more difficult to ignore. To deny.

"Dad?"

"What was that?" I asked, feeling as if I'd been caught.

"I asked if you want to grab lunch together."

He winked at one of the physical therapists who passed. Jude had always been a bit of a flirt. Flaunting his wealth and charm. He reminded me of my cousin Jasper. And I worried that, like Jasper, Jude would never grow out of it.

"I'd love to." I wrapped my arm around his shoulder, and we walked back through the tunnel.

This was a huge reason why I loved my job. Because I got to do something I loved with my son. We were building something together. This wasn't just about family, but about a legacy. My grandfather, Huxley Graham, had always instilled that in us. And Jude was a big part of that.

"Dad?"

"Yeah?"

"I think it's really nice what you're trying to do for Kendall."

Talk about twisting the guilt knife.

"Thanks. She's a sweet girl, and she's been through a lot." I waved to the team doctor as we passed her in the hall. "Are we still on for dinner with Chrissy and her parents this weekend?"

I wanted to verify our plans, but also…I was curious. Would Jude have a change of heart about Chrissy now that Kendall was back in the picture?

"Yep. I was going to ask if you wanted to host and show off the new house, but…"

"With Kendall there, it could be awkward," I said, finishing his thought.

"And you're still interviewing chefs, right?"

I nodded. I'd had the Hartwell Agency send a few chefs to the house. I loved cooking, but I didn't always have the time. Plus, I figured Kendall would let me feed her if she thought she was doing something to help me. If she thought it was about interviewing chefs, not spending time together.

"Why don't we go out to eat?" I offered. "I'll ask Graham to reserve a table at 76." It was one of the restaurants at the Huxley Grand, and the food was phenomenal.

"Sounds great. Maybe Chrissy and I will get a room afterward. I think she's expecting something to celebrate our anniversary."

"How long has it been?"

"Two months."

"Oh, um—" I cleared my throat so I wouldn't laugh. "Congratulations."

"What about you?" Jude asked, turning his gaze on me.

"What about me?"

"Are you going to bring a date to dinner?" He nudged me.

"Nah." I smiled. "I'm more interested in spending time with you and getting to know Chrissy."

"When was the last time you went on a date?" he asked.

"What's with the sudden interest in my love life?" I teased, elbowing him back.

"I just—" He gave my shoulder a squeeze. "I want you to be happy."

"I am happy," I said. Though I appreciated his concern, I wondered where this was coming from. "I have a great family. A fabulous house. Amazing cars. A career I love."

But my response to Jude's comment made me realize how thin the veneer was. I'd filled my life with activities and accolades to avoid the feeling of emptiness always lurking just beneath the surface. Because despite everything I'd achieved, it still felt as if something was missing.

"But you're alone," Jude said.

"There's a difference between being alone and being lonely," I said, though the words had felt hollow lately.

"Yeah, but…" Jude sighed, and I was surprised by how

introspective he suddenly seemed. "What's the point of it all if not to share it with someone?"

I locked my arm around his neck. "That's what I have you for."

I was only half joking. He *was* my legacy. Him and the Leatherbacks. The team was an extension of my family.

Jude shook his head. "You know what I mean, Dad. Mom remarried years ago."

"You think I should get remarried?" Where was this coming from? Jude's mom and I had been divorced for over a decade.

"I'm not saying that. But I think you should find someone who makes you happy."

Easier said than done. The woman who made me happy was… I pushed away the thought. It didn't matter.

While Jude grabbed his jacket, I checked my emails. There was a new one from the Hartwell Agency. Staci wanted to check in about the chefs and see how much longer I'd need Kendall. Staci ended her email by asking if I was pleased with their service.

I thought about Kendall and just how much she pleased me.

And I knew Jude was right. It was time to get Kendall out of my house and into a more suitable role. Something that would help her but wouldn't provide so much temptation for me.

CHAPTER SEVEN

Kendall

"Argh." I mashed on the keyboard to my laptop. "Not again."

Knox rapped on my doorframe, and I jerked my head up from my laptop. The tutoring website had kicked me out just before I'd finished trying to upload my students' graded assignments for a third time.

I was frustrated with how unpredictable the website had been lately. Not to mention the complete lack of IT support. It was affecting both my schedule and my income.

"Everything okay?" Knox asked.

I sighed and set my laptop aside. "Yeah. It's fine."

"You sure?" he asked, brow furrowed with concern. Why did he have to be so sexy?

"It will be," I said, my bad mood vanishing at the sight of him. I smiled and admired the way the blue of his button-down shirt brought out the color of his eyes. "You look nice."

"Thanks." It was then I noticed he had two ties—one slung over each shoulder. "Dinner with Jude and…"

"And…?" I leaned back against the headboard, enjoying the way his eyes tracked my every move. Right now, he was staring at my throat. My lips. His gaze like a laser beam intent on the destruction of my underwear.

"And Chrissy," he finally said.

"It's okay to talk about Jude and his new girlfriend," I said, standing from the bed and stretching. "I'm happy for him."

"You are?" Knox asked, stepping closer, his bare feet padding on the floor.

"Of course I am."

I placed my hands on Knox's chest, using the ties as a pretext to touch him. I'd found myself doing that more and more lately—finding excuses to touch him.

He often sought my opinion. And not just on ties. Over the past few weeks, he'd come to me for an opinion on things regarding the house. On requests from charities. He'd ask my thoughts on how the team was doing or how our opponents were shaping up. I'd never felt so valued.

"Hmm." I picked up one of the ties and held it to his neckline. I placed it back on his shoulder then did the same with the other, taking my time to evaluate each one. My eyes pinged between his shoulders, his lips, and his eyes.

"Which do you prefer?" he asked.

They both looked great. Knox always looked amazing. He could be wearing an old, ratty shirt and jeans, and he'd still look hot.

I held the first one up to his neck again. This time, he leaned forward, his Adam's apple grazing my knuckles when he swallowed, his breath caressing my face as he exhaled. I let out a shaky exhale of my own, feeling as if I might combust from his proximity and the way he was looking at me.

When I continued to evaluate the ties, he said, "I may not be home until late, but I'm happy to bring some food home for you."

"Thanks, but I'll probably just have something light."

"You sure?" he asked.

I'd never felt so cared for, and I knew a big part of that was thanks to Knox. Looking back, I realized he'd always tried to make me feel welcome.

Any time we'd gone on the yacht last summer, he'd always ensured that my favorite snacks were stocked. One time, he'd had the chef at a Michelin-star restaurant change the entire tasting menu to accommodate my dairy sensitivity. Knox had always gone out of his way to make sure I was comfortable and enjoying myself. In the past, I'd told myself it was because I was dating his son. But now...I wasn't so sure.

"Positive," I said. "You should enjoy yourself."

"I know how much you love their flourless chocolate cake." He arched one eyebrow, tempting me—and not just with the promise of cake.

I moaned, thinking of the decadent dessert. "I just can't figure out their secret. There's no dairy, but it's so rich."

When I realized he was staring at my lips, I added, "Sorry. I shouldn't keep you. I'd hate to make you late for dinner."

"Does that mean you've picked a tie?"

"This one," I said, holding up the winner.

He took it from me and went over to my floor-length mirror, buttoning the top button of his shirt and then setting to work tying the tie. I studied his hands, his movements fluid and dexterous. Sexy.

Even though his attention was on the tie, I could feel his eyes on me. Watching me in the mirror as he finished dressing. It felt...strangely intimate.

"All right," he said, turning to face me. "Good?"

"Good," I said, though it was so much more than good. "I'll walk you out."

He placed his hand on my lower back, ushering me down the hall. As I admired the newly hung artwork, I realized how comfortable I'd become. Every day, this felt more like my home and less like a job.

I knew I'd have to move out at some point, and I knew that day was coming sooner than later. But the idea filled me with a sense of dread. I'd miss this beautiful house and all the wonderful staff who had become my friends. More than anything else, I'd miss Knox.

"Thank you for sorting the mail," Knox said.

"Of course."

I liked doing little things to make his life easier. He was always doing things for others, even if they didn't realize it. For the longest time, I'd thought Jude was behind the peonies—my favorite—in our hotel rooms when we stayed at Huxley Grand properties for the Leatherback's away games. And while it had seemed slightly out of character for Jude, I would've never guessed his dad was behind them.

It was only more recently that I'd made the connection. Knox had done so many kind and considerate things for me. But it was when the pink peonies—and only ever pink peonies—had started showing up on the dining table here at the house that I'd put it together. Knox had been behind it all along.

And in some small way, taking care of the house, helping him, felt like paying him back. Not that he'd ever made me feel like I owed him anything. More that…I'd realized Knox was so busy taking care of others that I wondered if he knew what it was like to have someone do something nice for him. Take care of him.

And the more things I did for Knox, the more I realized that pleasing him pleased me. I could envision other ways to give Knox pleasure, but I quickly shut down that line of thought.

Knox was my boss. And my ex's father. Hoping for

anything more was wildly unrealistic and inappropriate, not to mention wrong.

A FEW DAYS PASSED, AND NOTHING HAD CHANGED. KNOX'S dinner with Jude and Chrissy had gone well. And I was still crushing on my boss.

I headed inside and opened a few packages before checking the inventory on some of the household products. With Knox spending more time at the house, I'd wanted to make sure he was comfortable. And since I was doing less actual house-sitting, I'd taken it upon myself to adopt more of a house manager role to compensate for it. Plus, I was still tutoring him in Spanish, though that was fun.

I taught a few classes online, but there'd been a drop in enrollment the past few weeks. Students had complained about the website not working. I wished I had answers for them, but I was just as frustrated as they were.

After I'd finished, I headed down to Knox's office. The door was open, and he sat behind his desk, concentrating on the computer screen. The late-afternoon sunlight glinted off his hair, especially the silver strands near his temples and in his beard.

I studied him, thinking about how he was always leaving his mark. Whether it was on a personal level—all the nice things he did for me—or through the Leatherbacks.

After purchasing the team years ago, he'd changed the name and revamped the entire brand so it would be more inclusive. As part of its mission, the team donated a portion of its ticket sales to a conservation fund that helped both leatherback turtles and other marine wildlife.

And then there were the community outreach projects. Since moving in, I'd gained even more insight about Knox and the team, and he was just as active off the field as the players were on it. He regularly attended charity functions, and not just fancy galas that raised money. He went on hospital visits with the players. He organized for the unsold concessions from the stadium to be donated to local food banks.

The man was incredible. A powerhouse. And I'd never met anyone quite like him.

"Are you just going to stand there and watch me?" he teased, smiling as his eyes remained focused on the screen.

In the past, his question would've made me jump. But during the time we'd spent together, something had shifted. I felt more comfortable teasing him. I found myself pushing back. Pushing the boundaries in ways I wouldn't have before or with anyone else.

"Maybe." I grinned, placing the mail and the keys to the Range Rover on his desk.

He regarded me over his laptop then removed his glasses and set them on the desk with a sigh. "I thought I told you to keep these," he said, referring to the keys.

I'd started driving his SUV a few weeks ago. He'd asked me to pick something up across town, and he didn't think the item would fit in my trunk. Since then, he'd told me to take the Range Rover every time I went out, and not just when I was running errands for him.

"I know." I left the keys where they were. "But I have a car."

He eyed me skeptically.

"What?" I asked, unafraid to challenge him. I enjoyed doing it—just to see how he'd respond.

During the time I'd spent with Knox, I'd realized a few things. Yes, maybe Emmy was right that I didn't let people—

okay, men—in. But I'd never met a man who made me feel safe enough to do so. Not fully.

Things hadn't worked out with Jude, not because I'd planned to move. That was simply the excuse. The true reason was that I'd never felt secure in our relationship, partly because of my past. But a big part of that was Jude's personality. He was flirtatious. And when I'd finally broached the subject, he'd been dismissive of my comments.

But Knox... Knox encouraged me to speak my mind. He made me feel safe to express my opinion and not just about rugs or things that affected the team. About everything. Which was why I wasn't afraid to stand my ground on the car or anything else when it came to him.

"Kendall..." He leaned back in his chair, resting his ankle on his knee. "We talked about this. Your car is barely running, and it isn't safe."

It wasn't the first time he'd said as much.

"You'll take the Range Rover," he said in a tone that left no room for argument.

"But it's yours," I said, not backing down.

"Not anymore."

I tilted my head. "What are you talking about?"

He smirked just as the sound of a large truck backing up caught my attention. I frowned and rushed over to the window, watching as a tow truck started to drive off with my car attached to it.

My eyes went wide. "What the hell?"

I ran for the door, but Knox said, "It's too late."

"You can't just..." I sputtered, hands on my hips. "You can't just take my car. You stole my car!"

"No." He regarded me slowly, like a lion watching its prey. "I replaced the hunk of scrap metal you called a car with something much safer and more reliable."

"But it was mine." I stared at the empty driveway still in

disbelief. "And what about..." I shook my head. "What about the stuff I had inside?"

Not that it had been much, but still.

"I personally removed everything of yours," he said. "And I put it in your new car."

"But..." I squeezed my eyes shut, wondering when he'd taken my keys. How long had he been planning this? "You had no right to do that," I sputtered, simultaneously annoyed by his actions and overwhelmed by his generosity. "I didn't ask you to do that."

"I know." The corner of his mouth tilted upward. "But I wanted to."

He removed a piece of paper from the drawer to his desk and slid it and the keys across the surface to me. When I looked at the paper, I realized it was the car title. He'd literally given me the Range Rover.

"It would please me very much," he said, "if you would accept my gift."

"You've left me little choice," I grumbled.

But I had to admit, it was a relief to have a safer car. One that wouldn't leave me stranded on the side of the road when I was trying to get Mom to an appointment she couldn't miss. That had happened just last week. So even though I wished Knox would've talked to me about it first, I realized I should've been thanking him, not scolding him.

"Thank you." I placed my hand over his, and it was then he peered up at me. His gaze darted from my eyes to my lips then down to my shirt.

I moved closer, leaning against his desk. Wanting him to see more of me. *Want* more from me. Because he made me feel seen in a way no one else had.

"You're welcome."

"Look," I sighed. "I'm sorry if I came across as ungrateful.

I appreciate it more than you could know. But…" How could I say this without coming out and saying it?

"But what?"

"I know this is going to sound ridiculous, but I don't want to get used to it."

He furrowed his brow. "Get used to what?"

"You know…" I made a show of looking around, taking in the luxury and splendor that surrounded me. "All this. I'll be moving out soon." At least, I assumed so. We hadn't discussed the termination of the placement, but we both knew it was looming.

He steepled his fingers and regarded me over the top of them. "I see."

But I wasn't sure he did. Knox may not act entitled, but he'd been raised with money. He was one of the heirs to a freaking billion-dollar hotel fortune. He'd never *not* had money.

"That's actually something I want to discuss."

The abrupt change of topic was jarring, but I leaned my hip against the desk, trying not to let my anxiety show. "That sounds ominous."

He shook his head. "It's about an opportunity."

I quirked my brow, my mind going all sorts of places. "What kind of opportunity?"

"One I'd like to discuss over dinner. Are you hungry?" he asked, though he was the one with the ravenous look in his eyes. It warmed me to the core, and I shifted as if that would somehow ease the ache.

Nothing eased the ache.

Not my fingers. Not my vibrator. It was as if I walked around in a constant state of arousal. I often wondered if Knox knew just how keyed up my body was. How I burned for him.

I lifted a shoulder. "A little."

"Good," he said with a wolfish smile.

"Is there a dress code?" I asked.

When Knox had gone out to dinner the other night, he'd been wearing a sport jacket. If that was a regular Tuesday evening for him, I had no idea what to expect.

"Wear whatever you like," he said, standing from his desk and rounding it.

I needed more information. He'd said it was an "opportunity." Did that mean it was a business dinner? Would there be other guests? Would Jude be there?

God, I hope not.

I felt bad enough that I had a crush on my boss. Anytime Jude was near, it only made me feel worse about the fact that my boss was also my ex's dad.

Still, I couldn't resist asking, "What would you *like* for me to wear?"

Knox shook his head, his attention on the floor. "Answering that question will only get me into trouble."

I stilled, his words reverberating through me like a tuning fork that had been struck. Did he...was he saying what I thought he was? We'd been dancing around this tension for weeks, and I thought I might combust.

It had never been like this with Jude. Not even in the beginning. And while I didn't want to compare the two men, at times, I realized just how much every other man I'd been with paled in comparison to Knox. Even his son.

Bad, Kendall. So, so bad.

But when Knox's eyes lingered on my lips, all I could think was how *good* it would feel. To give in to him. To this... this *thing* growing between us.

"What?" he asked, tilting his head to the side. "Is there something in my teeth?" He made the goofiest expression, and I immediately burst out laughing.

"No." I gave him a gentle shove. "Your teeth are perfect."

TEMPTATION

Just like everything about you.

"So, you'll join me?" he asked, taking my hand in his. The one I'd used to shove him. And I was surprised he seemed almost…shy. "On the back patio."

"I'll be there," I whispered, feeling as if we were sharing a secret.

"Good." We held each other's gaze longer than was necessary. "It'll just be us. So wear whatever you want."

I nodded then headed up to my room to agonize over what to wear. Finally, I gave up and decided to text Emmy.

> Hey. Need your opinion on an outfit.

> Emmy: Ooh. For a date?

I debated a moment then responded.

> Me: I'm not sure what it is.

My phone immediately rang, and I answered it. "Hey."

"Give me all the details. Where are you going? Who are you going with?"

"I'm—" I stared at the closet, shuffling through my options while trying to keep my voice low. "Knox and I are having dinner at the house."

"Alone?" she asked.

"Mm-hmm." I didn't want to say too much and risk him overhearing. The walls were thick, and it was a big house, but still…

"Is he nearby?"

I shook my head then remembered she couldn't see me. "No. But he's home, so I don't want to talk too loud in case the sound carries."

"Is this a date?" she asked.

"No." I lowered my voice to a whisper. "He said he wants

to discuss an opportunity."

"What kind of *opportunity*?" Her inflection suggested something more.

"I don't know." I flopped down on the bed, wishing I had more answers. She was asking all the same questions I'd been asking myself. "Which is why I need outfit help."

"Do you think he's going to ask you to sleep with him?"

"I-I—"

I wanted to tell her that was absurd. And yet…I clenched my thighs together. I shouldn't like the idea of that as much as I did.

"Ooh. But you want him to," she said.

"I—" I hesitated, not even sure what to say. "I'll admit I'm attracted to him. But it can't go any further than that."

"Maybe it should. Maybe that's why you're calling me. For reassurance."

"Emmy," I hissed, hating how right she was. "Will you please just help me with my outfit?"

"I can only help you if you're honest about your goals. Are you trying to look professional or sexy?"

I rolled my bottom lip between my teeth then said, "Maybe a little of both."

"Yas, girl!" she squealed. And then she turned serious, telling me exactly what to wear and how to style my hair. Before hanging up, she said, "Ooh. I'm so excited!"

Just as I said, "I think I'm going to be sick."

"Have *fun*," Emmy said before we ended the call. "Live a little for once in your life. Just don't fuck up our free tickets to the Leatherbacks."

"Fine," I huffed, but I was laughing. "I'll do my best."

We'd settled on a lavender-colored dress that was soft and gauzy. It was dressy but comfortable. It was relatively modest in front—just a hint of cleavage. But it dipped low in the back, revealing a huge expanse of skin. I took my time curling my hair and braiding part of it so it would rest over one shoulder.

When I headed downstairs, Knox was already waiting. He stood with his back to me, his attention on the sunset. His hands were in his pockets, and I tracked his form from his shoulders to his tapered waist to his powerful legs.

"Hey," I said, joining him. Looking out at the sky from the same vantage point.

"Hey." I could hear the smile in his voice. "Come. Sit," he said, pulling out a chair for me. He placed his hand on my back, lingering a moment before sliding down my bare skin. "You look beautiful."

I admired the flowers—pink peonies, of course—and the chilled wine as I tried to calm my nerves from his words and his touch. Knox and I always found small ways to touch each other, but this felt…different.

What am I doing?

"Thank you," I said, taking a seat. Feeling his presence, the connection between us, even as he stood behind me, just out of reach.

"My pleasure," he said, joining me. "I would've prepared dinner, but I thought we could both use the night off."

The back door opened, and a waiter stepped out, a plate of salad in each hand. He served us without a word, and then he was gone.

"Wow," I said. "Thank you. That's very thoughtful. I suppose that means you finally decided on a chef."

He nodded. "Yes. You were right. Javier was the best choice."

I preened, pleased he'd accepted my advice yet again. That he continually sought it out, wanting my opinion.

Our conversation turned to other matters—the team, soccer, everything. Well, almost everything. Neither of us mentioned Jude.

When the salad plate was cleared and the entrée arrived, Knox turned to the waiter. "Thank you. That will be all."

The man nodded and took his leave. I assumed he'd let the other staff know that they were dismissed for the night. Leaving me completely alone with Knox.

He lifted his wineglass, and I joined him for a toast. "Thank you for taking such good care of the house. And me."

"Absolutely," I said, feeling both gratified and sad as I sipped the wine. This was clearly goodbye.

"Have you enjoyed working with me?" he asked.

I was surprised not only by his question but by the way in which he'd phrased it. Even though I might have been here to do a job, he always made it seem as if we were equals. He'd never treated me as anything but.

"Very much," I said.

His eyes lingered on my lips, hanging on my every word. "Would you want to continue working with me?"

I leaned back in my chair and laughed as I ran a hand through my hair. "Knox, you obviously don't need a house sitter. You haven't for a while."

"Damn." His lopsided grin made my stomach quiver with anticipation. "You caught me."

"Yes." I rolled my eyes. "And while I appreciate you letting me stay on as long as I have, we both knew this day was coming."

"Which is why I wanted to talk with you. I contacted the Hartwell Agency to officially end the house-sitting placement since I plan to move in next week."

I nodded, wondering where he was going with this. Was he going to ask me to sleep with him? Was that the "opportunity," as Emmy had suggested?

I shook away the thought and tried to focus on what Knox was saying.

"I'd like to continue to have you tutor me in Spanish," he

said. "And I want to hire you as my personal assistant to manage some charity projects for the Leatherbacks."

"You do?" I tried not to frown.

"You sound...surprised." He tilted his head to the side. "Disappointed, perhaps?"

"No. No." I waved my hands in front of me, telling myself to slow down on the wine. "I mean, yes, I'm surprised. And I'm flattered—" I took a breath. "But I'm not sure that's a good idea."

"Because of Jude?" he asked.

I nodded, figuring that was easier than admitting the truth. Knox might no longer be my boss—at least for the moment. But he was still Jude's dad.

"Jude actually suggested I hire you for this position."

I jerked my head back. "He did?"

I'd seen Jude a few times over the past few weeks. He was as friendly as ever. But I was still surprised that he'd suggest such a thing.

"Mm." Knox sipped his wine. "He did. He knows how much I've enjoyed working with you, and he thinks we're good together."

He did? Does?

"You'd get free tickets to the games," Knox continued.

"You already give me free tickets," I teased, though I didn't expect that to last much longer now that my placement was over.

A pair of tickets had appeared on my nightstand every week since that first night in his kitchen. Emerson and I had been taking full advantage of them. The Leatherbacks were on a roll this season, and my mom was thrilled that I was living life again.

She was certainly living life again. She was still undergoing treatment and tired easily, but she'd started dating Joe. For the first time in a while, life felt almost...normal.

Knox narrowed his eyes at me. "Well, if you want that to continue, then I suggest you take the job."

I laughed. "Mm-hmm."

He sighed, his shoulders slumping. "Please? I need someone I can rely on. Someone I can trust. And I can't think of anyone better for the position."

He was selling it a little too hard. Not that I didn't know my worth, but the fact that Knox had prolonged the house-sitting gig so I'd have extra income made me wonder if he was offering me this new position for the same reason. *Pity.*

"Thanks, but I don't want a pity job."

"Pity job?" He scoffed, and I immediately realized my mistake. Knox expected excellence, and the offer wasn't made out of pity but kindness. "I wouldn't hire you unless I had faith in you. And, trust me—" he leaned in, his eyes darkening "—I am going to work you hard."

Holy shit. The images that raced through my mind at his statement. Knox taking me from behind, my hair clasped in his fist. Me riding his...

"Kendall?" he asked.

I bit my lip and dipped my head. Could he tell that my mind had gone down a completely unprofessional path?

"Can I think about it?" I asked, wondering how I could possibly continue working with Knox and resist this insane pull.

Surely it wasn't one-sided, was it?

Part of me wanted to believe it was, because then it would be nothing more than a childish infatuation with my boss. But another part of me knew the feeling was mutual. Knew Knox longed for me the way I burned for him. And that staying anywhere near him was asking for trouble.

"Absolutely," he said. "But we have a charity event coming up, and I need you." Had I imagined the seductive tone to his voice?

I nodded and turned my attention to the pool. Stared out at the water in an attempt to compose myself.

After a moment passed, he said, "Kendall? Can I ask you something?"

"Sure," I said.

"You know this has Jude's blessing, yet you remain hesitant. Does that have anything to do with me?"

"I, um—" I fidgeted with the hem of my skirt. "I'm not sure I should answer."

"Because you think I won't like your answer?"

"Mm." I shook my head, trying hard not to laugh. "No. Not exactly."

"Do you want to know what I think?" he asked.

I hesitated a moment then nodded. I was weak when it came to this man. How much longer could I resist?

"I think you're smart and kind. Selfless and caring."

I dipped my head and smiled. "Thank you."

"But I've always known you were incredible."

I lifted my head. "Thank you," I said again, stunned.

Knox had said nothing about my physical appearance and everything about my heart. It was as if he saw me. Not the version of Kendall everyone else saw, but the true me.

"And while I know you could do this job in your sleep, and you have dreams that are so much bigger than this, I'm confident you could do a lot of good in this role. Because every time you help someone, I see the way you light up. Whether it's taking a sandwich to Vincent..."

I opened my mouth. *He'd seen that?*

He smirked. "Or baking one of the garden crew a nut-free, vegan cake for their birthday. You like celebrating people. And that's why I think you'd be perfect to help with this."

"Wow." I blinked a few times, my resistance melting away the longer he spoke. "I don't know what to say."

"I'm not going to pressure you into anything. But I'd love to have you on my team."

"Okay," I said. "I'll consider it." How could I not after a speech like that? I mean...*wow*.

"Our lives on this planet are short, but the legacy we leave behind can last forever."

I nodded, knowing how important legacy was to Knox. And how right he was.

His honesty encouraged me to be vulnerable. For the moment, he wasn't my boss. He was just a man. Someone I respected and admired, not because of what he'd accomplished but because of the type of person he was.

So with a shaky breath, I asked, "Do you want to know what I think?"

He leaned forward, and the pull between us intensified. "Very much."

I smiled, forcing myself to say the words I'd been thinking since...well, forever. "I've always thought you were a good man. Kind and handsome."

"Thank you." He tugged at the collar of his shirt.

"Now you're the one who sounds disappointed."

He chuckled. "Handsome is nice. But it feels like—well, what if I were to call you 'cute'?"

I wrinkled my nose.

"Exactly," he said, smoothing a hand down his beard.

"Well, excuse me, but it was the only semi-appropriate compliment I could come up with."

He leaned forward, his voice deeper. "And what if I don't want you to be appropriate?"

"Knox..."

"Sorry. It's late. I should...I should go." He stood quickly, nearly toppling his chair. "Too much wine turns me into a foolish old man."

If the wine was making anyone foolish, it was me. I'd

been flirting with him all evening. Flirting with the idea of being with him, even when I knew it was impossible.

"Knox," I said again, standing. "You're neither of those things. But I'm..." I shook my head and turned away. "Never mind."

"No." I heard the rustle of his clothes as he stepped closer. "Tell me what you were going to say." The heat from his body radiated off him. I felt his hand as if it were a feather grazing my back.

I took a deep breath, his presence giving me strength, the wine making me brazen. My placement was over. Technically, he wasn't my boss anymore. At least not right now. I hadn't accepted his job offer; we weren't breaking any rules.

"Do you want to know the real reason why I'm hesitant to accept?" I asked.

I wasn't considering the position, not really. Between the Hartwell Agency and my online tutoring, I could get by. At least, I thought I could. If enrollment continued to drop because of the tutoring company's incompetence, I might have to look at other options.

And yeah, maybe those jobs weren't as stable or exciting as what Knox was offering, but they were flexible. And with my mom's health, I valued flexibility.

"Yes," he said from behind me. It was almost easier not to face him when I said this.

"Because sometimes—" This was it. I was going to go for it. "Sometimes, I wish you weren't my boss."

"And why's that?" he asked, his tone betraying nothing.

"I think you know why." I stared at the pool and the way the water lapped at the edges, even as my heart raced.

"I need to hear you say it." He placed his hands on my shoulders and turned me to face him. "Tell me, Kendall. Why do you wish I weren't your boss?"

CHAPTER EIGHT

Knox

Kendall stared up at me, her eyes full of questions. She pulled her lower lip between her teeth and shook her head. Fuck me, she was gorgeous, her lavender dress somehow making her seem ethereal.

"Kendall," I rasped. "Technically, I'm not your boss anymore. Not tonight anyway." I lifted my hand but then lowered it before I could touch her. "And you're no longer my employee."

"But you're still Jude's dad," she said.

"Is that what this is about?" I asked, frowning. "Because he'll tell you the same thing I did earlier. He wants you to take this position with the team."

"He wouldn't if he knew…" She drew in a jagged breath, and I waited for her to finish that thought. Seconds felt like hours until she said, "If he knew the types of thoughts I've been having about you."

I stilled, feeling as if everything had built up to this moment. I'd waited too long to act before and had missed out. This might be my last shot. My only chance.

"What types of thoughts?" I asked, hoping I was right.

Hoping she wanted me as badly as I wanted her.

She dipped her head. "It's... They're inappropriate."

Her candor encouraged me to proceed despite all the reasons not to.

"If I had a dollar for every time I've had an inappropriate thought about you, I'd be a billionaire."

She laughed. "You *are* a billionaire."

"Okay. If I had to pay a dollar every time I had an inappropriate thought about you, I'd have no money left."

Her eyes searched mine. "You would?"

I nodded. "I think about you all the time. When I go to bed, you're the last thing on my mind. When I wake up, you're the first. These past few months have been a test of my willpower, and I'm not sure how much longer I can resist the—" I gestured to her "—temptation. Resist you."

I was practically panting, my heart racing at my confession. It felt as if the organ was surging forward, trying to leave my chest as I awaited her response.

She closed her eyes, her lashes fluttering as if my confession pained her. "I know, but..." Then she opened her eyes slowly and nibbled on her lower lip, tantalizing me even as I prepared myself to be ripped in two. "We can't."

I nodded, the air between us swirling with tension. "You're right," I said, but that didn't stop me from stepping closer. "We shouldn't."

"Exactly," she said, leaning closer, leaning in to me.

That was it—the truth. It was finally out there, and I felt both better and worse.

Kendall wanted me, and I wanted her. But we couldn't be together.

We could *never* be together. At least, not in any meaningful way.

"What if..." She shook her head and backed away slowly.

"No. I should. Yeah. I should go—" She hooked her thumb over her shoulder. "Before we do something we'll regret."

I watched her turn and leave, but I couldn't let her go. I didn't care that she was younger. That she'd dated my son. Nothing mattered in that moment but this woman. Because when I was with her, it was as if the world stopped.

Before she reached the back door, I called, "Wait."

She paused but didn't turn to face me. Her shoulders were hunched with tension, and I knew how she felt because I was damn near ready to explode myself.

"What if...we could have tonight?" I asked, finishing her unspoken question from earlier.

She let out an exhale, her shoulders relaxing as she turned to face me. "Yeah. But that's impossible, right?"

I shook my head, stepping closer. "Maybe tonight is the one night that this—" I gestured between us "—could be possible."

"Tonight, we're no longer boss and employee," she said, as if trying to convince herself this was okay. "But what about tomorrow?"

I placed my finger to her lips. "Tomorrow isn't guaranteed." She, of all people, knew that. "So, tell me, Kendall. What do you want?"

She kissed my finger, and my body came alive from that simple touch. I stared, enraptured by her lips, especially when they parted slightly. Inviting me in.

I slid one finger into her mouth, then another, my dick hardening at the warmth. The wetness enveloping me. I groaned, imagining her doing the same thing to my cock.

"Kendall," I groaned, enjoying the way her eyes darkened with lust.

I removed my fingers, trailing them down her chin. Her neck. To the top of her dress. Her nipples pebbled against the material; they'd been distracting me all night.

"Go for a swim with me?" she asked, almost shyly.

"What?" I blurted, still trying to unscramble my brain.

"A swim," she said, stepping away from me. Grasping the hem of her dress and pulling it over her head in one smooth movement.

I stared at her, mouth agape. Her body was beautiful in the moonlight, the shadows only accentuating her delicious curves.

"What are you—" I clenched my fists, forcing myself to remain rooted to the spot despite the overwhelming desire to move closer. To touch her.

All she wore was a lacy lavender thong, the rest of her body revealed to me. *She* was baring herself to me.

"I'm seizing the day. Or...I guess, the night." She shrugged, a sexy little smirk playing at her lips.

"Kendall," I groaned.

This woman was going to be the death of me. But I'd been the one to push that line. To dip a toe in the forbidden. And now she was going to jump right into the deep end.

She turned and sauntered toward the water, my eyes never leaving her form. When she reached the edge, she flashed me the sweetest smile over her shoulder. And then she dove in, barely making a splash.

When she popped back up, she was grinning. Her skin was wet, her hair even darker against her skin.

"Are you just going to stand there and watch?" she teased, reminding me of earlier, in my office.

My mind conjured up an entirely different image. One where she was laid out on my bed, touching herself. And I was enjoying the show.

Even so, I didn't need to be asked again. I couldn't strip out of my clothes fast enough. My hands were shaking as I attempted to unbutton my shirt. It didn't take long for me to give up and rip it open, buttons flying onto the grass. I peeled it off, then shucked my pants and kicked them aside but followed her lead and kept my boxers on. Her eyes roamed my body with appreciation, lingering on the muscles of my stomach and then dipping lower still. My cock ached from her attention.

She crooked her finger, and it felt as if there were a string tied from it to me. And she was dragging me toward her. Pulling me even further under her spell.

I took a deep breath and dove into the pool, only resurfacing when I was mere inches from her. The water was warm against my already heated skin. The lights from beneath the surface gave me glimpses of her form, and I waited to see what she'd do. What she wanted. She had to take the lead in this.

When she splashed me, I reared back in surprise. And then I leaned my head back to the sky, and I laughed. Only Kendall.

I returned my attention to her, narrowing my eyes. "You're going to pay for that."

"Oh yeah?" she taunted, as if she wanted me to punish her. And then she took off.

She was fast. I'd seen her swimming laps often enough to know that she was an agile swimmer. But she wasn't fast enough to escape me.

I caught up to her quickly, tugging her leg. Pulling her to me. We surfaced, and she placed her hands on my shoulders, her touch like a jolt of electricity against my bare skin. My cock was already standing at attention, and I wondered if she realized what she did to me. The power she held over me.

She squirmed against me, her breasts crushed against my chest, my body hyperaware of her every move. Of the feel of her warm skin against mine as she giggled and writhed against me.

Finally, I decided to tickle her. Only then did she stop fighting. She was too busy laughing to try to get away.

I loved seeing her let go. Have fun. I loved that she felt comfortable enough with me to relax.

She wrapped her legs around my waist, and I held her close. My cock was desperate for her, seeking her heat and nudging her entrance through the thin material of her thong.

Then slowly, her laughter subsided. And everything became serious again. Tenuous.

"Tell me what you want," I said, waiting for her command. Her request. In that moment, I would've given her anything.

She peered up at me, water dripping down her forehead and over her lips. I wanted nothing more than to kiss her. Claim her.

"Kiss me." The words were said so softly, I wondered if I'd imagined them. As if I'd somehow willed her to say them.

I slid my hand into her hair, using the other to grip her hip and pull her closer to me. To line us up so our bodies connected the way my mouth ached for hers. And still, it wasn't enough.

Would it ever be enough?

One kiss certainly wouldn't be. And I was positive one night wouldn't either. But that was all we had.

"I know this is a bad idea," I said, inhaling her coconut scent. Wondering if she tasted as good as I imagined. "But I can't seem to think clearly when it comes to you."

"I know." Her throat bobbed as I kissed down the column of her neck. "God, I know."

I kissed her cheekbones, tasting the chlorine on her skin mixed with the flavor of her. The corners of her eyes. Her forehead. I wanted to kiss every inch of her. Slowly. And then I wanted to do it all again.

I fully intended to savor this moment. Because if all we

had was this night, I needed to make it count. Especially since I'd been dreaming of kissing Kendall for over a year.

"But I can't stop myself," I said as I closed in on her lips.

"No one can ever know," she whispered.

We both knew there was one person in particular who couldn't know, but I pushed thoughts of Jude from my mind. I was too far gone at this point. I'd wanted this for too long to hold back anymore.

"No one," I said in a solemn tone.

"Knox." She tightened her grip on my shoulders.

"Yeah?"

"Kiss me." She panted. "*Please.*"

"Oh." I brushed my nose against hers. "I plan on doing a hell of a lot more than just kissing you. But I've waited too long to rush this moment."

"Wha—"

I silenced her question with a kiss. Answering would only lead to more trouble.

Her lips parted, her mouth opening to me. Welcoming me in, making me feel more at home than I ever had anywhere else.

She tasted like berries. Like the wine we'd consumed, and yet a flavor unique to her. I craved her, craved the sexy little sounds she made as I roamed her body with my hands. Craved the feel of her skin on mine.

To be able to touch her like this. To pretend she was mine. It was heaven and hell all at once because I knew it was only temporary.

But I had until tomorrow, and I intended to make the most of it.

"You feel…" I swallowed hard. "So good."

"So do you," she said, wrapping her arms around my neck, molding herself to my chest.

I'd never experienced so many sensations simultaneously; it was nearly overwhelming. The warmth of her body. The water flowing around us. But the most prominent, the most constant, was our connection. It was heaven.

"Fuck, *mi cielo*. Your body is perfection." I slid my hands down her back and over her ass, holding her even closer to me.

I used my grip to glide her up and down my shaft. She was driving me fucking crazy. And judging from the sounds she made and the way she angled her hips toward me, she felt the same.

"*Mi cielo?*" She smiled, knowing I was using the Spanish term for "my heaven." We'd talked about it in my lesson just the other day.

"Yes," I sighed. "Wanting you has been heaven and hell."

"I know." She moaned, arching her back as she writhed against me. "But wasn't it worth it to feel like this?"

I kept at it, enjoying the friction. The heat and closeness of her body. The way she responded to me. "Yes. I'm tempted to slip these panties aside to see just how tight your pussy is. If it's the paradise I've imagined."

"Yes." Her breathing was ragged. "Please, Knox."

My dirty promises seemed to drive her even wilder. "And then I'd bury myself deep, feeling the way your walls clench around my cock."

She clawed at my back, our movements turning frantic. If we kept this up, I was going to come too quickly.

"Not yet," I said, more to myself.

With her legs still wrapped around my waist, I waded through the water until we reached the stairs. "What are you doing?" she asked. "Where are we going?"

When I started ascending the steps, she shivered and held on tighter. "Knox?"

"I need to taste you." I set her on the side of the pool.

"I—that's..." She tried to slink back into the water. "It's okay. You don't have to do that."

I tilted my head to the side, wondering why she'd suddenly clammed up. "Do you not want me to?"

"It's just..." She focused on something in the distance. "Most guys don't like doing that."

I didn't want to think about the other guys she might be referring to. I didn't want to picture her with anyone but me.

I'd never had such a possessive streak with other women. But Kendall brought out this side of me. She made me want to claim her, want to know that I was the only man she wanted.

"I wouldn't offer if I didn't want to do it," I said, resting her legs on my shoulders, pulling her closer to my mouth. "And I want to, very much."

When I kissed my way up her inner thigh, she shuddered and seemed to finally relax. She rested her elbows on one of the stairs, tilting her head back to the sky.

She was so achingly beautiful it made my chest hurt to look at her, to know that this was all I'd ever have with her. One glimpse of paradise and then back to reality.

"Tell me if you want me to stop. Or if there's something you like. Or don't," I said, focusing on this moment instead.

She nodded, and I peeled her panties aside, baring her to me. Her pussy—like the rest of her—was beautiful. Pink and wet. Begging to be licked.

I pried her apart, blowing on the sensitive skin. She shivered, her stomach muscles clenching. I growled, loving her reaction. Loving how responsive she was to me.

"You like that?" I asked.

"Mm-hmm." She said it lazily, her body relaxing for me. Opening to me. Just like she had over the past few months. "Your beard...your *everything* feels so good."

I leaned forward and licked up her slit. One taste, and I

was already hooked. I couldn't get enough of her as I licked and flicked and sucked. And she seemed just as keen for me to continue—digging her fingers into my hair. She dragged her nails against my scalp as her body wound tighter and tighter, approaching her climax.

"Knox," she gasped, riding my face. Writhing from my touch. From *my* mouth.

It was *my* name on her lips, and I'd never felt so fucking proud.

"That's it, *mi cielo*," I said, using my fingers to pleasure her. "Give it to me. Give me everything."

And as I watched Kendall's orgasm barrel through her, I realized just how fucked I was. Because I didn't just want her pleasure; I wanted her heart.

CHAPTER NINE

Kendall

"Oh god," I gasped.

I flopped back against the stairs, sending ripples through the pool as shock waves continued to rock my body. Even as the water turned calmer, the waves gently lapping at my skin, my body felt as if it had been torn apart in the best possible way.

I'd never had someone touch me like Knox had. Never had a man look at me with such devotion while absolutely devouring me. It was... It made me feel so powerful. So desired.

"You're cold," he said, sounding almost angry. But his expression was one of concern.

I didn't realize I was shivering until he mentioned it. I'd been so lost in the sensations, in him, that nothing else seemed to affect me anymore. Not the weather nor the fact that he was my ex's father.

It was as if we'd entered this bubble, where time and rules ceased to exist. Where there were no consequences. Where we could be together, and we could have what we wanted.

I knew that wasn't true.

I knew this was only for tonight.

But for once, I'd decided to do something for me. Not because I felt like I "should." Not because it was what Knox wanted or it was the opposite of what Jude would want. But because it was what *I* wanted.

And this was definitely what I wanted. Knox was what I wanted.

He cradled me in his arms, lifting me out of the pool with care. Treating me as if I was the most precious thing in the world. Tonight—and anytime I was in Knox's presence—it felt as if I were.

Mi cielo. My heaven.

He'd certainly taken me to outer space with that orgasm. I wasn't sure I'd ever come so hard. I'd literally seen stars.

And his kiss. God, I could get lost in his kiss. Everything about him commanding yet gentle. Taking while giving.

Knox grabbed a large, fluffy towel and draped it over me before carrying me into the house and up the stairs to his bedroom. He kept glancing down at me as if he couldn't fully believe this was happening. Neither could I.

He placed me on his bathroom counter before switching on the shower. His boxers clung to his skin, leaving little to the imagination. And while he checked the water temperature, I checked out his ass. The round, sculpted muscles showing his strength. Strength he'd used to hold me in the pool. To carry me up the stairs to his room. He was such a powerful man, and yet he'd only ever made me feel safe. Cherished.

Steam billowed out the top of the shower, and Knox stood before me. Opening the towel, helping me stand so he could peel off my underwear.

"You are so fucking gorgeous," he said, spinning me slowly until I faced the mirror. "So fucking mine." At least that was what it sounded like he said as he trailed his fingers over my spine and down my ass.

As I watched us in the mirror, I felt like his. I *wanted* to be his. And not just for tonight.

But it was all we had.

So I stayed there a moment, reveling in the look of appreciation on his face. This magnificent man wanted me. Knox Crawford wanted me.

I turned to face him, hooking my fingers in his boxers. And then I dragged them over his hips. Down his legs as I kneeled before him. His cock bobbed toward me, hard and proud.

I peered up at Knox, and his eyes were hooded. Full of lust and longing, and I was dying to taste him.

I gripped his shaft, gently guiding him to my mouth. I swirled my tongue around his tip, feeling the bulge of his vein. Exploring the crown as it slipped between my lips.

He groaned, and I'd never heard a sound more feral. It was clear from the way he clenched his fists at his sides that he was losing control. I liked the idea. I wanted to make him unravel.

So I decided to test his limits. I smiled up at him, teasing him again with my tongue. He tangled his hand in my hair, letting me play for a minute before pulling me to my feet.

"In the shower." He guided me toward the entrance. "Now."

I stumbled into the shower, the warm spray instantly relaxing my muscles. I hadn't realized how cold I was until I felt the heat of the water.

Knox joined me, pumping shampoo into his palm then rubbing his hands together. "Turn. Let me take care of you."

I turned so my back was to him, moaning with appreciation when he massaged it into my scalp. Between the orgasm earlier and now this, I was going to melt into a puddle on the floor.

He kept at it for a while, never seeming to be in any rush. For a man who owned a successful pro soccer team and was involved in countless philanthropic efforts, he always seemed to have time for me.

When he finished, he turned me gently. Kissing me slowly and deeply while the shower washed the soap away.

"Hi." I smiled up at him when he pulled back and cupped my face.

"Hey." He grinned, tracing my jaw.

The moment felt tender and precious, like the soap bubbles swirling the drain. They were beautiful, but they only lasted a moment.

I didn't want to think about that. I didn't want to think of anything but right here. Right now.

So I guided him to the shower bench, grabbing the shampoo and lathering his hair. All the while, he ran his hands over my body. Exploring. Caressing. Teasing.

When his hair was finished, and my body was clean, he washed himself quickly.

"Let's get out," he said, rinsing his body then stepping out of the shower.

I pouted when he wrapped a towel around his waist. "But I wanted to wash you."

"Another time."

But there likely wouldn't be another time, which only upset me more.

"Come on, Kendall." He grabbed a plush white robe and held it open for me. "Be a good girl and get out."

I'd always been a "good girl." I always followed the rules. I always did what I was supposed to. And I was sick of it.

I didn't want to submit or obey. I wanted to rebel.

And even though being with Knox was its own sort of

rebellion, I felt as if I'd barely stepped into my power. Into embracing my desires.

Knox had always encouraged me to express my opinion, especially with him. He'd made me feel safe to do so. Which was why I felt comfortable saying, "Maybe I don't want to be a good girl," even as I got a thrill from that small act of defiance.

"Kendall," he chided.

I hesitated a moment, testing the boundaries. Pushing myself to stand up for my wishes. To assert my needs. Then I switched off the water, stepping out of the shower on my terms and into his arms.

"Yes, Daddy," I said, mostly in jest.

He turned me so my back was to the shower, pinning me against the glass. "Don't call me that."

His expression was murderous, and it only made me want to tease him more.

"Would you prefer, 'Sir'?" I joked, relishing this newfound boldness.

"Kendall," he growled, and I tried my hardest not to laugh.

"Okay. So, you're not a fan of that either." I ducked beneath his arm and darted toward the door. "How about 'my king'? Or *'mi rey,'* if you prefer?"

Oh my god. If Emmy could see me now. She'd die.

"Kendall," Knox called again, his footsteps steady and loud as they pounded against the floor. "Don't make me spank you."

I ran around to the other side of the bed, putting the mattress between us. He glared at me over the top, and I laughed in return.

"If you want to spank me," I said, breathless from laughter, "you'll have to catch me first."

He narrowed his eyes. But we both knew how much he

delighted in a challenge. "Oh, I will. I'll even give you a head start."

I took off before he could say "Go," heading down the hall as fast as my feet would carry me. My heart was pounding so loud I could barely hear him counting, but it didn't matter. He was fast. He was determined. And he would catch me.

But that didn't mean I'd make it easy for him.

I raced down the hall, rushing down the stairs. I craned my head from side to side, wondering if I should hide. If I should keep running. I didn't have much time, so I darted toward his office.

"Better run faster," he taunted, his deep voice seeming to come from both everywhere and nowhere in particular.

I wasn't sure I'd ever been more aroused. I could feel the desire pooling in my core. I ached for Knox's touch. And then his arms were around my waist.

"Gotcha." His voice was deeper, more gravelly. His beard tickling my jaw.

I laughed, struggling against him. Though, to be honest, I'd wanted him to catch me. He easily lifted me in the air, dropping me over his shoulder. My head hung down by his terry-clad ass. His arms banded around my thighs.

He slapped my ass over the robe, and it was hard enough to sting. But he kept his palm there, soothing me with his touch. For a moment, I froze, both intensely aroused and a little nervous.

I trusted Knox. I wouldn't have started a game like this if I didn't. But this was new territory, and I didn't know what to expect. It honestly made it kind of fun.

I smiled to myself. I was finally letting go. Having fun. And it was all because Knox made me feel comfortable enough to play.

"Put me down." I struggled against him.

He slapped my ass again, then rubbed circles over the spot. "I'll put you down when I'm ready."

I wouldn't have expected this side of him, and yet, it didn't surprise me. What surprised me more was how much I liked it.

With the men in my past, we'd never teased and taunted like this. We hadn't played games or explored power dynamics. But for the first time—with Knox—I felt...free. Free to be myself. Free to express the desires of my heart.

He set me on his desk, leaning over me. Our breathing ragged. Our bodies drawn together, as always. Yet he didn't touch me, at least not at first.

Instead, he sank into the chair, resting his arms behind his head. Legs spread wide. Cock straining against the towel.

Mm. He liked this as much as I did.

"Touch yourself," he commanded.

I fluttered my fingers at the base of my neck, my skin heated from his words. That hardly seemed like a punishment. So, I slid my hand down my chest, dipping inside my robe.

"Spread your legs." His eyes glittered with darkness, and he lowered his arms. "Let me see how wet you are for me."

I did as he asked, loving the way his attention was focused on me. Loving the way he licked his lips and gripped the arms of the chair. I felt powerful. In control.

"That's it," he said, watching me touch my clit. Squeeze my breasts. I was getting off on the idea of getting him off.

"Are you going to call me 'Daddy' again?" he asked.

I considered it a moment then said, "No." I'd relented because that was what *I* wanted. Not because it was what he'd demanded.

"Good. Now come here." He opened his towel and pulled me onto his lap.

His skin was warm. His legs strong. His cock insistent.

"I can't tell you how many times I've imagined this. *You*," I admitted, as I rocked on top of him. His erection slid between my folds, dangerously close to plunging inside me. We were being reckless, but it felt too good to stop.

"These past few weeks?" he asked, tightening his grip on my hips. Guiding my movements.

I shook my head, tilting it back when he tugged open my robe and began playing with my nipples. "Oh god, Knox."

"Before?" he asked with a lilt to his voice, and I struggled to follow the conversation. The sensations he was provoking inside me were too good. Too distracting.

I nodded slowly. His answering groan rumbled through me, vibrating deep in my core.

"Since when?" He kissed down my neck, his beard scraping my skin, leaving a trail of sparks in his wake.

When I didn't answer, he grasped my throat lightly. "Tell me, Kendall. How long have you fantasized about me?"

I met his eyes and finally gathered the courage to admit the truth. "Since always. But you were… And I was…" I trailed off, too embarrassed to admit any more. Too afraid I'd already said too much.

"With Jude," he finished for me, loosening his hold.

I nodded, but it was more than that. More than Jude. Yes, I'd been dating Knox's son, but he was…well, him. Knox was hot, older, magnetic. He'd always seemed so unattainable.

I nodded slowly, accepting the easy explanation. "Yes."

I feared that would be the end of it, but then he returned his gaze to mine, his eyes hooded. Lust poured through us like the wine that had flowed earlier in the evening.

Did that… Had what I'd said turned him on?

"You might have been his," he said, his eyes intent on mine. "But I saw you first. I wanted you first."

He gripped my hips, pulling me back down onto his lap,

letting me feel again just how much he wanted me. I gasped when his hardness nudged against my core.

"You did?"

"Do you remember the night we met?" he asked.

"At the party on your yacht?" I remembered it vividly.

Jude had invited his buddy, Cade, Emmy, and some of our other friends to the party. Emmy had dragged me along. It was the first time I'd met Jude. But before I'd ever set eyes on him, I'd seen Knox.

Powerful. Charismatic. Handsome. His world was so different from mine, he might as well have lived in a different universe.

Knox nodded. "That fucking neon-green swimsuit." He dropped his head to his chest. "And then you started talking to me about soccer."

I laughed, stunned that he remembered what I'd been wearing. That he remembered *me*. "That's what did it, huh?"

"That's what did it." He captured my lips in a searing kiss.

"So you were attracted to me because I love soccer?" I teased.

"I was attracted to *you*." He tucked my hair behind my ear. "Surely you noticed."

"I-I—" I stuttered. "I had no idea."

If only I'd known…

"The entire time, I imagined what it would be like to touch you. Kiss you." He slid his hands beneath my robe, caressing my ass. "I can't tell you how many times I dreamed of pulling aside those flimsy bottoms and sinking into you."

I shivered from his words. From the desire that practically oozed from his voice. "I'm sure it didn't take much. I was practically naked, and my nipples were hard anytime you were around."

He gripped my hips, rocking up and against me. "That was for me?"

I nodded, remembering how attracted I'd been to Knox from the moment I'd seen him standing at the railing. I hadn't known who he was. I hadn't known he was the owner of the Leatherbacks or that he had a son. The realization hadn't come until later. Until after I'd started dating Jude.

But I didn't want to think about Jude. I was too far gone at this point. Too tired of ignoring my wants and needs for a man who'd never put me first.

"What else did you think about?" I asked, reveling in Knox's confession.

"What it would be like to suck them." Knox slid his hands up my ribs, cupping my breasts.

I gasped, arching my back, my nipples aching for him to do just that. "Yes. *Please.*"

He tugged the robe aside, baring my breast to him. He stared at me as if I were the most decadent dessert, and then he kissed the underside of my breast, his touch featherlight, his beard gently scraping my skin in the most delicious of ways. He continued to tease and torture me, showering my skin with attention but never touching my nipple. Until finally, he pulled one into his mouth, and I nearly came undone.

"Oh god," I said, shivering from his touch. "That feels...so good."

His cocky grin told me he was as pleased by my reaction as I was by his ministrations. And the way his hard-on dug into me promised so much more to come.

"Even better than I'd hoped," he said.

I angled my head back and moaned as he continued lapping and sucking, using his teeth against my skin. I'd never had someone show my nipples so much attention, and my pleasure was building, wound so tight I thought I might explode from that alone. I hadn't thought it possible—at least not for me. But when I allowed myself to relax and receive the pleasure Knox was intent on giving me, I found the precipice growing closer and closer.

"And then last summer..." He trailed off, and I knew he was avoiding mentioning Jude.

So I picked up the thread, going back to that moment in time. Rewriting our story with Knox. "You'd walk around shirtless. Your tanned skin glistening..." I gasped when he added his fingers to my clit.

"You wanted me," he said. It wasn't a question. We were too lost in the fantasy to care.

"I wanted you." I took a shaky breath. "I wanted you to slide your hand beneath my swimsuit and touch me like you are now."

"Did you?" he rasped.

I wasn't sure whether I had then or I wanted to now, but I was enjoying myself too much to question it.

I pulled my bottom lip between my teeth and moaned both in answer to his question and from what he was doing to me. I writhed on his lap, enjoying the look of desire in his eyes. Loving the fact that he seemed just as out of control as I felt.

I leaned forward, grazing the shell of his ear with my teeth. "I need you inside me, Knox. *Now.*"

He grabbed a condom from the desk drawer and unwrapped it before sliding it down his cock. And then he guided me to his tip then paused. As with so many other things, he waited for me to take the lead. I sank down onto him slowly, both of us groaning in unison, months of pent-up tension finally being released.

"*Mi cielo,*" he sighed, a look of serene contentment overtaking his expression.

"*Cielo,*" I agreed, reveling in the way our bodies fit together.

CHAPTER TEN

Knox

"God, you're sexy," I rasped, wanting Kendall to come. *Needing* her to come. I was barely holding on as she writhed on my lap.

And she was close. It was clear from the way color bloomed on her chest to the way her pussy gripped my cock. She dug her nails into my shoulders, and I stood with her in my arms. Lowering her gently onto the desk.

Thank fuck Jasper had foisted some condoms on me that night at the club all those months ago. I knew he'd intended for me to use them to get over the Leatherback's loss, but I hadn't. And I'd shoved them in this drawer, where they'd sat, unopened. Until now.

"That's it," I said, using my thumb to stroke her clit. Rubbing in circles while I watched the point where our bodies connected. Where I disappeared and she began.

But it was more than the physical connection. I felt it on an emotional level too. I'd always felt it with her, but I'd tried to deny it for so long.

"Knox," she gasped, propping herself up on her elbows. "Oh god." She leaned her head back.

"Eyes on me, Kendall," I demanded, needing to know she was with me. Only ever me.

She lifted her head, her gaze pinned on mine, my hand on her chest. Her hand on my cheek. Deepening that connection.

I leaned in to kiss her, fusing my mouth to hers. Wishing it could always be like this—tongues tangling. Bodies linked. *Paradise.*

I'd called her *mi cielo* on instinct, but I couldn't think of a more fitting description for Kendall. She was my escape. My salvation.

And being with her—like this—was bliss. I'd never felt as contented and whole as I did with her. Being able to give her pleasure brought me more joy than I could've expected—both in and out of the bedroom.

She placed her hand to my cheek. "Knox. Yes." She dug her heels into my ass, spurring me on as she gasped, "Harder."

We clung to each other, and I watched as she was overcome with pleasure once more. As her body tensed and released. As she gave in.

I didn't want it to end, but I couldn't hold back anymore. I sank into her again and again, letting loose until there was nothing left to give. Until I finally slumped over her, my heart racing, a sheen of sweat on my skin.

I lay there a moment then finally pulled back and swept her hair away from her face, trying to assess what she was thinking.

She shook her head, her eyes still glazed. "I can't believe we just did that."

My heart clenched painfully. *Did she regret it?*

But then she smiled and placed her palm over my heart, quieting my fears.

"Come on." I straightened then grabbed her hand, pulling her up. "Let's go upstairs."

"Good." She yawned. "I could use some sleep."

I gave her ass a satisfying slap. "There will be none of that."

She giggled and pulled on the robe, swaying as she did so. I scooped her into my arms and carried her back up the stairs to my room.

Okay, maybe we'd sleep some. But if we only had one night, I planned to make the most of my time with her. And I certainly did. Waking her with my head between her legs. Another time, I woke to her mouth around my cock. I lost count of the number of times I made her come.

Now it was morning, and last night had been…incredible. One of the best nights of my life. And while I knew it was a one-time deal, I wasn't ready for it to end. The sun might be peeking over the horizon, but as long as Kendall was in my bed—in my arms—I wasn't going to let her go.

At least, I hadn't intended to any time soon. I turned and frowned at the empty pillow next to me, the down still indented from her head.

I heard rustling from down the hall, so I grabbed a pair of athletic shorts and pulled them on. When I made it to the door to Kendall's room, she was frantically pulling on a pair of yoga pants.

"What's the matter?" I asked, glancing at the clock. It was early. Too early. "What's going on?"

She jolted but quickly resumed getting dressed. Was she freaking out about what we'd done? Did she regret it? Or had something else happened?

"Kendall." I stood before her, blocking her path. "Talk to me."

"I—" She hesitated, looking anywhere but at me. "I need to leave. I have to go."

"Go where?" I asked, hating the idea, but especially when she seemed so upset.

"My mom—" She shook her head. "She was admitted to the hospital."

I pulled her into my arms, holding her to my chest. We stayed that way for a moment, and I pressed a kiss to the top of her head. "I'll make breakfast while you shower, and then I'll take you up there."

"I—" She pulled away. "I can't. I have to go."

"Okay. I'll just put on a shirt and grab my things." I moved to leave.

"Please." She rolled her bottom lip between her teeth. "You have to stop being so nice to me. You're making this harder than it already is."

"Making what harder?" I frowned.

"Everything." She said the word with such a sense of finality. "We both know I can't stay. And after last night—" She shook her head, not meeting my eyes. "Well, I appreciate everything you've done for me. I appreciate it more than you could ever know."

She straightened, and I furrowed my brow. I sensed I wouldn't like what she had to say next.

I rubbed the back of my neck. "Why do I feel like you're saying goodbye?"

She pressed her lips together then said, "Because I am."

"Kendall," I sighed, trying to make sense of everything. "What about the job?"

She shook her head. "I can't take it. We both know I can't."

"Because of last night," I said. It wasn't really a question.

I'd known last night would change things, but I'd never expected her to pull away.

"Because of everything." She pulled a shirt over her head, paying me no more attention. I stood there, feeling helpless as I watched her.

When she zipped her tote bag and stood, I took it from her. I followed her down the stairs, hating everything about this. She headed for her car, but I headed for mine.

"Hop in." I opened the passenger door. "I'll drive."

"Thanks, but no." She tried to take the bag from me. But when it was clear I wouldn't budge, she narrowed her eyes at me.

I placed my hand on the small of her back, steering her toward the passenger door of the Maserati. "That wasn't a request." She glared up at me, but I stood my ground. "Get in."

She took a steadying breath. "I can take care of myself."

"I know you can," I huffed, frustrated beyond belief. With her. But mostly with the situation. "But it's okay to let people help you. It's okay to let them in." *To let me in.*

"I've already wasted enough time," she said, ducking beneath my arm. She slid into the Range Rover, shutting the door quickly and firing up the engine.

Unbelievable.

She rolled down the window before she reached the gate. "I'm sorry. I have to go. I'll get my stuff later."

Vincent popped his head out of the guard shack. But when he saw my face, he quickly disappeared once more.

I gnashed my teeth and watched as her car disappeared into the distance. I debated going after her, but I had a feeling that would only upset her more. So, I went inside and showered, trying to make sense of it all. Kendall's decisions. My own. Everything.

When I caught sight of the backyard, my eyes went wide. Kendall's dress and my shirt and pants were strewn across the grass. I picked them up, tossing my shirt in the trash before dropping the other garments into my laundry bin.

I checked my phone again and again throughout the morning, but there were no missed text messages or calls from Kendall. I'd reached out to her, letting her know to call if she needed anything. But judging from this morning and her continued silence, I had a feeling she wouldn't.

She'd been in my bed only a few hours ago, and now she was gone.

Perhaps I should've been relieved. With other women, I would've been. But all I felt was a gaping hole. A realization that everything had changed and nothing would be the same. And the idea of my life without Kendall felt even emptier than it had before.

When the security alarm chimed three times then twice, I jogged toward the front door. "Kendall. Oh, thank god," I said in a rush.

But when I rounded the corner to the foyer, it wasn't Kendall. It was Jude.

"Dad?" He scanned my features. "Is everything okay?"

"Um. Hey, Jude." I cleared my throat. My heart was fucking racing, and I thought I was going to be sick. "What are you doing here?"

He tilted his head to the side. "You invited me over for brunch. So we could look over the numbers for the team. Remember?"

Fuck. Fuck!

"That's right." I clapped a hand on his shoulder and ushered him inside, my gut twisting with guilt. "Come in. Come in."

"You seem...flustered." His expression betrayed concern. "Are you sure you're okay?"

"I, uh—" I shoved my hands into my pockets. What a fucking mess.

I felt guilty as fuck about what I'd done. And I knew Jude would lose it if he ever found out. And then there was Kendall. I was unsettled by how we'd left things this morning. She'd been in such a rush. And I worried about her and her mom.

But I couldn't tell Jude all that, so I said, "I'm worried about Kendall. Her mom was admitted to the hospital."

"I hope everything's okay," Jude said. "When I talked to Emmy recently, she said Kendall's mom was going in for another round of treatment soon, but she'd been doing well."

"Hopefully this is only a minor setback," I said.

"Yeah." He grabbed a glass from the cupboard and filled it with orange juice. "They've been through a lot. That's why I'm really hoping Kendall will take the job with the Leatherbacks."

"Not likely," I said.

"Really? I thought she'd be excited about it. Seems like it'd be right up her alley."

I shook my head, trying to maintain a calm façade. "It's not what she wants."

"She told you that?" he asked. When I nodded, he said, "When? I thought you were going to offer her the position last night."

"I did. And she declined it." This morning. After I'd slept with her. I took a deep breath, feeling completely out of control.

Jude set his glass down on the counter with more force than was necessary. "Well, we'll just have to change her mind, won't we?" He smoothed his palms over the surface.

"Jude." I rubbed a hand over my face, wondering what the hell I'd been thinking. "I don't think she's going to change her mind."

"So, that's it? You're really just going to let her go?" he asked, and I wondered if he regretted letting her go months ago.

"You did," I said, hoping to remind him of that fact. And

then immediately regretting it. I sounded like a jealous asshole, and I was lashing out at my son, of all people.

His shoulders slumped. "That was different."

"It's just a job. Kendall's a smart, capable young woman. I'm sure she'll find what she's looking for." *It just isn't me.*

"It's not *just* a job. I heard from a mutual friend that she needs the money."

I furrowed my brow. "What are you talking about?"

"Her mom hasn't been able to work for months. Kendall's been taking care of her and paying their bills. And you know as well as I do that medical expenses aren't cheap."

I nodded, thinking of how much the Leatherbacks spent on health care.

Kendall was carrying so much more than I'd realized.

"She never mentioned it," I said.

"Yeah, well, you know how she is. But I'll convince her." He leaned across the counter. "So, do you want to go out for brunch or stay in?"

I lifted a shoulder, still processing everything Jude had told me. "My chef asked for the morning off at the last minute. But if it's all the same to you, I'd rather stay in."

Brunch in LA wasn't *just* a meal out. It was a chance to be seen. And after the morning I'd had, I was in no mood to put on a smile and keep up appearances. Trying to act normal in front of Jude was challenging enough.

"Fine," he said. "As long as you cook."

"Deal." He was a terrible cook. Probably because he thought it was an annoyance, where I found it relaxing.

"You start the omelets, and I'll grab your laptop."

"Sounds good." I headed for the fridge and started pulling out ingredients.

A moment later, it hit me. He'd headed toward my office. The office where I'd taken Kendall on my desk.

My eyes widened in panic, and I scrambled down the hall. "Jude, wait."

"Whoa. Ho. Ho. Someone had a wild night," Jude said as I skidded to a stop in front of the door.

Papers were still scattered on the floor. My pen cup had been knocked over, the contents strewn across the desk. My usually tidy office was a disaster, much like my thoughts.

And then I watched in horror as Jude used the end of a pen to indicate the discarded condom wrapper that had fallen just beside the trash can. He gave me a pointed look. "Care to explain this?"

"No." I turned for the door, needing to get out of there. Away from the evidence of last night.

It was both a painful reminder of the power Kendall had over me and the fact that I'd betrayed my son in the most unthinkable of ways. In that moment, I was hit with the full force of what I'd done, and I nearly vomited on the $40,000 rug Kendall had helped me choose for the office.

"And all this time," Jude said, his footsteps shuffling down the hall behind me, "I thought maybe you were secretly holding out hope that you and Mom would get back together."

"What?" I jerked back my head. "No." I barked out a laugh, mostly to cover just how uncomfortable I was. "We're definitely better off as friends." I stilled, turning my attention back to him as it dawned on me. "Why? Do you wish we'd get back together?"

"No." He laughed. "I guess I wondered if that was why you never date. Because you're still hung up on Mom."

I closed my eyes and pinched the bridge of my nose. If he only knew…

"I love your mom, but I like our relationship as it is. We're better as friends."

"So, who was your lady friend?" he asked.

"A gentleman…"

"You were with a guy?" He smirked. "Interesting."

I rolled my eyes in an effort to hide my discomfort. I was worried Jude would put the pieces together and realize what I'd done. Who I'd been with.

"I know. I know." He held up his hands. "A gentleman never kisses and tells. Just answer one question." I tried to school my face into a neutral expression as I waited. "Is it serious?"

I shook my head, forcing out the words, "It's—" I blew out a breath. "Nothing."

Because it could never be anything more than last night. One perfect night that never should've happened.

CHAPTER ELEVEN

Kendall

I lifted my shirt to my nose, inhaling the scent of Knox's cologne. It smelled like vacation. Like freedom and fun. Like comfort.

He always made me feel so safe. And even just having this small token of his was calming. It grounded me, blocking out the smell of antiseptic.

God, I hate hospitals.

I peered over at my mom. She was sleeping peacefully, and her vitals looked good. She'd been admitted early this morning for an infection, and after testing, they'd discovered she had mono.

Unbelievable.

I wanted to blame Joe, but I knew he felt terrible. Besides, he'd been the one to convince her to come to the hospital. And he'd been at her side the entire time.

The doctors assured me she would recover, but we hadn't had a scare like this since the beginning. It didn't matter that Joe was here. I should've been with her. I should've been paying better attention so it wouldn't have reached this point.

But I'd been distracted. Wrapped up in Knox. And not just last night.

God. Last night.

The memory of it filled me with equal parts pleasure and guilt. It was empowering and liberating. And also so, *so* wrong. Part of me still couldn't believe what I'd done.

I'd slept with my boss. Well, technically, my former boss. But even more than that, I'd slept with Jude's dad. I'd slept with two men who were related—first the son, and now his father.

What the hell is wrong with me?

"Kendall," Joe said, placing his hand on my shoulder. "Why don't you go home? Get some breakfast or a shower."

"I'm fine," I snapped, then immediately regretted it. "Sorry. I'm—" I rubbed my eyes. "I didn't get much sleep last night." And I *hated* hospitals.

"I know." He rubbed a hand over his face, his eyes on Mom. And I realized Joe had lost sleep for an entirely different reason. Which only made me feel worse for not being there for her.

"I shouldn't have snapped at you. I know you're only trying to help. I'm just—" I blew out a breath. I wasn't used to this—having someone be there for us. Be there for Mom. "I'm worried about her."

And how we were going to afford this. Between her medical debt and my student loans, we were barely keeping our heads above water. The placement with Knox had been nice while it had lasted, but now that was over.

Hopefully the Hartwell Agency would find something else, but there was no knowing how long that would take. And with how unpredictable the tutoring website had been lately, I couldn't depend on that either.

Maybe I should've taken Knox up on his job offer.

"She's going to be okay," Joe said with more confidence than I felt. "She has to."

The way he looked at her, with such intensity and devotion, I realized it was the way Knox looked at me. My heart clenched painfully in my chest, and I sank down onto the chair and placed my head in my hands.

A headache had been building all morning. And I had a feeling no amount of coffee would cure what ailed me. This was more than an "orgasm hangover," as Emmy would've called it.

Last night was... Well, it was only supposed to be for one night, but what a night it had been. The culmination of months of tension. The realization that it had been so much more than just sex.

Which was exactly why I'd left.

Why I'd turned down the job.

Why I couldn't see Knox again.

Granted, I'd freaked out. But I knew I'd made the right decision. Because it would be too painful to know what it was like to be with him while trying to accept that it could never happen again.

And Jude... God. *Jude.* There was no way I could ever face him after last night.

It was best to end things now. To leave. Before someone got hurt.

Before *I* got hurt.

"Kendall," Joe said, careful to keep his voice low. "If you won't go home, at least go to the cafeteria."

"Okay." I stood, knowing he was right. "Do you want anything?"

"I'll get something later," he said.

I nodded and wandered down the hall in a zombie-like state. My phone buzzed with a new message, but I didn't even bother glancing at the screen. Knox had texted me on and off throughout the morning, and I didn't know how to respond.

What I really needed was to talk to Emmy. So I headed to the cafeteria to grab some breakfast and call her about... well, everything. I was on my way there when I spotted Jude. He was carrying a vase of flowers and scanning the hallway.

I panicked, my heart racing. I tried to turn to go a different way, but it was too late. He'd already spotted me, and he was smiling.

"Kendall. I'm so glad I found you."

"Jude?" I gaped at him, wondering if I was delusional. Was the universe mocking me? "What are you doing here?"

"I wanted to come check on you. And bring these to your mom." He held up an enormous vase of flowers. Cheerful and bright, just like her.

"That's so sweet of you. But..." I frowned. "How did you know we were here?"

"I had brunch with Dad this morning, and he mentioned that your mom was admitted. So I checked on social media."

I lifted my chin but stayed silent. I wondered if Knox had mentioned anything else.

I was still processing everything when Jude opened his arm for a side hug. I hesitated. Hugging Jude after sleeping with Knox just felt...wrong.

"I, um, haven't showered." I tucked my hair behind my ear.

And I slept with your dad.

"I like it when you're dirty." He winked, which only made me feel worse. About sleeping with Knox. About the way Jude was flirting with me, despite having a girlfriend. "Get over here."

The walls were pressing in on me, the drab color making my temples throb and pulse. And the fact that I still hadn't hugged Jude was getting increasingly awkward. So, seeing no other option, I stepped into his open embrace.

"Sorry." I gave him a hug, feeling as if I were somehow betraying Knox even though I didn't owe him anything. "My manners seem to have gone missing."

Along with my morals.

Why did I feel worse about hugging Jude than having sex with his dad?

Jude chuckled, giving me a quick squeeze. "I get it. If it were my dad in the hospital..." He shook his head, and bile rose in my throat.

Oh god. If Jude knew the truth...

"Ken?" Jude asked, placing his hand on my lower back. "Are you okay? You're white as a sheet."

"I'm—" I tried to push down my guilt. "I was headed to grab a bite to eat."

"Let me drop these off in your mom's room, and I'll go with you."

"No, that's—"

"I insist," he said, and I could tell he wasn't going to budge. "Besides, these hallways are so serpentine. I could use a guide, or I fear I'll never make it out alive," he joked.

I let out a deep sigh and walked back to Mom's room, this time with Jude and his bouquet. Mom was still asleep, and Joe was dozing in the chair beside her, their hands locked. Jude smiled and set the flowers on the windowsill before sneaking back out to join me in the hall.

"They're cute."

"He's a good guy," I said. "I'm not sure I've ever seen her this happy."

"I wish my dad could find someone who made him happy like that," Jude said. "Though..." He hesitated.

"What?" I asked.

He shook his head. "No. I probably shouldn't tell you."

"Tell me what?" I asked, concern for Knox overriding my better judgment.

"It's just..." He leaned in. "I found a torn condom wrapper in his office."

I held a hand to my stomach, my eyes going wide. *Oh god. I'm going to be sick.*

"Come on." He wrapped his arm around my shoulder, perhaps realizing the horror on my face. "I shouldn't have mentioned it. And I'm sure you'll feel better once we get some food in you."

During the walk, he asked about my mom. About how I was holding up. He was kind and friendly, and I realized that maybe I'd underestimated him. Maybe he would've been there for me if I'd let him. He was here now, despite the fact that we'd broken up.

"Why are you being so nice to me?" I finally asked when we sat down at a table, a stack of waffles on my tray. At least they smelled good.

Or maybe I was just *that* hungry that even hospital cafeteria food seemed appealing. I hadn't eaten since dinner last night. Was it any wonder I was starving after the workout Knox had given me?

"Because I care about you, Ken," Jude said, flashing me a genuine smile. "Isn't it obvious?"

"But we broke up," I said, confused. My head and my heart were all over the place.

"It was amicable. And exes can still be friends." He grabbed a piece of bacon from my plate and took a bite. "I mean, look at my parents."

"True." I nodded, dipping my waffle into the syrup.

I'd always admired the way Jude's parents interacted. They might have been divorced, but they'd remained friends. They'd prioritized their family dynamic even though they were no longer married.

"And to be totally honest, I might have also had a selfish motive for coming here," he said.

I frowned, dreading the direction of the conversation. Instead of saying anything, I shoved a big piece of waffle in my mouth.

"Why did you turn down the job?"

"Jude..." I let out a sigh. I really did not have the energy for this. I decided the universe wasn't mocking me, but rather punishing me.

"Is it because of me?"

"No." I stared at my plate.

"Is it because of Dad? I know he can be demanding sometimes, but he'll be good to you."

Oh, how I knew that. I had firsthand knowledge. I squeezed my thighs together, remembering how empowered I'd felt. How nice it had been to do something for myself for once.

"Kendall?" he asked.

I shook my head. "Your dad is great."

Too great. That was the problem.

"Look—" Jude took my hand in his. "I know it's not your dream job, but it's a good opportunity. It's stable and pays well. You'd get free tickets to the games. And I'm sure Dad would be flexible with your schedule."

I sighed, wishing I could accept. "I know, but..."

He held up a hand. "You've had a crazy morning. Take some more time to think about it before you make a decision."

"I don't need more time," I said, pushing my food around the plate. "I'm not going to change my mind."

My phone chimed with an incoming text message from Emmy. When I saw the screen, I frowned at the link she'd sent.

"What is it?" Jude asked, then leaned over, reading my

screen. "Holy shit."

I squeezed my eyes shut. This was a nightmare. It had to be. Any minute, I'd wake up and realize none of it was real.

But when I opened my eyes again, the news article was still sitting there. The tutoring website had been shut down, pending a federal investigation. And I was out of a job.

"Seems like a message from the universe," Jude said.

I rolled my eyes. "Or it's just bad luck."

"Well, then it's *lucky*—" he nudged me with his elbow "—I came here to offer you a job."

"I have a job. The tutoring gig wasn't my only income source." Just my main one. My stomach clenched.

"The Hartwell Agency?" He shook his head with a laugh. "Do you really want to keep working there?"

"What?" I spat, annoyed with his attitude. Not all of us were sons of billionaires. "It's not good enough for you?"

"It's not good enough for *you*." His eyes pierced mine. "I mean, some of the guys joke that it's the Hard-On Agency. That Hartwell is basically a glorified escort service."

Wow. Even if it wasn't true, I'd fed right into that stereotype. My fork clattered against the plate, and I nearly choked. Jude patted me on the back and slid my water closer.

"You okay?"

"Mm-hmm." I placed a hand to my chest, still trying to catch my breath. "Yep." I swallowed, but it went down like glass.

Once I'd caught my breath, I said, "The Hartwell Agency is reputable. Kings and sultans use them to staff their castles."

He dropped his head. "I'm sorry. I shouldn't joke about something like that. But what we're offering you is so much better. Why would you turn that down?"

I studied him. "Why is it so important to you that I take the job?"

"Because my dad could really use the help. And I get the feeling so could you." His smile was gentle.

I didn't know what to say. Jude was right; I needed the money. But it wasn't that simple. He didn't realize what he was asking.

Then again, maybe I was making this into a bigger deal than it needed to be. Jude and I got along, despite the fact that we used to date. And Knox and I had been professional the past few months, despite our insane chemistry.

Besides, I was moving out of Knox's house. I wouldn't have to see him all the time. And anytime I did, we'd be at the office. With other staff. With Jude.

If Knox and his ex could get along so well after being married and having a son, surely we could handle this. *Right?*

"I'm—" I dropped my head, resignation settling in. "Fine. I'll do it. I'll take the job. But—" I held up a finger when he opened his mouth to speak. "*Only* until he finds a suitable replacement, or I get another full-time placement from Hartwell."

"Fine. Great." Jude was clearly pleased he'd gotten his way. "You won't regret it."

I wasn't so sure about that. But I kept that thought to myself.

CHAPTER TWELVE

Knox

I stood with Jude and some of the players from the team while we waited for the event to begin. The Leatherbacks and I would be visiting with kids undergoing treatment at a local hospital. We'd pass out swag and take pictures, basically have fun and take their minds off things for a little while.

Kendall was busy making the final arrangements with the staff, and I couldn't stop thinking about her. About our night together.

I'd barely seen her since then, apart from the occasional meeting at the office. And even then, she seemed to be avoiding me as much as possible. She'd accepted the job via email. HR had expedited the hiring process.

Kendall had officially moved out of my house, and I told myself it was both necessary and for the best. She was my employee—again. And we'd agreed it couldn't happen *again*. Hell, it shouldn't have happened in the first place.

Jude turned to me with a smile, and I felt even shittier for what I'd done. It would be so much easier if I didn't have to see her every day.

But he'd pushed Kendall to take the job. She'd agreed. And now here we were.

"Who pissed in your oatmeal?" he asked.

"Jude," I chided, hoping none of the staff had overheard his crude comment.

"What? You're the one with the grimace. I thought you loved these events."

"I do," I said. Events with kids were my favorite. They were hilarious and just such a joy.

But they were bittersweet because they reminded me of when Jude was little. I'd barely graduated college when he was born. I hadn't had as much time as I'd wanted to focus on being a dad. And spending time with the kids made me remember just how much I'd always wanted more children.

Tori had been opposed. Even with the help of nannies, she'd said it was too much. She didn't want to wreck her body and have to get back in shape again. And I hadn't pushed because I'd seen the toll the pregnancy had taken on her—especially her mental health.

"What, then?" Jude asked. "Are you worried Kendall won't pull it off?"

I crossed my arms over my chest. "I have full faith in Kendall."

It was myself I didn't trust. Especially when it came to her.

She'd been working with the Leatherbacks for a week, and it had been a struggle to act professionally. To pretend as if nothing had ever happened between us. To ignore my desire to pull her into my arms and do it all again.

"Well?" Jude asked, nudging me.

I kept my eyes trained ahead. "It's nothing."

The door opened, and Kendall came in to greet the players. While she was laughing with a few of them, a man with a hospital badge approached her.

"Kendall." The man hugged her, and my blood surged with possessiveness. I hated it. I hated his hands on her. And I hated my reaction to it.

Was this what it was going to be like from now on?

Standing by. Watching from the sidelines as she moved on with someone else.

I rubbed my chest. Sleeping with Kendall had been ill-advised and short-sighted. I both hated myself for giving in, and would willingly do so again.

Because every time I looked at her, I was reminded of how things could be. I remembered the ecstasy and contentment and connection that I'd felt with her. And I wanted more of it.

"Good to see you," he told her, smiling.

"You too, Timothy." Her tone was genuine, and she practically fucking radiated. It didn't matter that she was in a room full of celebrities; she always captured the attention of anyone lucky enough to be near her. "Thanks for all your help making this event a success."

"Are you kidding? This is all you." He winked, and I shoved my fists in my pocket so no one would see how hard I was clenching them.

She laughed and patted his shoulder. "We make a good team."

When her eyes darted to me, Timothy's attention followed. "Knox." She smiled. "This is Timothy. He's the hospital's point person for the event."

I held out my hand to shake his, maintaining eye contact but keeping my grip even. "Nice to meet you."

"The pleasure is all mine, Mr. Crawford." He grinned. As if he hadn't just been lusting after my woman.

But she wasn't mine.

When Kendall placed her hand on my arm, the contact

soothed me enough to relax. Enough to remember why we were here. And how many eyes might be watching.

"Please," I said, flashing Timothy a warm smile, "call me Knox."

"Well, Knox." He smiled. "We're all very excited for your visit. Do you want to brief the team, Kendall?"

She explained the schedule and asked if there were any questions. She was a natural.

I couldn't stop staring at her. The way her lips parted when she spoke. The sight of her dress clinging to her breasts before flaring out over her hips.

I hadn't even realized she'd finished talking until Jude nudged me. "She's captivating, isn't she?"

You have no idea.

"She's so much more talented than this job," I said.

"Yes, but at least we get to keep her for now." I watched my son out of the corner of my eye, wondering if he wanted another chance with her.

But as he walked off to join some of the players, I reminded myself that Jude was with Chrissy. And they seemed happy together. She and Jude seemed like a good fit.

Our group headed down the hall to the patient wing. Just before we entered, Kendall held up her phone. "You guys go ahead. I have to take this."

I frowned as she turned and darted back down the hall in the direction we'd come. Her skin was pale, her expression drawn. And I worried that the call was about her mother.

I held the door open for the players, waiting until they'd all passed through before turning to follow Kendall. Her hair whipped behind her as she rushed down the hall and disappeared into the bathroom.

I waited for her to come out, and when time stretched on, I began to worry even more. When I couldn't take it any longer, I knocked on the restroom door. "Kendall? It's Knox. Are you okay?"

"Be out in a minute," she called in a cheery voice. But I wasn't buying it.

I leaned against the wall and waited. The door eventually opened, and she nearly collided with me.

"Hey." I grasped her biceps. She seemed more than a little shaken up. "What's wrong? Is your mom okay?"

"Yes." She jerked her head back. "Why?"

"Because you took a call. And you looked concerned. So I…"

She pasted on a bright smile that I saw right through and said, "I'm fine."

I narrowed my eyes at her. "Kendall."

She huffed. "I'm not a big fan of hospitals."

I didn't know many people who were, but she seemed more affected by it. "Because of your mom?"

She nodded. "Because of the smells. The sounds." She shuddered. "It reminds me of all the times I've had to wait for my mom. Wondering whether she'd survive the surgery or not. Worried about the future."

"Why didn't you tell me?" More importantly, why hadn't that crossed my mind?

When she'd told me she didn't need to attend the event after I'd insisted, I'd thought she'd been afraid of intruding. Selfishly, I'd wanted her by my side. And I'd wanted her to see the fruition of her hard work. If only I'd realized… I should've realized.

Her skin was still just as pale as it had been before, and she looked as if she might be sick.

I leaned in, rubbing circles on her back. I told myself I was merely comforting a colleague, but it was a lie. "Do you want to leave?"

"No." She frowned and shook her head. "Of course not."

She straightened, pressing her shoulders back. "I'll be fine. I just... For some reason, it's affecting me more today. I think maybe because I know the patients are kids. And I didn't get enough sleep because I wanted to make this the best day ever for them."

My heart softened. Of course she had.

But when she took a step forward, she seemed to sway. There was no way she was ready to join the others. I peeked inside the bathroom and noticed it was a single stall with a large bench.

"Knox," she hissed when I grabbed her arm, ushering her inside. "What are you doing?"

"I know you say you'll be fine. And I know you're tough. But it's not going to be 'the best day ever' if you faint in front of them. You're not ready to go in there. Not like this." I guided her to the bench then locked the door.

"B-but—" She sputtered. "We're... This..." Her eyes went wide. At least she no longer looked like she was going to be sick.

"No one saw us," I said. "If that's what you're worried about."

She nodded. Her shoulders relaxed. After a moment, she closed her eyes and leaned her head back against the wall. "I'm sorry. I just need a minute. And maybe some breakfast. And then I'll be fine."

"You haven't eaten?" I asked. When she shook her head, I cursed under my breath. "Why not?"

"I was too nervous about making sure the event was a success. And I worried about traffic. And..."

"Let's get you something to eat," I said.

"What?" She jerked her head back. "We can't just leave. Especially not you."

Of course I could. And I would. I would do whatever the fuck it took to make sure Kendall was okay. That thought should've scared me, but if anything, it only felt right.

"As your boss—" I shoved my hands in my pockets "—I think you should go home."

Her eyes shifted, green slits of fury flecked with gold. "No."

"Kendall," I growled.

She stood and placed her hands on her hips, this conversation having the complete opposite effect of what I'd intended. I'd wanted to help her relax. I'd wanted to assure her that she'd done her job and she could leave.

Yet she was standing her ground.

I shouldn't have been surprised. Hell, I'd always encouraged her to speak her mind. If I hadn't been so annoyed by her stubbornness, I would've been proud of her.

"I want to stay. If these kids can endure all that they do just to survive," she said, eyes blazing with passion, "I sure as heck can handle this."

I bit back a smile, admiring her determination. Admiring her fire, despite her discomfort. But as much as I respected her dedication, I was more concerned with taking care of her.

"Should I threaten to fire you?" I asked, mostly in jest. Part of me wanted to fire her because then she'd no longer be off-limits. Well, at least, she'd no longer be off-limits for *that* reason.

She stepped closer, closing the distance between us. "Maybe I should quit."

Tension crackled between us. I pushed her, and she challenged me.

"Am I really that terrible to work for?" I asked, my voice low as I searched her expression. Her breathing was shallow, and I would've killed to know what she was thinking.

"No. Yes. Ugh." She turned and threw her hands in the air.

"This is all your fault." She started pacing, her heels clicking against the tile floor.

I furrowed my brow. "How is this *my* fault?"

"If you weren't so...so..." Her cheeks were pink, and I would've laughed if she weren't so flustered, if I didn't feel that same frustration, that same longing, too.

"So...what?" I asked. We'd been dancing around this all week. It was time to just get it out there.

"Amazing," she spat the word like it was a bad thing. "This wouldn't be so difficult."

"You know what's difficult?" I asked, my chest rising and falling more rapidly the closer I got to her. "Knowing what you feel like but not being able to touch you. Pretending I feel *nothing* when I want you so badly, I ache."

She stepped closer, placing her hands on my chest. "Knox." She peered up at me, her hazel eyes questioning. Wanting.

I was already close to my breaking point, and I didn't know how much more I could take.

"Kendall." I clenched my hands at my sides so I wouldn't touch her. I closed my eyes and took a steadying breath. She was temptation personified. She was going to be my damnation.

But when I opened them again, all I saw were her beautiful eyes peering up at me. And in that moment, everything else faded away. "*Mi cielo.*"

"Touch me, Knox. Please," she whispered. It was my undoing.

"If I touch you," I rasped, my control so damn close to snapping, "I won't be able to stop."

"Maybe I don't want to stop." Her swallow echoed against the tile walls, and I was taken back to that night. To the way she'd swallowed my cock. Then my come. "Maybe I'm tired of trying to fight this."

I grabbed her hips without thinking. Instinctively knowing exactly where to place my hands. My body came alive from her touch, as if I'd been denied oxygen. She was the air I breathed, and I needed more.

I slid my hands up her waist, her rib cage, stopping just below her breasts. I wanted to kiss her. I wanted to taste her again. Consume her the way she consumed my thoughts.

She was such a fucking distraction.

"Even if this is a bad idea," she whispered, echoing my words from our night together. I cupped her cheek, wondering if she was referring to this moment or our relationship.

"Is it?" I asked, leaning in and touching my nose to hers. "Because it's the only thing that feels right."

"I know," she groaned, moving closer still, until our lips nearly touched. Our breath mingling. "Staying away from you has been torture. But we can't..."

I leaned in, caging her in my arms. How could something so wrong feel so right? "We already did."

"You know what I mean," she said, as I ran my nose down her cheek, behind her ear. Taking her coconut scent deep into my lungs and trying to memorize it. "It's different now. I'm your employee. And I need this job."

I had a plan for that. But right now... "I. Need. You," I spoke the words beside her ear, each one revealing just how unraveled I'd become.

"I need you too," she said, breaking the last thread of my resistance.

So much for keeping my distance.

So much for the rules.

I turned her so her back was to me, hands braced on the wall. The position perfectly showcased her form, drawing my eyes up from her heels to her ass to her gorgeous waterfall of hair that flowed down her back. I slid my hand over her stomach until I was cupping her mound.

"Knox." My name was a moan, a plea as she arched back into me. Pressing her ass against my hard-on.

I glanced back at the door to confirm it was locked. Even knowing how risky this was, I couldn't stop touching her. Wanting her.

"This was what you wanted, wasn't it?" I asked, stilling my hand. Waiting for confirmation to proceed.

"I—" She let out a shaky breath. "Yes."

I caressed her thigh, lifting her skirt until I could access her panties. But she wasn't wearing any.

"Naughty girl," I said, gripping her hip. "Were you secretly hoping for this?"

"Maybe." It sounded as if she was biting her lip, trying to keep quiet.

"You wanted me to fuck this sweet pussy," I said, sliding my fingers through her slick folds. All the while, I kissed her neck, her shoulder, anywhere I could reach.

"*Yes*," she gasped, arching back into me. I held her tight, not wanting to give her an inch. Not wanting to let her go. "Yes, Knox. Fuck me."

She whimpered when I increased my pressure, concentrating on the sensitive nub. Her hips were rocking now, and she was trying to hump my hand. I fucking loved how wild she was.

"Will you stop torturing me now?" she begged.

"*Mi cielo*," I said, slipping my other hand into her hair and fisting it. I pulled gently, tilting her head back so her face was angled toward mine. "You've tortured me since the moment I laid eyes on you. I'm only just getting started."

"This—" She shook her head. "No. This is it. The last time. We'll get each other out of our systems once and for all."

I chuckled, the sound dark as it echoed off the tile walls. I didn't think that would be possible. At least not for me.

I couldn't do it. I wasn't going to let her walk away from me again.

I didn't know what that meant for our future, but I refused to have a repeat of our first time together. So, I removed my hand, licking it clean before putting her skirt back in place.

She tilted her head back, her lips extra pouty. "What are you doing?"

With more restraint than I thought possible, I said, "Later."

She turned to face me, skin still flushed. "What do you mean—*later*?"

"We're going to talk about this more later. At my house," I said, knowing I was taking a risk. Knowing it was going to be fucking painful to try to ignore this hard-on until then. "Tomorrow night. Over dinner."

I didn't want to wait that long. I didn't want to give her even more time to change her mind. But I was supposed to attend a business dinner tonight with the MLS commissioner and some of the other team owners, and it was an engagement I could not break.

Besides, if Kendall came over tomorrow night, I could give her my full attention. We could spend the weekend together. I was already imagining it, in detail.

But then she placed her hands on her hips. "And what if I say no?"

"Do you want another orgasm?"

She narrowed her eyes at me. "You play dirty, Crawford."

"No, Kendall." I took her chin in my hand. "I play to win." I adjusted myself and headed for the door. "And I'll be waiting for you."

She muttered something under her breath that sounded a

lot like, "Cocky bastard," but I merely smiled and continued on, pumping some hand sanitizer and rubbing my hands together before I left.

When I reached the patient wing, I could hear the excitement bubbling out. I grabbed some of the team gear we'd brought to give away and started making the rounds. The kids were adorable, and their parents seemed just as giddy about our visit.

I took pictures of them with the players and laughed when some of the guys attempted to put on a puppet show. Jude was busy with some of the other kids, and I was relieved he didn't seem to have noticed my absence.

I didn't know what Kendall and I were going to do about my son, but staying away from her wasn't working. Maybe I should've been stronger. Maybe I should've tried harder. But I was so tired of fighting it.

Kendall entered a minute later, her expression betraying nothing of what had just transpired between us. She took a seat at a table where some kids were crafting, eagerly joining in the efforts despite her distaste for hospitals.

I admired how she threw herself into the job. How she dedicated herself to making sure the event ran smoothly, and participated as well.

She said something, and the kids erupted into laughter. They adored her. Hell, who wouldn't?

Kendall and I had never talked about children, but it was clear she delighted in them, as did I. She would be a great mom someday—if that was what she wanted. But I couldn't be the person to give it to her.

CHAPTER THIRTEEN

Kendall

"You okay?" Emerson asked as she rolled up her yoga mat beside me. "You seem distracted today."

"Yeah," I exhaled slowly, staring at the ceiling. My mind still spinning. My body on overdrive.

We'd just finished a class with our favorite instructor, and going through the poses had helped me feel calmer and more centered. But only marginally so. My mind was still on Knox. On what he'd said yesterday, when we were at the hospital for the Leatherbacks event.

I'd been hoping to tell Emmy about everything with Knox, but she'd been out of town. And now, I didn't even know where to start.

He was hot. It was forbidden. We were a secret. And it needed to stay that way.

So, I contemplated what to say. I'd slept with Knox once. I could still brush it off as a mistake.

But in my heart, it didn't feel like a mistake. At least, if I ignored the fact that I'd dated his son. I'd *slept with* his son.

That was the part that always made me cringe.

But I couldn't *not* tell Emmy. She was my best friend. And

she would never think less of me, even if I was totally judging myself for sleeping with my ex's dad.

I opened my mouth to tell her, but before I could speak, she asked, "How's your mom doing?"

"Better, thanks," I said, shoving down my confession. At least for the moment. "Joe hasn't left her side."

"Aw. That's sweet."

I kneeled and started rolling my own mat. "It would be if I didn't have a front-row air mattress to their budding romance."

She frowned. "It sucks that you had to move out of Knox's and back into her living room."

"Hopefully it's only temporary," I said, though I had no idea how I could justify the expense of moving out of Mom's. But hey, maybe the Hartwell Agency would come through with another house-sitting placement. Even if it seemed like a long shot.

"You've been through a lot. Not just the past year, but the past few weeks," she said, placing her hand on my shoulder. "Your placement ended, your mom was in the hospital, your tutoring gig was..." She shook her head. "Well, I didn't see that one coming."

"Neither did I," I said, still trying to wrap my mind around the fact that the tutoring website was being investigated for fraud.

Maybe I should've realized something sketchy was going on. For weeks, I'd been annoyed with the lack of customer service and the declining enrollment. But I'd assumed it was a temporary glitch. It sucked that I wasn't going to be paid for the last month. But at least I wouldn't have to testify or be involved going forward.

"I suppose it's not all bad." She smiled. "You got a new job with the Leatherbacks."

"True," I said, taking my time to smooth out any wrinkles

before setting the mat in the bin with the others. She continued talking as we grabbed our shoes, but my mind was stuck on my new job. It was fulfilling. And I loved working with the team, even if it was a struggle to focus anytime Knox was near.

"Kendall?" Emmy asked.

"Hm?" I glanced up.

"I asked how you like your new job."

She'd given me the perfect opening to talk about Knox. I decided to ease into it.

"It's good." I nodded. "Well, mostly."

"I thought the event went well."

"I—" I sighed. "Yeah."

"Well, don't be too hard on yourself. You only just started. I'm sure it'll get easier once you learn the ropes."

We walked in silence a moment, the pressure building within me with every step closer to the juice bar. We were nearly to the counter when I blurted, "It's not about learning the ropes. I did…something. Something really bad."

She turned to me slowly, her eyes widening. We'd been friends long enough that I knew she was connecting the dots. "Something or *someone*?"

"Next," called the guy behind the counter.

"Oh. My. God," Emmy gasped, grabbing my arm. "Shut. Up."

"*Next*," the guy said again, this time more insistent.

"Emmy." I prodded her. "It's our turn."

"I'll take a raspberry lychee," Emmy rattled off our order, barely taking her eyes off me. "And she wants an apple kale." She tapped her card and paid before I could even process what she'd done.

"It was my turn to pay," I said, though I knew she wouldn't let me pay anyway. She never did.

"Who cares about that." She pulled me aside while we

waited for our order. "I can't believe you're sleeping with your boss."

My cheeks heated. "Emmy!" I hissed, my gaze darting around the shop. "Keep your voice down."

The fewer people who knew, the better. There was more than just my job at stake. Knox's relationship with his son. Hell, his plans for the team.

When they called Emmy's name, I quickly grabbed our juices from the counter. Then I steered her toward a table on the sidewalk, and she slumped down in the chair across from me.

"Oh my god. I thought you'd deny it. Or tell me I was wrong. Not...not..." She leaned across the table, her eyes searching my face. "It's really true?"

I opened my mouth, but instead of trying to shut it down, I whisper-hissed, "You can't tell *anyone.*"

"*Holy.* Fuck," she said, dragging out the syllables.

But then her shock morphed into something else, and she looked downright giddy. Hell, I felt giddy when I thought about Knox. Well, when I didn't feel sick about what this would do to Jude and how it could all blow up in my face.

"Wow." She shook her head. "Just wow..."

I wasn't sure I'd ever seen Emmy speechless. Or at least, I'd never been the cause of it.

"You're such a rule-follower." Her tone was one of exasperation, but it was clear from her expression that she was impressed. "And when you finally decide to break them..."

"I know." I covered my face with my hands. "God, I know. It's terrible."

"Is it, though?" She smirked. "I mean... How's the sex?"

I rolled my eyes but laughed all the same. "Emmy," I chided.

"I'm serious, Kendall." She leaned forward, wearing an earnest expression. "I want to know."

"It's... He's..." My cheeks heated. "Amazing."

"Better than it was with Jude?" She held her reusable straw to her mouth and took a dainty sip.

I cringed. "Seriously, Emmy? God!"

"What?" She shrugged, leaning back in her chair. "I'm sure you've thought about it. How could you not compare the two?"

"Honestly—" I huffed. "I spend most of my time actively trying *not* to think about just that."

She shook her head. "Well, I can genuinely say I *never* saw this coming. Mostly because I figured you'd never allow it. But I always suspected Knox had the hots for you."

"You did not!" I slapped her arm playfully, relieved to have finally told her.

"I did," she said with a solemn expression. "Anytime you were near, his eyes never left you."

Even though Knox had admitted as much, it shocked me that Emmy had seen it too. How had I never realized it?

"Since when?" I asked, dying to hear more.

She rested her elbow on the table and dropped her head in her hand. "Since always."

Did Jude know?

"Why didn't you tell me?"

"Um, hello." She jiggled her head. "You were dating his son."

What could I say to that? It was true, but I also wasn't going to admit that she was right. Mostly because Knox had told me that in confidence. It felt too personal. Too intimate.

"You better hope Jude never finds out. He would flip his shit."

I cringed. "I know."

"Do you remember how bad it was when Cade got the same watch as him?"

I groaned and shook my head. I'd tried to block that incident out of my mind. But the moment she mentioned it, it came zipping back.

Jude had finally gotten a Breguet watch that he'd been coveting. And when his best friend, Cade, had shown up with the same watch, Jude had been livid. He hadn't spoken to Cade for days. It was all so immature.

"*You're* the watch," Emerson said, pointing at me.

"Gee. Thanks," I said in a wry tone.

"At least you know Knox doesn't view you as arm candy."

"What makes you say that?"

"By definition, arm candy is something you show off. But he's sneaking around with you."

"It only happened once." Though, we'd come close to having sex in the bathroom yesterday. At a work function.

"So far." She gave me a meaningful look.

"I—" I hung my head. I couldn't keep doing this. I couldn't keep pretending that nothing had happened with Knox. I couldn't keep denying how I felt about him. "Yeah."

She arched an eyebrow. "What does that mean?"

"He wants me to come over tonight. To discuss it."

She barked out a laugh as I stood. "You mean to fuck."

"Emerson!" I widened my eyes, begging her to keep her voice down.

"Oh, come on. We both know that's what he really meant." She stood as well and tossed her cup in the trash. "So, are you going?"

"I—" I shrugged. "I'm not sure."

I still hadn't decided what I was going to do about Knox, even as I rolled up to the gated entrance to his home.

The sun was setting behind the house, the silhouette of the palm trees stark against a cotton-candy pink sky. I hadn't let Knox know I was coming because I still hadn't committed to myself that I was going through with this.

My mind kept going back to that sense of being empowered. Of doing what I wanted—for me. And deep down, I knew I wanted to feel that way again. I wanted to be with Knox again.

"Miss Kendall." Vincent smiled, leaning out of the window of the guard shack. "It's so nice to see you."

"You too, Vincent. How have you been?"

"Good. It hasn't been the same here without you."

I smiled. "Thanks. I've missed everyone."

He nodded and opened the gate, allowing me through. I parked in the driveway and stared up at Knox's house, accepting my decision, even if I didn't know where we went from here.

I took a few deep breaths and rang the doorbell. It swung open a moment later, Knox looking as delectable as ever. His hair was still wet as if fresh from the shower, and his smile was warm.

"Come in," he said, opening the door wider to let me in.

I merely nodded, my words failing me. I was too nervous. I didn't know what to expect or what I even wanted. Well, I knew what I wanted. I just didn't know if it was possible.

Knox seemed to believe so.

"Can I get you something to drink?" he asked. "Water? Wine?"

"Whiskey, please," I said, needing something strong to calm my nerves.

He smiled. "Sure."

I followed him into the living room, noticing the new drapes. "These turned out great," I said, running a hand down the material.

"Thanks. Lauren did a great job."

"Yes," I said. "She really did."

"Here." He handed me a tumbler filled with amber liquid. The ice clinked against the glass as our fingers brushed, and I was tempted to remove one of the cubes and run it along my skin just to try to cool myself down.

I lifted my glass to his as he held his out for a toast, but I couldn't seem to form words in his presence. He looked incredible. And this felt insane. And...

"You were amazing yesterday," he said, sipping his drink. "The event ran smoothly and exceeded all expectations, especially considering you had to take it over on such short notice."

"Thank you," I said, appreciating his praise. And yet feeling as if there was a formality to his words that hadn't been there before. "A lot of the legwork had been done for me, so—"

"No, Kendall." His expression was serious. "Don't downplay your role. *You* pulled it all together at the end. And *you* made it special."

"Thank you," I said. "So did you. The kids seemed to have a blast."

He nodded, taking a seat in one of the chairs. I didn't know what to do with myself, so I perched on the arm of the sofa.

When the silence stretched on and I couldn't take it anymore, I finally asked, "Knox, is everything okay?"

"I—" He shook his head. "I know I asked you to come here, but I was wrong. *This* is wrong."

I scoffed. "Um. What happened to—" I pitched my voice low in a terrible attempt to mimic Knox's. "'It's the only thing that feels right'?"

He groaned but said nothing. The silence stretched on for so long that, finally, I stood.

"Right," I said, embarrassed that I'd come. I wasn't going to be yanked around. I grabbed my purse then headed for the door.

And then I paused. In the past, or with other men, I

would've stayed quiet. I would've let it go. But Knox had always encouraged me to speak my mind, and I wasn't going to hold back now.

I turned to face him, resolved to find out the truth. "I don't understand. What changed since yesterday? Where's the man who was determined to be with me and would let nothing stand in his way? The man who said he needed me. And made me believe it was true."

"It was—*is*—true," he said, his expression one of agony.

"Then tell me what's different," I demanded. "I mean, what happened to playing to win?"

"Don't you get it, Kendall? When it comes to us, everyone loses."

I softened, remembering how much was at stake—for all of us. "Is this about your relationship with Jude?"

"Yes," he sighed. "And no. I just..." He smoothed his beard. "Look. Seeing you with the kids at the event, well, it got me thinking. And you should be with someone younger. Someone whose life goals are more aligned with your own."

I wanted to laugh. At this point, I wasn't sure I had any life goals. But I wasn't going to tell Knox that because I knew it would only piss him off.

Instead, I inched closer. Needing to touch him. Reassure him.

"I'm too old for you," he said as if trying to warn me off.

I barked out a laugh. "Are you kidding? I don't think most people would bat an eye at our age difference. Now, the fact that I dated your son...that may raise some eyebrows. But you being older than me—"

"Not just a little older," he interrupted. "I'm twenty *years* older than you."

I waved away the distinction. "No one cares. And it's a moot point. No one is going to know about us anyway."

"Maybe *I* care," he roared. "Maybe I want people to know

about us. But do you know what that would do to Jude? To you?"

"To me?" I asked, trying to understand.

"I'm only trying to protect you."

"That's not your job," I said. "I'm a big girl. I can take care of myself."

"I know that." He cupped my cheek, and I leaned into his touch. "But maybe I like taking care of you."

"Then take care of me," I said, wrapping my arms around his neck, sensing his resistance waning. I waited until his eyes met mine. "Like this. Because you're the only person who can give me what I want."

He evaluated me a moment. "This is really what you want?"

"Yes, Knox. *This* is what I want."

He leaned closer until our noses were touching. Our foreheads kissing. So much energy bounced between us as he gazed into my eyes, the tension growing until it finally snapped.

Then everything happened in a blur of movement and passion as we lost ourselves in the kiss. In each other. Giving and taking exactly what we wanted, over and over again.

CHAPTER FOURTEEN

Knox

Weeks flew by in the blink of an eye—a blur of work, soccer, and Kendall. Every spare moment I had, I spent with her. She'd stayed over almost every night for the past few weeks, but I hated the reality that crashed down on me at the start of each day. Because then we'd go back to the office, back to pretending there was nothing between us. We might be sneaking around, but I wanted her with me all the time.

The sun was barely cresting the horizon when Kendall rolled out of bed. I groaned, tugging on her hand. "Don't go."

"I have to. All my stuff is at my mom's." She leaned back over and kissed me, her hair caressing my skin. "But I'll be back later."

"You wouldn't have to leave at all if you'd just move in."

"Right." She laughed, but I wasn't joking.

I was still traveling regularly for games. And when I wasn't, I wanted her at my house. In my bed. In my arms.

I still worried that she'd want children someday, but I realized that was a conversation for the future. Right now, we were happy. And that was all that mattered. The question of our future—and what that would mean for my relationship with Jude—would have to wait.

"I'm serious." I tucked her hair behind her ear. I'd flown home late last night—as soon as the game had ended—just so I wouldn't have to spend another night without her. "Think about it."

"About what?" she asked, placing her hand on my bare chest.

Fuck, she was gorgeous. Her full lips pink and pouty. Her skin warm and welcoming. I didn't ever want her to leave.

"Moving in with me," I said.

Surely this hadn't come as a surprise. She practically lived here already. I'd even had my stylist add new clothes to Kendall's side of the closet so she wouldn't have to pack a bag. Shockingly, she hadn't put up much of a fight about it. Probably because I'd persuaded her with a few orgasms.

"And how are we going to explain that to Jude? To my mom?"

"You could tell her you got another house-sitting placement with the Hartwell Agency." I didn't like the idea of asking Kendall to lie. But for now, it felt as if we didn't have a choice. At least until I figured out how to handle this with my son.

"And Jude?" she pushed.

I lifted a shoulder, trying to convey nonchalance despite a twinge of anxiety. "We'll tell him you're moving in to the pool house."

She scrunched up her face. It would've been adorable except I knew it meant she was going to try to refuse. "So... another lie."

"Just for now."

Just until I figured out how to tell Jude. Until I was confident Kendall would be in favor of the idea.

"Mm-hmm." She pushed off the bed and started getting dressed.

Before she pulled her shirt over her head, I hooked my arms around her waist and hauled her back into bed with me. I rolled on top of her, pinning her in place.

"Knox!" She giggled, struggling to free herself from my hold. "Let me go."

"Say you'll stay," I demanded.

"I *can't*. I have yoga with Emmy."

I kissed her neck. Her clavicle. She sighed. Melted.

"You know what I mean," I rasped against her skin.

"I love that you asked, but I don't see how it could possibly work."

"We'll figure it out," I said. "Just like we've figured everything else out. Together."

She cupped my jaw, thumb brushing my lower lip as those hazel eyes sparkled up at me. "Together, huh?"

"Yes." I slid between her thighs, thrusting in the crevice created by her skin. "*Together.*"

"Knox," she moaned, arching into me. "I can't."

"Yes." I gnashed my teeth. "And you will."

"You can't just make it so," she protested, even as her body relaxed from my touch.

I met her eyes as I inched higher, my cock slipping between her wet folds but not breaching her core. "Watch me."

"No," she said, gnashing her teeth, fighting the pleasure even as it built.

"Yes," I said, punishing her with my pace.

"No," she said again, and I pinned her hands above her head.

I kissed my way down her chest, taking one nipple then the other in my mouth. "I *will* change your mind."

"We'll—" She gasped as I pushed one finger inside her. "See."

I smirked, taking her words as a challenge. And then I used everything within my power to convince her to stay.

"Have fun tonight," Kendall said, peering up at me from the couch.

She looked as if she belonged there. Probably because she did. She'd played a role in many of the final design decisions. The details that had really brought it all together.

It had been weeks since I'd asked her to move in. She'd never outright agreed, but she stayed here every night. And she'd brought over more of her things from her mom's.

"I will." I grinned. "Because you're going with me."

Tonight was the annual gala to celebrate the Leatherbacks and support our charitable endeavors, and it was being hosted at the Huxley Grand. It was a huge, star-studded event, and there was one person in particular I wanted Kendall to meet. But first, I needed to convince her to go with me.

"What?" She jerked her head back. "You're kidding, right?"

I sank down beside her. "I want you there with me, *mi cielo*."

It bothered me that we couldn't go on a real date like an ordinary couple, so this was the best solution I'd come up with. For now, anyway.

"But..."

I cut off her protest with a look, knowing what she was

about to say. I didn't want to hear Jude's name. He'd dated her once, for six months.

Besides, he was with Chrissy now. And while they'd be attending the event tonight, Jude would understand if I brought Kendall along. This could technically fall within her job description, even if it was a bit of a stretch. Somehow, I didn't think he'd mind.

"It's a work event," I said. "And your boss demands your attendance."

"And if *my boss*—" her tone was saccharine "—wished to make my attendance mandatory, he should've given me more notice so I could've found a suitable dress or gotten my nails done."

"*Mi cielo.*" I placed my finger to her lips. "You don't have to worry about a thing."

Her eyes widened then narrowed. "Knox. What did you do?"

"You'll see." I leaned in, smiling against her lips before kissing her thoroughly. I couldn't wait to see her reaction. I'd been planning this for weeks, and it had been difficult to keep it a surprise. But I knew the payoff would be worth it.

As soon as we entered the penthouse suite at the Huxley Grand, Kendall's eyes went wide. She seemed to be taking it all in, from the glittering chandeliers to the floor-to-ceiling views of downtown Los Angeles.

"What's all this?" Kendall asked, glancing around at the living room where several racks of designer gowns were now on display.

"My stylist will be here soon. Choose whatever you like. And a glam squad will help you get ready."

"Yeah, but…" She shook her head, and when she started to back away, I knew she realized this was all for her.

I stepped closer, rubbing my hands up and down her

arms. Holding her in place. "Nope. I don't want to hear any arguments."

"But—"

I kissed her, holding her close. "It would please me very much to dress you in a beautiful gown."

She sighed in resignation, her shoulders relaxing. I knew she enjoyed pleasing me. And I had a feeling she was just being stubborn about the gown. I'd seen the way her eyes had lit up when she'd entered the room.

There was a knock at the door, and I went to answer it.

"Good afternoon," Jay said, entering with his usual panache. His team followed behind.

I stepped back to let him see Kendall, wanting her to step into the spotlight. Into her power.

"Ooh. Your picture didn't do you justice," Jay gushed, sizing Kendall up.

"Picture?" She sounded confused and a bit wary, but he was too busy assessing her from all angles. Admiring her curves. If he weren't so good at his job—and so happily married—I would've fired him on the spot.

"Well, I'll leave you to it." I headed for the door, but not before pressing my lips to Kendall's cheek. "Have fun."

Kendall's face froze, and I could feel the waves of panic rolling off her.

"Are you okay?" I kept my voice low, brushing her hair over her shoulder.

"Shouldn't you...? Do they...?" she whispered, glancing around furtively.

"They'll be discreet," I assured her, knowing I should probably be less affectionate around others. Especially since Jude didn't know about Kendall and me yet. Something I was hoping to change soon.

I hated lying to my son. And while I feared his reaction, I was sick of living in this constant state of secrecy.

"Would you like final say, Mr. Crawford?" Jay asked, clearly delighted at the prospect of dressing Kendall.

"I trust Kendall to make a good decision."

"Still," she said, twisting her hands. "I'd like to hear your opinion since I've never attended an event—" she gulped "—quite like this."

"Of course." I took a seat on the couch, watching as she and Jay sifted through the racks of designer dresses.

He told her about the designers and the construction of some of the garments. She listened intently, asking questions and telling him about her preferences. Finally, they narrowed it down to three dresses to try on and then disappeared to the bedroom down the hall.

I checked my emails on my phone and waited for her to reappear. When she did, it was with a swish of fabric. And when I gazed up at her, my heart nearly stopped.

The champagne-colored dress looked as if it had been painted onto her body. It sparkled when she moved, and I couldn't take my eyes off her. Off the way it dipped low on her chest, revealing a large expanse of skin. Or clung to her hips, the subtle pattern of the sequins only accentuating her incredible curves.

"Leave us," I said without taking my eyes off Kendall.

Jay and his team left the room, but the tension between Kendall and me remained.

"Turn," I said in a gruff tone, standing.

She did as I asked, and I reveled in the sight of her. She was gorgeous. Absolutely gorgeous—both inside and out. And she was mine.

"What do you think?" she asked in a quiet voice as I stalked toward her.

"I think it's going to be impossible to keep my eyes—or my hands—off you." I was salivating just looking at her.

She dipped her head, but she couldn't hide the slight downturn of her lips. "I wish you didn't have to."

I trailed my finger down her sternum, and she shivered. "What do you think of the dress?"

She peered down at the material and smiled. "It's beautiful."

"No." I placed my finger beneath her chin and lifted her gaze to mine. *"You're* beautiful."

I pressed my lips to hers, intending to give her a quick peck. But it soon turned heated. Kendall gripped my shirt, our hips pressed together. My hands splayed over her ass.

"Knock. Knock," Jay called in a chipper tone.

I gnashed my teeth and turned away. Focusing on the skyline while I silently willed my hard-on to disappear.

"Did you want to try on any of the others, or shall we proceed with this dress?" Jay asked. Even with my back turned, I knew his question was directed at me.

I looked at Kendall over my shoulder. This was her decision, not mine. I wanted her to feel as confident and beautiful as she was. "Up to you, *mi cielo.*"

"Yes!" She beamed. "I love this dress."

"Well, that was easy." Jay rubbed his hands together. "Now for shoes and accessories."

"I have some business to attend to," I said, pressing my lips to Kendall's cheek. "I'll see you in a bit."

She nodded, seeming much more at ease now. Though the fact that Jay had given her a glass of champagne certainly helped. He was gushing over the dress, and he'd rolled out a ton of shoes. I chuckled to myself, the door closing behind me.

I made some calls and checked in with the event planner, Juliana Wright. Everything was running smoothly, not that I'd expected otherwise. She was meticulous.

I went to Jasper's hotel room to shower and change into

my tux, then grabbed one final surprise before heading back up to the penthouse.

"She's all yours," Jay said as I exited the elevator to the top floor. His team had taken the rejected garments down the staff elevator, and I couldn't wait to see Kendall.

"Thank you, Jay."

He stepped closer, adjusting my tie. "This Tom Ford looks divine on you."

"You always make me look good." I appreciated his eye for design.

"Thank you," he said, sincerity ringing in his voice. "I'm always happy to style you—and, now, Kendall. Though, I guess I've already been styling her, considering all the clothes we filled your closet with."

I nodded. "Yes, and I'd appreciate your continued discretion."

He mimed zipping his lips. "You got it, boss. It was nice to finally meet her in person. She's a rarity in Hollywood. Gorgeous and authentic." He shook his head, but he wasn't telling me anything I didn't already know. "She is going to slay."

"I don't doubt it." I took a step forward, eager to see her.

He placed a hand to my chest, eyeing me up and down. "Whoa there, cowboy."

I stilled. "What?"

"Do *not* fuck up my masterpiece," he said with a stern expression as I continued past him. "I mean it, Crawford," he called.

I chuckled but continued down the hall, swiping the keycard to the suite. The lock disengaged, and I swung the door open. And there she stood, her hair in waves down her back.

She peered out at the city, her dress glittering like the sunset on the beach. A promise of forever. *My* forever.

"My god." I drank in the sight of her, scarcely able to form words. Jay hadn't been exaggerating when he'd referred to Kendall as a masterpiece.

She slowly turned to face me. Her eyes scanned me from head to toe, an appreciative smile spreading over her face. "Wow."

"I changed my mind," I said, stepping closer. Careful to keep my next surprise hidden behind my back. "We're not going."

She laughed, smoothing her hands down my lapels. "Mm. Tempting. But it gives us something to look forward to for later."

"I like the sound of that." As beautiful as she looked, I couldn't wait to muss her up. To smear her lipstick and tousle her hair. "Now for the final touch."

She furrowed her brow, and I removed the velvet box from behind my back and held it between us. Her eyes went comically wide when I opened the lid to reveal the contents.

"Oh. My. God." Her attention was glued to the diamond necklace and matching earrings. "Please tell me these are costume pieces."

I shook my head and gestured for her to turn. She faced the skyline, our reflection visible in the window. I trailed the necklace up her chest, enjoying the way she shivered in response.

I secured the clasp and pressed my lips to her shoulder. "There. Perfect."

She lifted her hand to the necklace, grazing the pendant with her fingers. The pattern matched the earrings exactly, with a round cut diamond at the top, followed by a cluster of four stones that created the illusion of an X, leading to a large, pear-shaped stone at the bottom. It was more subtle than I would've preferred, but it was more suited to her tastes. And they were the best quality and clarity money could buy.

"These are on loan, right?"

I waited until she met my gaze in the reflection. "They're all yours."

Just like my heart.

But I wasn't going to tell her that. Not yet anyway. She wasn't ready to hear it. But one day, I'd tell her my heart belonged to her, just like the diamonds adorning her skin.

CHAPTER FIFTEEN

Kendall

"I still can't believe you got to meet David freaking Beckham," Emmy said, shaking her head.

She grabbed some bags from the trunk, loading up her arms. She was between nanny placements, so she had some time off. And since Mom had just gone through her sixth—and hopefully final—round of treatment, we'd gone to pick up some groceries for her.

"I know." I laughed. "I still can't believe it myself."

I'd known it was going to be a star-studded event, but to meet David Beckham? *No.* Not just *meet* him but sit next to him at dinner? It was a dream come true.

Knox and I had talked to him and Victoria about soccer and traveling. She'd admired my dress, and I couldn't believe I'd been able to speak in their presence.

It had almost felt like a real date. Like we were a normal couple, apart from the fact that we were hiding our true relationship from everyone. But that hadn't stopped Knox from putting his hand on my leg beneath the table. Even Jude's presence at the event hadn't prevented our stolen glances and whispered promises.

But it was all so far removed from my normal life, it was laughable. Looking at me today—yoga pants and an oversized tee—no one would've guessed where I'd been just a few nights ago. I could scarcely believe it myself, though my diamond earrings and necklace were certainly a good reminder. They were beautiful, if a bit much for everyday wear. At least, for the types of things I tended to do in my daily life.

"Was Becks as hot in person as he looks in pictures?" Emmy asked as we loaded into the elevator.

I shook my head. "Hotter."

"Oh, I bet Knox loved hearing that." She cackled.

I'd kept that thought to myself. David Beckham might be hot, but I only wanted Knox.

"Jude was there, right?" she asked.

We arrived at Mom's floor, and I held the door open with my hip, allowing Emmy to pass by. "Yeah. And his girlfriend, Chrissy."

At first, I'd been nervous that Jude would be upset Knox had brought me as his date, but Knox had explained that it was good for me to see how the event was run. And Jude had been so busy fawning over all the other celebrities in attendance, he'd barely paid us any attention.

"She totally looks like a clone of you," Emmy said. "Though obviously, you're prettier."

"And *obviously*, you're biased." I laughed, setting the bags on the kitchen counter. "Not that it's a competition."

She pursed her lips, considering. "Maybe not to you."

"What's that supposed to mean?" I asked, unloading groceries and sorting them into piles for the pantry or fridge.

"Oh, come on, Kendall. Everything's a competition with Jude. Always has been."

I hoped she was wrong. Even though we both knew it was

in Jude's nature to be competitive, Chrissy seemed so sweet. And I got the impression she really cared about Jude.

"It doesn't matter. I'm not with Jude anymore. And Chrissy was really nice."

"Oh my god. Oh my *god!*" My mom's voice grew louder with each word.

My heart racing, I rushed into her bedroom. "Mom?" She was standing at her dresser, a piece of paper in hand. "Are you okay?"

She'd been doing well since the treatment. And Joe had been a huge support. Even so, Knox had insisted I take the day off. He knew I'd want to be there for my mom, to help with anything she might need. She seemed okay—at least physically—but my heart was still pumping adrenaline through my system.

"Am I okay?" She turned to me with a smile on her face and tears in her eyes. "Kendall—" She held the letter out to me with shaking hands. "Look, sweetheart. A miracle."

The treatment center logo was at the top of the page. And the letter went on to inform us that my mom's treatment past and future had been paid in full.

My eyes widened. "What?" I flipped it over. "When did you get this?"

I'd brought the mail in earlier, but I hadn't had a chance to go through it.

She took it back from me, scanning the contents again as if she couldn't possibly believe it was true. "I can't believe Jude did this."

"Jude?" I jerked my head back.

She furrowed her brow. "Who else would it be?"

"I-I—" I promptly shut my mouth. I knew exactly who our anonymous benefactor could be, and it sure as shit wasn't Jude.

"Please tell him thank you. Oh—" She held the letter to her chest. "This is incredible. I told you he loved you."

I wasn't sure whether to laugh or cry. And while I was grateful to Knox, he should've talked to me first. Now my mom thought...

I grabbed my keys and headed for the door.

"Where are you going?" My mom's attention snapped to me as I took the letter from her dresser, but she looked so happy that I couldn't burst her bubble.

I'd let her believe the bill had been paid, but I couldn't allow Knox to do that for us. He'd already given me so much. This was...too much. First the Range Rover, then the clothes, the jewelry, and now this?

God, I felt sick even thinking about the amount of money he'd just handed over. Without a second thought. For me.

"Kendall?"

"Work," I blurted, knowing it wasn't a total lie, unlike the rest of my life. "Emmy's here if you need anything. I'll be back later."

When I returned to the kitchen, Emmy had finished putting away the groceries. "Everything okay?"

"It will be. Can you stay with my mom for a little bit?"

"Of course."

"Thanks," I said then darted for the elevator.

When I arrived at the stadium, I took the elevator straight to the top floor. "Hey, Kendall," Brenda, Knox's receptionist, called.

"Hi!" I waved at her and smiled, hoping she couldn't tell it was forced. I strode into Knox's office without knocking, closing the door behind me.

"Hey." He grinned, standing. "This is an unexpected surprise."

"Mm," I said, unamused. "I suppose it's only fair after the surprise I received today."

He tilted his head to the side, leaning his hip against the desk. "A good surprise, I hope."

I slid the letter from the treatment center across his desk. "What were you thinking? Paying off my mom's medical expenses."

He straightened, ignoring the letter and coming over to me. "Kendall." He rubbed his hands up and down my arms. The motion was soothing. Momentarily distracting me from what I wanted to say. "The money means nothing to me. But you…" He placed his finger beneath my chin, lifting my head so I was forced to meet his gaze. "You mean everything to me."

I sucked in a jagged breath. Hearing him say those words while looking at me with such intensity, well, I wasn't sure I could handle it.

And I knew he expected nothing in return. It was one of the kindest things anyone had ever done for me. And it wasn't about the amount spent; it was the fact that he'd wanted to do something to alleviate my stress. To make my life easier. Even if it wasn't his responsibility.

"Knox…" I shook my head, taking a step back. Taking a breath. "It's—*this* is too much."

"You know I'd do anything for you—or your mom. So what's really bothering you? Is this about the money or something else?"

All of it, but I found myself saying, "I told Emmy about us."

"I figured," he said. "And I'm glad you have someone you can trust to confide in."

I appreciated that. But… How was I going to tell him this? "My mom thinks Jude paid her medical bills," I blurted.

"What?" He jerked his head back. "Why?"

"Because she thinks we're back together."

A muscle in his neck twitched, and he crossed his arms over his chest. "Why did you tell her you were with Jude?"

I threw up my hands. "I didn't! *He* came to the hospital and brought her flowers when she got mono. And *she* assumed he paid her bill."

Knox frowned. "I'm glad Jude's been a good friend, but I don't like the idea of your mom hoping you'll give him another chance."

I massaged my temples, a headache brewing. This was such a mess. The secrecy was wearing on me. I hadn't realized just how much until the other night at the gala. Until now.

I let my hands fall to my sides, slumping in exhaustion. "I've tried to tell her it's not happening, but it's not like I can tell her about us," I said. "If only I'd never…"

"Dated him?" Knox asked quietly.

I nodded, hating that I couldn't avoid bringing Jude into the conversation. Whether we mentioned him or not, the guilt was still there. He would always be part of the equation because he was Knox's son.

Knox pushed away from the desk and grasped my chin, his blue eyes piercing in their intensity. "You may have dated him first, but you always belonged to *me*."

I was frustrated with our situation and the fact that we could only ever be a secret. And I was mad at myself for falling for him. But all I wanted right now—all I needed—was for him to kiss me. To distract me from my frustrations and my fears. To make me feel whole in the way only he could.

My eyes fluttered closed, and I waited for Knox to kiss me. To claim me with his mouth as he had with his words.

But instead, he tightened his grip on my chin and rasped, "Say it."

"Say what?" I asked, peering up at him.

"Tell me you're mine."

"I'm yours." I gasped when he grabbed my ass with his free hand, pulling me into him. Letting me feel his desire.

"Good." He rested his hands on my waist. "Now prove it."

My body ignited, incredibly turned on by his words. "Here? Now?"

We'd always been very careful in our interactions at the office, never wanting anyone to suspect the true nature of our relationship.

"Yes." The black of his pupils nearly eclipsed the blue of his iris. "Did you really think you could storm into my office in those fucking pants and not provoke me?"

I glanced down, only then remembering what I was wearing. Yoga pants and a T-shirt. I sighed, wishing I'd thought this through. Wishing I'd been more professional.

"And why aren't you wearing my earrings?" he asked, turning me so my back was to him. "And my necklace."

He held me to him with one arm, using his free hand to rub me through my pants.

Oh god.

"God isn't here," he said, making me realize I'd said the words aloud. "I am. And it damn well better be my name on your lips when you come."

My mouth went dry at his words, loving the way he could be both possessive and gentle. Demanding and loving.

My eyes darted to the door, knowing it could open at any moment. "This is dangerous."

"I. Don't. Fucking. Care," he growled, sliding his hand inside my pants. His gentle touch contradicted the harshness of his tone. "And the fact that you're this wet says you don't either."

"*Knox*," I gasped when he speared me with his fingers.

He worked me into a frenzy, the pleasure building fast and furious. I couldn't control it, any more than I could my feelings for this man. I was on a high-speed express train. Trying to stop this orgasm was as pointless as trying to stop myself from falling for Knox. So I let go. But before I could cry out, he covered my mouth with his hand.

He spun me, pushing me back onto the desk and pulling my pants down over my hips. I didn't know what had gotten into him, but I liked it.

He spread my legs wide before standing back to admire the view. "*Mi cielo.*" He rubbed a hand over his beard, the other pressing down on his cock. "How did I get so lucky?"

I scoffed, admiring the incredible man before me. "I'm the one who's lucky."

"Don't move," he demanded as he went to the door.

"Where are you going?" I asked, embarrassed that the question almost came out as a whimper. This man made me desperate for him.

He locked the door then returned to me, a look of pure determination and lust on his striking face. He knelt to the floor, strong hands gripping my bare thighs, his head between my legs. He was about to devour me when my phone rang.

"I should—" I pushed up on my elbows.

He glared at me over my mound. "You should stay here and let me take care of you."

"What if it's my mom?" I asked, worry lancing me.

He grabbed my phone from my purse, but when he saw the name on the screen, he clenched his jaw. "Why is Jude calling you?"

"Maybe it's something about work," I said as it rang again.

"He knows you have the day off." His tone was flat, though I sensed anger beneath the surface.

I shrugged, exasperated. "Then maybe he's calling to check on my mom."

"Does he do that often?" he asked, his hands flexing on my thighs.

"I—" I swallowed, glancing at the screen. Wondering if I should answer it. Wondering if Jude was in the building. If he'd catch me in the arms of his dad.

"Answer it," Knox said, hitting the button to connect the call before I could disagree or try to stop him.

"He-hello." I cleared my throat, nerves working their way through my system. I glared at Knox. What the hell was he thinking?

"Kendall?" Jude's concern was evident in his tone. "Are you okay?"

Knox leaned forward and nuzzled my already sensitive clit, making me draw a sharp breath. I'd barely recovered from the last orgasm, and I had a feeling he was determined to kill me with pleasure. It didn't sound like a terrible way to go.

My head fell back as he licked up my slit, and I bit the inside of my cheek to hold back a moan. "Yeah?"

Damn. Knox was making it difficult to think, let alone speak. The flicks of his tongue were distracting. As was the way he was looking at me, intent on my pleasure.

"I was calling to see how your mom's doing."

"Oh, um—" Knox inserted a finger, and I bucked my hips, nearly knocking his keyboard off the desk. "She's. Good." The words came out breathy and strange.

"Are you sure you're okay?" Jude asked, clearly concerned.

"Ahhh—" I gripped the edge of the desk when Knox curled his finger, hitting that magical spot. "Yeah. Just...*busy*."

"Okay. I'll swing by later with some dinner."

"Mm-hmm." I leaned my head back, the sensations overtaking me until Knox bit the inside of my thigh. My eyes darted to his, and he shook his head, a dark look in his eyes.

"What?" I mouthed.

"No dinner," he mouthed back.

I nearly groaned with frustration. I wanted Knox to stop teasing me, withholding my orgasm. And I didn't understand why he was so upset. Jude was just being nice; it didn't mean anything. Did it?

"I-I—" I struggled to compose myself and my thoughts. "That's really sweet of you, Jude. But totally not necessary."

"Don't be silly. I'm happy to do it."

Knox stood and unzipped his pants, removing his cock. I loved the way he slicked the tip through my juices, no barriers remaining. After the gala, Knox hadn't wanted to use condoms anymore, and I had readily agreed since I was on the pill.

His eyes held a challenge, a dare. His message was clear. If I wanted him inside me, I needed to convince Jude to leave me alone. To let me go.

"I—" I scrambled for a plausible excuse. Something believable. "I don't think my mom's up for visitors."

Knox nodded, inching his way inside me. I never felt as full or as complete as when we connected like this.

"Perhaps another time soon, then," Jude said, completely oblivious to the fact that his dad was fucking me on the other end of the phone.

"Thanks," I said in a rush. "Gotta go." And then I disconnected the call as quickly as possible.

"Good girl," Knox said, smoothing his hand down my sternum.

I narrowed my eyes at him. "Do you want me to call you the 'D' word?" I asked, knowing how much he hated being called "Daddy."

"Only if you want me to gag you with my cock." His eyes were wild.

That didn't sound like too much of a punishment to me.

"What has gotten into you?" I demanded, frowning as I

pushed up on my elbows and locked my legs around Knox's hips.

"You." He dragged his thumb down my lips, his eyes following the progression. "*You* make me crazy. Now show me how pretty you look when you come on my cock."

He picked up the pace, covering my mouth with his. Deepening our connection. Making me want him even more.

When I came, I nearly fell off the desk, his thrusts hard and relentless. And there was no doubt about it—I was his.

CHAPTER SIXTEEN

Kendall

Emmy was standing outside the restaurant when I pulled up. The valet opened the door for me, and Emmy's eyes danced with laughter when she spotted me climbing out of the Range Rover in one of my new designer outfits. I shot her a look as I took the ticket from the valet and met her on the sidewalk.

"First the Range Rover, and now the designer duds?" she asked. "What did he do to convince you this time? Burn your old clothes?"

"Ha-ha," I deadpanned. She knew all about Knox having my car towed. "No, but if he does, I swear to god…"

"Ooh. Feisty. I like this new side of you." She smirked.

"Come on." I linked my arm through hers. But deep down, I liked this new side of me too.

It wasn't about the luxury car or the designer clothes that kept appearing on my side of the closet. It was about Knox. I knew the gifts were his way of telling me he cared. And despite how nice all the presents were, the only thing I really wanted was him.

"*Rough* day at the office?" She waggled her eyebrows.

I rolled my eyes. "Seriously, Emmy?"

"What?" She shrugged.

"That was bad. Even for you."

She stared at me with mock outrage. "Hey!"

"Drinks," I said, giving her a pointed stare. "We're here to celebrate your new placement."

She frowned. "Not sure it's worth celebrating."

The inside of the restaurant was loud, so I waited until we'd been seated and ordered drinks to broach the topic again. "So…what happened?"

She flopped back in the booth with a groan. "I don't want to talk about it."

"Why not?" I asked.

"Because he's a pain in the ass, and I want to quit. But I won't." She straightened. "Because I'm a *professional*, and his daughter is freaking adorable."

"Who is it?" I asked, my curiosity growing.

"I'm not supposed to say, but…" She lowered her voice. "I'm sure you'll find out anyway since it's Nate."

"Knox's brother, Nate?" I asked, surprised.

"One and the same."

"I've only interacted with him a few times, but he always seemed nice."

"Yeah, well—" She huffed and downed some of her drink. "Maybe to you."

I arched an eyebrow. "What does that mean?" When she didn't answer, I prodded. "Does it have something to do with him being your celebrity crush?"

"He's *not* my crush," she insisted, though her pink cheeks said otherwise.

"Um." I held up a finger. "Pretty sure he spent the last five years in the top three of your celebrity fuck-it list."

She leaned closer. "Maybe he was before, but he isn't

anymore. And if you ever tell him or Knox that..." She ground her jaw.

"Okay. Okay." I held up my hands. "Wow."

"I'm sorry," she huffed. "It was a *long* day. But hopefully I won't have to interact with him as much going forward."

"Mm-hmm." I had a feeling her opinion on that would change. At least I hoped so. "Which appetizer do you want?"

She closed her menu with a huff, setting it on the table as the waiter arrived. "We'll take the shrimp, please."

"Absolutely," he said and then disappeared again after taking the rest of our order.

"How crazy is it that we were placed with brothers?" she asked.

"Well, they both have money, and businesses like Hartwell thrive off personal recommendations."

"Yes, but I guess it's got me thinking about brothers."

Where was she going with this?

"How cool would it be if we married into the same family?"

I grinned, loving the sound of it. "Then we'd legit be family."

"We already *are* family," she teased. But then she started laughing, clutching her stomach as her eyes watered. "Oh my god."

"What's so funny?"

"It's just—" She was laughing so hard she could barely breathe, let alone speak. She held up a hand. "I'm sorry." And then she burst out laughing again.

"Come on, Emmy." My face broke into a smile. I didn't know what was so funny, but her laughter was infectious. "Tell me."

"Well—" She covered her mouth with her hand. Then she schooled her features into a neutral expression, or tried to anyway. "If you married Knox, you'd be Jude's stepmom.

Your ex—" she dissolved into a fit of giggles "—would be your stepson."

My stomach soured, even as the waiter delivered our appetizer then left. "First of all..." I held a hand to my stomach. "Gross. And secondly, Knox and I aren't getting married."

I knew she was joking. But the fact that it was so wildly unrealistic hurt.

Emmy patted my hand while wearing a sympathetic expression. "Maybe not, but I get the feeling Knox is serious about you."

I hedged, fiddling with my empty glass. "I know I'm basically living with him, but...marriage?" I shook my head. All the while, I tried to ignore the pang of longing I felt at the idea of not having to hide our relationship. But instead getting to celebrate it.

"Girl, he's taking a *huge* risk by being with you." When I frowned, she added, "With Jude. And Knox doesn't seem like the type of man who would jeopardize his relationship with his son for a mere fling."

"Maybe not, but it's not like we're planning to tell Jude about us."

"Kendall." She smiled gently. "He's in love with you."

I popped a bite of shrimp into my mouth. "You haven't even seen us together."

"I don't need to. He paid your mom's medical expenses." She ticked off one finger. She lifted a second. "He gave you a freaking Range Rover."

"He—" I opened my mouth to protest, but she beat me to it.

"Took you to a star-studded gala. Bought you a diamond necklace and earrings. Introduced you to David Beckham..."

"He's a billionaire, and he likes being generous," I said as the waiter arrived with fresh drinks.

But even I knew that was a lie. Knox wasn't just generous with his money. When it came to me, he was generous with his time. Something he'd struggled with in the past apparently. Jude had told me it was one of the big reasons his parents had divorced.

"And you're in love with him too," she said, delivering the fatal blow.

I dropped my head in my hands, unable to deny it. "Yeah."

"Yeah?" she gasped. "Holy shit. I can't believe you admitted it."

"I'm crazy about him."

"What are you going to do about Jude?"

I groaned. "I don't know. And I don't know how Knox feels because I'm afraid to ask him."

She dipped a piece of shrimp in the sauce and took a large bite, moaning around it. "It's probably a talk the two of you should have."

I gnawed on my lip. "I know, but what we have is good. So, *so* good. And I don't want to ruin that."

She grinned.

"What?" I asked.

"Does that mean you can see a future with Knox?"

I took a deep breath and let the sounds of the restaurant fade to a din as I contemplated her question. Could I see a future with Knox? I wanted to think we could be happy together long-term, but it was difficult to see past the fact that I'd dated his son.

"Jude would hate it," I finally said, knowing a future with Knox was nothing more than a daydream. And wishing otherwise was futile.

"You're right about that," she said. But instead of feeling vindicated by her confirmation, it only depressed me further.

The meal arrived, and conversation changed to other matters. After dinner, we headed back to Knox's. Emmy was the only person who knew I'd moved in, but she'd never tell anyone.

We'd just changed into pj's and settled on the couch when my phone pinged with an incoming text. I grabbed it from the coffee table, smiling when my code name for Knox popped up. "D" for "Daddy." It made me laugh every time.

> D: Did you have fun with Emerson?

Traveling for the games was hectic, but Knox always texted me throughout the day. Even when we were just down the hall at the office. But especially when he was out of town.

I switched on the TV, navigating to the pregame show and hoping for any glimpse of Knox. He'd barely been gone a day, and I missed him more than I should. More than I had any right to. Did Knox realize how crazy I was about him?

> Aren't you supposed to be getting ready for the game?

It was partially asked in jest. But I also didn't want to be a distraction. I knew how much the team meant to him.

It wasn't just about the money. The Leatherbacks were an extension of his family. He was deeply invested in the success of the team and every person who worked for him. It was one of the things I loved most about him.

"You're texting him now, aren't you?" Emmy asked, plopping down beside me.

"Yeah." I smiled down at my phone as it vibrated in my hand.

> D: It's not like I have to warm up or stretch.

I laughed, grateful he couldn't see me right now. I

burrowed deeper into the pillows, thinking about Knox and love and…well, how empty the house felt without him.

With Emmy here, it felt less cavernous and hollow. But it was as if Knox's personality brought it to life. As if he filled the rooms, infusing them with his presence.

The Leatherbacks lost the coin toss, and their opponent decided to kick off first. The game started, and Emmy and I settled in to watch. The Leatherbacks were playing well. We'd just scored the first point when it hit me—a sharp stomach cramp.

"Are you okay?" Emmy asked, placing her hand on my back as I leaned forward.

"I—" My stomach gurgled, and then I broke out in a cold sweat. "No." I tried to focus on my breathing. Something, anything but the way my stomach roiled and cramped.

I hated the sensation of being both hot and cold. It was disconcerting and only made the nausea rolling through me worse. Like a cold front meeting a warm front inside my body. I had a feeling something destructive was coming.

"Oh god." I stood and stumbled toward the nearest bathroom, desperate to reach it before something awful happened.

I barely made it to the toilet before emptying the contents of my stomach into the basin. I quickly flushed it and squeezed my eyes shut, my body feeling as if it were curling in on itself. I took a few breaths then threw up again, finally slumping against the wall.

"Kendall?" Emmy asked, peeking her head inside.

My phone buzzed again, but I ignored it.

"Are you feeling okay?" I asked.

"Yeah. But you look—" She shook her head and grimaced.

"Do you think I could have food poisoning?"

She opened her phone and started typing. As she listed off more symptoms, they continued to match up.

"But I don't get it. We shared the appetizer," I said. "And I tried your meal."

"Yeah, but I didn't try any of yours."

"Thank goodness," I moaned, clutching my stomach.

"Hopefully you'll feel better quickly," she said, grabbing a washcloth from beneath the sink and wetting it before handing it to me.

"What did the website say?"

She winced. "Twenty-four to forty-eight hours?" Then she straightened, handing the washcloth to me. "But you never know—maybe it will be over sooner."

I groaned both at the idea and how I felt. I clutched my stomach and rushed over to the toilet again. I'd just washed my hands when my phone buzzed again. I held it out to Emmy.

"Will you please answer Knox? I—" I slumped against the wall. "I can't."

And I knew if I didn't, he'd worry. And the last thing I wanted was to distract him from the game.

She left to search for some bottled water. I moaned, wishing I could just be done with this. The pain. The throwing up.

"Food poisoning sucks," I croaked as she returned, holding out a bottle to me. "No. I can't."

"What about something with electrolytes?"

Even the mere suggestion made me nauseous. "How's the game going?"

She laughed. "You want to know about the game? Now?"

"Yes." I crawled toward the door to the bathroom, hoping to hear about the plays. The score. "I need a distraction."

"Let's get you back on the couch," she said. "I'll get you a trash can."

I grunted. I could barely lift my head, let alone comprehend the idea of going as far as the couch. So, she relented and told me about the plays.

I must have fallen asleep in the bathroom, because the next thing I knew, someone was lifting me from the floor. Knox, judging from the warm and summer scent of his cologne that surrounded me as he cradled me in his arms.

"Knox?" I whispered, my voice hoarse.

My body was so weak. My limbs exhausted. And the nausea that had been kept at bay was resurfacing once more.

"What time is it?" I murmured, too exhausted to even open my eyes. "Where's Emmy?"

I could hear the TV in the distance, an announcer talking about the postgame highlights. *No.* I tried to concentrate on what he was saying. If I wasn't mistaken, the game was still going.

"She's asleep on the couch," Knox said. "I'm glad she called me."

"But...but..." I tried to make sense of everything as he carried me up the stairs.

"Shh, *mi cielo*. I've got you." He placed me gently on the bed.

He smoothed his hand down my hair, and it felt so good. The way he stroked me. Cared for me.

"But you're supposed to be in San Jose. For the game."

He caressed my cheek. "You're more important."

I forced my eyes open, my throat aching from earlier. I wasn't even sure how to respond to that statement. For Knox to say I was more important than soccer. Than his legacy and his team...

This was more than him giving me a Range Rover or diamonds or even paying my mom's medical expenses. Knox had given up something that was more limited and precious than all the money in his bank account—his time. And he'd done it to be with me.

"Knox," I chided, loving that he'd done that for me, yet hating it at the same time.

"Kendall," he said, mimicking my tone.

He shifted, wrapping his other arm around me. As always, I slid into place. A perfect fit. As if we'd been made for each other.

"What's the point of having a private jet if I can't do what I want? And what I want..." He pulled me closer, gently. As if he knew my body—or perhaps my heart—was fragile at the moment. "...is to be with you."

I didn't want to spoil the moment, but the nausea was rising again. So I kicked off the covers and rushed to the bathroom. When I looked up after flushing the toilet, Knox was there. Watching me as he leaned against the doorframe, the skin beside his eyes wrinkled with concern.

I groaned and pulled my legs to my chest, debating which was worse—the intense stomach cramps or the fact that he was seeing me like this.

He turned on the sink. A moment later, he crouched beside me. He brushed my hair aside and then placed a cool washcloth on the back of my neck. His movements were gentle, reverent, despite the fact that he'd just watched me dry heave over the toilet.

"Thank you," I murmured, my nose stinging as I tried not to show just how touched I was by his concern. By his care.

"Of course. Have you had anything to eat or drink?"

I shuddered at the mere mention of food. "Not since dinner with Emmy."

"Be right back," he said.

He wasn't gone long, though I'd lost track of time in general. I worried how much of the game he'd missed. But selfishly, I was glad he'd come home early.

When he returned, he unscrewed the cap from a bottle of Ultim8 Hydr8 and held it out to me. "Here. Drink this. Slowly," he added. "The electrolytes will help. I don't want you to get dehydrated."

I squeezed my eyes shut. Even water sounded…*bleh*.

I shook my head quickly and regretted it immediately. "No." I held a hand to my throat, which was raw from throwing up.

He held it to my lips. "Slow sips. Take your time."

I pouted, but I knew he wouldn't relent.

"Come on, *mi cielo*," he pleaded, and I opened my mouth. He tilted the bottle ever so slowly, allowing me to drink at my pace. "That's it," he added in a gentle voice.

I slumped against the wall. This was exhausting and mortifying. And yet Knox acted as if it was no big deal. As if leaving a game early to hold my hair back while I puked my guts out was the only place he wanted to be. The only thing that really mattered to him.

I'd never felt less sexy or more loved.

"Do you want to stay in here a little longer, or are you ready to go back to bed?" he asked.

"I don't want to move," I said, afraid if I did, I'd throw up again.

"That's fine." He rubbed my back. "We can stay here as long as you need."

I laid my head in his lap, and he stroked my hair. At some point, I remembered him carrying me to the bed. Setting me down gently before joining me.

It felt like I was dreaming. But when he whispered, "Sweet dreams, *mi cielo*. I love you," as he pressed a kiss to my temple, I knew it was true.

CHAPTER SEVENTEEN

Knox

I watched Kendall as she slept, concentrating on the sound of her breathing. It grew measured and even, and it was only then that I started to relax a little. Only when she was in my arms, sleeping peacefully, that I could breathe again.

I hated seeing her like this. I hated worrying about her. I hated myself for falling for her, and yet, I wouldn't change it for the world. She was *mi cielo*, my heaven on earth. And I couldn't bear the thought of living without her.

Before Kendall, I'd been merely existing. Now, I felt as if I was truly alive. And watching her endure food poisoning had nearly killed me.

From the nightstand, my phone flashed with an incoming message, and I sighed. I wanted to ignore it, but I couldn't any longer. So, carefully as I could, I picked it up and swiped it open to review what I'd missed.

A few texts from the team press manager. A call from Jude. News stories flooding my screen about the team's win, followed by questions about my absence despite Jude's eloquent statement to the press after the game.

What did it say about me that I was willing to leave my team—my only son—to be with Kendall?

I could count the number of games I'd missed on one hand. I'd watched the game on my flight home, but nothing compared to experiencing it live. And even though I'd known my early departure would spark questions, I couldn't stay away from Kendall. Not when she'd needed me.

> Jude: Are you okay? Brenda said you had to leave then told me I was doing the press conference.

I set down my phone and dragged my hand through my hair. I'd have to answer Jude and deal with the rest of it at some point. But right now, all I wanted was to hold Kendall.

But the longer my phone sat there, Jude's message still unanswered, the guiltier I felt. So I picked up the phone and texted him.

> I'm good. And you did great, son.

Son.

I didn't feel like much of a father. Not when I'd left the game early to go home to *her*—the woman who held my heart in her hands. My son's ex.

I watched Kendall's sleeping form, her chest rising and falling with every breath. She was okay. She was going to be okay. I let out a slow, measured breath, trying to calm myself so I wouldn't wake her.

I needed to tell Jude.

Now wasn't the time, but I knew I couldn't expect to keep this a secret much longer. Hell, I was lucky we'd been able to as long as we had.

It wasn't fair to keep this from Jude. It wasn't fair to Kendall either. She deserved more.

But it would put everything I'd worked so hard for—not to mention my relationship with my son—at risk. I worried that Jude would resent me when he found out the truth. That he'd hate me.

> Jude: Are you sure you're okay?

> My praise isn't that rare, is it?

I resorted to humor because the truth was too painful. Too explosive, especially for a text message.

I told myself to treasure this moment. I had everything—another Leatherbacks win, a good relationship with my son, and Kendall in my arms. The moment felt fragile and precious.

I watched as three dots danced on the screen, appearing and disappearing. The same pattern again until finally disappearing altogether. I had a feeling he'd been pulled into another event for the team, and I trusted him to handle it.

Kendall needed me more. Or perhaps what was scarier to admit was that I needed her.

When I was with Kendall, she made me feel like the most important person in the world. She made me feel…valued. Loved.

She made me feel complete in a way that I hadn't felt since before my parents' death. Because as much as my grandparents had loved Nate, Graham, Jasper, Sloan, and me, they'd been running an empire and grappling with their own grief.

Kendall shifted against me, and I held on tighter. Scared to let her go. Scared of what the future would look like.

I lay there for what felt like hours, just watching her sleep. Trying to think of ways to get Jude to accept this. Accept *us*.

"Hey," Kendall said, smiling up at me as the sun crested the horizon. "You're really here."

I pressed a kiss to her forehead. "I'm really here."

"I can't believe you left the game early."

"I'd do it all again to be with you." I met her hazel eyes, hoping she knew just how much she meant to me. "Are you feeling any better?"

She nodded. "Thank you for taking care of me."

I pulled her into me, holding her close. "Anytime, *mi cielo.*"

"What were you thinking about?" she asked. "Earlier."

"Were you spying on me and pretending to be asleep?" I teased, unprepared for her question.

The corner of her mouth tipped up, and it was good to see her smile. "So…?"

"You should rest."

She propped her head up on one elbow, unwilling to back down. Silently encouraging me to continue.

I smoothed my beard. It was due for a trim. "I was thinking about my parents."

"What about them?" She placed her hand on my chest.

"I was just wondering how life would've been different if they hadn't died in the plane crash."

Her expression was one of compassion. "I'm sure that was… Well, I can't even imagine."

"It was just such a shock. And I can't fathom how my grandparents functioned, let alone ran a growing hotel business and raised five children."

"I'm sure they had help, right?" she asked.

"Yes, but they were always there for us. Or at least, as much as they could be. And sometimes I wonder if they stayed busy so they wouldn't have time to think about all they'd lost. And if, somehow, that was ingrained in me. This need to be productive. To constantly be doing something so I wouldn't have to feel that pain."

She placed her hand over my heart. "How does it make you feel to admit that?"

"It feels like…like it rings true. But also, like I don't want to live that way anymore."

"Why do you think that is?" she asked.

I smiled, setting my hand over hers as I turned to face her. "Because of you, *mi cielo*. Kendall," I said, pulling back to look at her. I took a calm, steadying breath. "I love you."

A silent tear rolled down her cheek, and I couldn't decipher what she was feeling. She swiped away her tears. "I love you too."

"Are those happy tears?" I asked, my voice wavering with hope.

She shook her head against my chest, her skin warm where her body was pressed to mine. "They're…" She sighed. "I don't know what they are."

I stilled. "Because of Jude."

She nodded.

I drew in a deep breath. "I think we should tell him."

She leaned back and gaped at me, eyes wide. "Knox. We can't."

"We have to," I said. I couldn't keep doing this to her. To us. "It's either that or we end things, and I don't have the strength to do that."

She chewed on her lip. "Yeah, but telling Jude?" She blew out a jagged breath. "That's…that's serious."

I took her hand in mine, our fingers dancing. "I'm serious about you. About us. I want us to be together. I'm tired of keeping this a secret. Of sneaking around. You deserve better."

And I'm too old for this shit.

"What about my mom?" she asked just as the house alarm chimed three times.

I frowned, wondering who Vincent would've let in. I stood and grabbed a shirt just as the double chime signaled a door had opened.

Emerson called out, "Oh. Hey, Jude."

I met Kendall's eyes, our faces mirror images of alarm. I might want to tell Jude about us, but not like this. Not without some preparation first.

"Jude's here?" Kendall hissed.

"I left the game early, without an explanation. He's probably worried."

"What are we going to do?" She scrambled around, looking for her clothes. "What the hell are we going to do?"

"Get dressed then meet me downstairs. I'll figure something out."

Finally, she nodded. "Okay."

"Okay." I pulled her to me, pressing a kiss to the top of her head. "It will be okay. Promise."

I pulled on my shirt and jogged toward the stairs. Jude was standing in the foyer with Emerson, and I silently thanked her for diverting him.

"Hey, Jude," I said.

"Dad, hey. I wanted to come by to check on you. But it—" he studied Emerson, a puzzled expression on his face "—looks like you have company."

"I was just hanging out with Kendall while you guys were gone for the game," Emerson said, and I was even more grateful that she knew about my relationship with Kendall. And, more importantly, she seemed willing to keep our secret.

Jude immediately perked up. "Kendall's here?" He glanced around as if searching for her, then his eyes landed on the doors to the backyard. "I'll just go say hi." He took a step in that direction, assuming she'd be in the pool house. Because that's where he thought she was living. *Shit.*

"I'm sure she'll...join us soon," Emerson said, perhaps realizing like I did that Jude would expect Kendall to be in the pool house. Not upstairs in my bedroom.

Jude opened his mouth, but I asked, "How about some breakfast?" I clapped a hand on his shoulder and steered him toward the kitchen. "You too, Emerson," I said over my shoulder.

"Great!" she squeaked. "I'd love some."

Javier was already in the kitchen, prepping various ingredients for the week. "Good morning."

"Morning, Javier. Could you whip us up some breakfast, please?"

"Eggs, bacon, pancakes, fruit?"

"That would be great. Thank you."

"Any allergies or food sensitivities I should be aware of? Besides Miss Kendall's dairy intolerance."

I turned to Emerson. "Emerson, anything you can't have or don't want?"

She shook her head. "Nope. But I will take a mimosa."

"Absolutely," Javier said. "It's a lovely morning. Would you like to eat your breakfast outside?"

"Great idea," I said and opened the doors to the back patio just as Kendall padded into the kitchen.

Javier brightened. "Good morning, Miss Kendall."

"Good morning, Javier." She smiled and then started conversing with him in Spanish.

They spoke quickly and fluidly. Thanks to Kendall's ongoing tutoring, I understood almost all of it.

"Hey, Ken," Jude said, giving her a hug. "How are you?"

"I'm good." Her skin was still pale, and her eyes were tired. But she looked better than she had last night. And for that, I was thankful.

Jude and Kendall chatted for a moment, and then she joined Emmy at the pool. They sat on the side and dipped their feet in the water.

"So, what happened last night?" Jude asked while Kendall and Emmy were absorbed in their own conversation. "You never leave the game early. I was worried about you."

"I know, and I'm sorry you were worried. But I had to take care of something."

He furrowed his brow. "What could be more important than the game? The team always comes first for you."

"I, uh—" I tugged on my neckline. "It was a personal matter."

"A personal matter?" Jude frowned, but then his eyes widened. "Wait. Does this have something to do with *her*?"

"Her?" I asked, my pulse skyrocketing as I tried to buy myself some time to formulate a response.

"Yeah." He lowered his voice. "You know—the woman you had sex with in your office."

I cleared my throat, grateful that Kendall seemed too absorbed in her conversation to pay us any attention. "Uh. Yeah, actually."

"Wow." He rocked on his heels. "I thought it wasn't serious."

"So did I."

He grinned. "That's great, Dad. I'm really happy for you. But...what happened last night? Is she okay?"

"Yeah," I smiled. "She seems to be doing much better now."

We fell silent for a moment, and then he blew out a breath. "I still can't believe you left the game—for a woman."

"One day," I said, "when you find the right person, you'll realize you'd do anything for them. Even things that once seemed unthinkable."

"Wow." He turned to me, smiling. "You really love her."

"Yeah." I rubbed the back of my neck. "I do."

"When can I meet her?"

"I don't know," I said, sweat trickling down my back. It

wasn't that warm out, but it felt as if the sun were beating down on me like a spotlight. "It's complicated."

"Is she married or something?" he asked.

"Or something," I said as Javier emerged from the house with several plates of food.

Jude's face brightened, and I braced myself for whatever crazy idea he was going to throw out. "We've been talking about taking the yacht out soon. You should bring her. We could have a party. Something low-key."

I huffed out a laugh. "Jude, with you, it's never low-key."

"I'm just saying, it would be a low-pressure environment for her to meet some of your friends and family. For me to meet her."

I was touched that my son was so invested in my happiness, but it only made me feel worse. "I don't know," I hedged as the four of us made our way to the table.

"We're taking the yacht out soon," Jude said to Kendall and Emerson. "You're invited, of course."

"Of course," Emerson teased, taking a seat next to Jude. Kendall was across from her.

"Now help me convince Dad that he should bring his girlfriend," Jude said, opening his napkin.

Kendall started coughing, choking on her water. Emerson patted her back.

"You okay?" Jude asked, while Emmy spoke to Kendall in calming tones.

I wanted to be the one comforting her, but I fisted my hands beneath the table instead. Kendall took a few slow sips of water, and I watched her closely, feeling helpless. Last night had been enough of a scare.

"Just—" Kendall wheezed, forcing a smile. "Yeah. Down the wrong pipe."

"Do you want some eggs and bacon?" Jude asked, holding the plate out for her.

"Oh, um—" She looked as if she might be sick. Her eyes darted to mine with a silent plea. "I'm not very hungry."

"Maybe some pancakes," I offered, knowing they'd be milder on her stomach.

She flashed me a grateful smile. "Yes. Thank you."

Jude continued talking about the yacht, and I was grateful to Emerson for listening. I was too concerned about Kendall to focus on much else. Needing to touch her, I placed my hand on her thigh beneath the table, and she jolted.

"You okay there?" Jude asked.

"Just a, um—" She glanced around. "I was startled by a bug."

"Did you know Dad was dating someone?" Jude asked Kendall.

She shoved a giant bite of pancake in her mouth and made a big show of chewing it. Emerson's eyes ping-ponged between the three of us like a cat at a tennis match. I figured she'd bust out the popcorn any minute—at least if she'd had some.

"I've done my best to be discreet," I said, hoping that answer would satisfy him.

"Does Graham know? Or Nate?" Jude asked, unwilling to drop it.

I shook my head, wishing Emerson would divert the conversation again. Wishing for an out.

"What about Jasper?" he asked.

"No. I haven't told anyone."

"Mm." He sipped his coffee. "Your secrecy is only making me more intrigued."

I laughed, though it sounded forced to my ears. "Jude, you're making this into a bigger deal than it needs to be."

"Then just tell me. Who is she?"

I wished he'd stop pushing. "I told you—it's complicated. I need to talk to her about it first."

Kendall finally relaxed, placing her hand over mine.

"I'll stop bugging you," he said. "But only if you promise to bring her on the yacht."

Kendall's eyes went wide, and I smoothed my thumb over her thigh. She quickly hid her surprise, and I tried to avoid the minefield we were navigating.

"We'll see," I said, hoping it would be enough to placate him for now.

CHAPTER EIGHTEEN

Kendall

The kitchen was clean. Emmy had already left, and I got the feeling Jude was only leaving because Knox had made some excuse about needing to check in on his "girlfriend." And Jude thought I was catching up on some things in the pool house.

Another lie. One of many.

So many that I'd lost count. How many lies had we told just this morning? Let alone the past few months. It was wearing on me.

"Thanks again for coming by to check on me," Knox said to Jude.

"Of course. I'm just glad everyone is okay."

They said something else, but I couldn't make it out. I was too busy wondering what Knox had told his son about his girlfriend. And how many more lies we'd tell. And if Jude would ever forgive us, especially Knox.

The alarm chimed twice in quick succession, letting me know that the front door had opened and closed. Which meant Jude was finally gone. I breathed a sigh of relief and slumped against the wall.

I wasn't sure which had been more exhausting. Battling food poisoning last night, or trying to act normal in front of Jude this morning.

Knox rounded the corner to the kitchen, narrowing his eyes when he spotted me. "Back to bed with you."

I shook my head, though nothing had ever sounded more appealing. I'd picked at breakfast. My stomach was calmer but by no means back to normal. And Jude's unexpected appearance certainly hadn't helped.

"Come on," Knox said, picking me up in one smooth movement.

I draped my arms around his neck and rested my head against his chest. His heartbeat was calm and steady, and it helped me relax.

By the time we reached the bedroom, I was exhausted even though he was doing all the heavy lifting. I was glad he'd insisted I go back to bed. I didn't have the energy for anything else.

Perhaps sensing that, he placed me gently on the bed. I sank into the plush mattress, missing him already, even though he was only a few feet away. My eyes drifted closed as he stripped out of his pants. I could hear the rustle of fabric as he removed his shirt before joining me in bed.

"How are you feeling?" he asked, touching me gently. First my forehead, as if he were checking my temperature. Then my cheek. My lips. My chin. All the while, his eyes scanned my face.

"I'm exhausted," I admitted, feeling a weariness that went down to the bone. I'd been up most of the night before—my body turning itself inside out. And this morning had been stressful beyond belief.

"Sleep, *mi cielo*." He smoothed his hand over my hair, his movements comforting. "Sleep."

When I woke again, the bed was empty. Knox had filled

my water bottle, and there were fresh peonies on the nightstand. I smiled and stretched, feeling a little better but still groggy. The palm trees were casting long shadows on the floor. A glance at my phone told me it was late afternoon, and I'd missed a few text messages from Emmy.

> Emmy: Whew. This morning was crazy. Are you okay?

> Emmy: I'm sure K is taking good care of you. But let me know if you need anything.

I smiled and sent back a quick text.

> Thanks, Em. I passed out after everyone left. I only just woke up.

> Emmy: I'm glad you got some rest.

> Me too. That was...a lot.

> Emmy: I'll say. What are you going to do about the yacht party?

I groaned. Part of me had hoped this morning was a figment of my imagination. A nightmare. It had certainly felt like one. But Emmy's texts reminded me that it wasn't. And I didn't know what the heck I was going to do.

> I don't know. Knox and I need to talk about it.

> Emmy: What do you want to do?

> I'm tired of lying, but I'm scared.

> Emmy: I have to say...you two are really cute together. He's good for you.

I smiled down at my phone, appreciating her approval more than she could know.

> Thanks, Em. That means the world to me.

Emmy: I'm just glad to see you happy.

> You're going to make me cry! And ditto.

> Talk later?

Emmy: Definitely.

I brushed my teeth and splashed some water on my face. My skin was still pale, but at least my stomach seemed to have calmed down. I wandered down the hallway, following the sound of Knox's voice to his office. When I peeked inside, he immediately smiled and waved me in.

I padded across the rug, and he said, "I'll call you back," to whoever was on the phone. He stood and rounded the desk, pulling me into his side. "Hey. You're up."

I nodded, reveling in his touch. Feeling safe in the warmth of his embrace. It was comforting in a way I'd never experienced, yet also terrifying. Knox had become such a part of my life, such a part of me, and I worried I was becoming too reliant on him.

"You okay?" he asked, rubbing gentle circles on my back.

I held on tighter, needing reassurance. No one had ever taken care of me apart from my mom. And even then, it had never been like this. Not that she didn't love me or didn't want to. But as a solo parent who was responsible for paying the bills and raising me on her own, she didn't have much time or energy for comfort and care. If she missed a callback, we didn't eat.

I didn't realize I was crying until Knox said, "Hey," in a gentle tone. "*Mi cielo.* What's wrong?"

He pulled back to look at me, drying my tears with his thumbs.

"What are we doing?" I blurted.

"Hugging," he said, intentionally misinterpreting my question.

"Knox," I chided. "You know what I mean. This morning—with Jude?" I shook my head. "God, I feel sick just thinking about it."

"I know." He hung his head, remorse written across his handsome features. "I know."

"That was too close," I said.

He guided me over to the chair. He sank down in it and pulled me onto his lap. "Agreed."

"You told him you're seeing someone?" I asked, still trying to piece it all together. I'd been so anxious at breakfast that I'd been concentrating on acting normal and not puking.

But then I remembered that morning in the hospital. Jude had come to visit my mom when she had mono, and he'd mentioned finding a discarded condom wrapper in his dad's office.

"He kept pushing. He wanted to know why I left the game early."

I rolled my lips between my teeth. "You shouldn't have done that."

He took my hand in his and placed them over his heart. His blue eyes were filled with endless love and devotion. "There was nowhere else I'd rather be."

I closed my eyes, the tears falling again.

"Mi cielo." He cupped my cheeks. "Tears again?"

"I'm scared."

"About what's going to happen with Jude?"

I nodded. "And about the future."

"What about the future?" he asked. "Do you have concerns about us? Is that why you're hesitant to tell Jude?"

"No. No." I smoothed my palm down his chest. "It has nothing to do with you and everything to do with me."

He rubbed his thumb over the back of my hand as those blue eyes stared intently at me. "What do you mean?"

"I've just—" I huffed. "I've never let someone in. Not truly. Not until you."

His smile was warm and reassuring. And it reminded me of all the reasons I loved him. If Knox was so sure about his faith in us that he was willing to risk his relationship with his son, then I could be brave enough to push past my own fears.

He gave my hand a comforting squeeze. "That doesn't sound like such a bad thing."

"It isn't. And…it is. Because it's scary to love someone as much as I do you. To know that you've given them your heart, and they could destroy you."

"Kendall." He leaned his forehead to mine. "I would never hurt you."

"I know that," I said. "I do. But I have a hard time picturing the future."

"With me or generally?" he asked.

"Mostly in general," I said. "I typically won't even let myself try to imagine it, for fear of being disappointed."

He frowned. "That makes me sad, *mi cielo*."

"I'm not trying to make you sad," I said. "I'm trying to be honest. In past relationships, I never let myself get invested enough to even try imagining a future together. But with you…" I cupped his cheek. "For the first time. I want to."

"I'm honored." He brought my hand to his mouth, kissing the back of it. "And it makes me indescribably happy that you're thinking about our future together."

I sensed hesitation on his part. "But…?"

He rubbed a hand over his mouth. "I didn't want to bring this up, but there's something you should know."

"Okay," I said, dragging out the word. My stomach was filled with nerves.

"Since we're talking about the future. *Our* future—" His eyes searched mine. "I think you should know that I don't intend to have any more children."

I would've joked that it was too soon to talk about children, but the fact that we were going to tell Jude changed things. Made them more serious. More...permanent in a way.

I wasn't sure what to think. But there was no need to decide anything now. Was there?

"Can we leave it open for future discussion? I mean, we haven't even told your current child about our relationship. Talking about future potential children seems premature."

"If only I were younger..." Knox shook his head, his expression one of longing and lament. "But I can't imagine having a baby at my age. I'm too old to start again."

"Psh." I rolled my eyes. "You're forty-seven. There are tons of celebrities who've had babies after fifty. Besides, I don't even know if I *want* children."

"That's just it," he said. "You don't *know*. And it wouldn't be fair of me to ask you to give that up. Especially when we both know this won't be easy."

"No," I said. "It won't. But I love *you*, Knox. I love who I am when I'm with you."

"I love you too, *mi cielo*. More than life itself. And I would give you the world, but I can't give you this."

Knox had always encouraged me to speak my mind. To challenge him. But I sensed he wouldn't budge on this.

"I don't need the world," I said, cupping his cheeks. "All I want is you."

He smiled, turning his head to kiss my palm. "What did I ever do to deserve you?" He placed more kisses on my palm, his scruff making me giggle.

"This isn't just about Jude, though," he said, turning more serious again. "People will talk."

"Does that concern you?" I asked. "What people will say about us?"

"I only worry how it will affect you. I've lived my entire life in the spotlight. And while I might not be a celebrity like Nate, people can be nasty."

I nodded. "It doesn't help that I dated your son."

"No, it certainly doesn't. I will do everything I can to shield you from it, but…"

"People will still talk," I said, knowing how this would look. How I'd be lambasted as a gold digger and worse.

"I want you to take some time to think about it," he said.

I shook my head. "I don't need more time. I know I want to be with you."

"Whew." I flopped back on my yoga mat. "That was intense."

"You know what was intense?" Emmy asked from her position on the floor beside me. "That breakfast with Jude."

"I know." I groaned. "He just kept pushing for answers. It was so awkward."

"Did you and Knox talk about it?"

"Yeah." I continued to stare at the ceiling.

"Come on." She stood and held out a hand. "You can tell me all about it at the juice bar. I'm buying."

"You always buy," I teased.

She lifted a shoulder as we slid into our shoes. After a short walk, we ordered our drinks then found a table outside.

"All right, girlfriend." She pulled a reusable travel straw out of a carrying case and pointed it at me. "Spill."

I laughed, already feeling more at ease. "Knox wants to tell him."

"What do you want?" she asked, and I could tell she was doing her best not to react.

"I don't want to tell Jude, but I want to be with Knox. And I'm tired of lying."

"Holy shit. I told you he loves you."

"You were right," I said, both miserable and elated by that fact.

"Considering the whole yacht party, I'm guessing Knox wants to break the news to Jude soon," she said.

"The sooner, the better."

"Is he pressuring you?" Emmy asked, frowning.

"No. No." I waved a hand through the air. "Nothing like that. I just…ugh. Once we do it, there's no going back."

"I know." She nodded. "And I know you love Knox, but, well, doesn't it seem a little fast?"

Emmy had always been so supportive of my relationship with Knox. So for her to ask if it was too soon was… Well, I hadn't expected that response from her.

My shoulders bunched. "I thought you were happy for me. You said he was good for me."

"He is. But how long have you even been together? How can you be sure this is what you'll want long-term? Because if you're going to tell Jude, you damn well better be sure."

I gnashed my teeth. For once, I wasn't running away, I was leaning in. And now Emmy was having second thoughts?

"I've known Knox for nearly two years," I said, hating the defensive tone to my voice.

"And for a decent chunk of that time, you were dating his

son. Then you didn't have any contact with him for six months."

"I thought you'd be happy for me. I thought you'd back me up. Not...try to talk me out of it."

She placed her hand over mine and smiled. "I want to make sure you're doing this on your timeline. Not Jude's. Not Knox's. But yours."

"I am! This is what I want. I know it's not the easiest path, but I love him and want to be with him."

She sank back in her chair with a smile. "Now I believe you."

I stared at her, mouth agape. "What? You were testing me?"

"No. But if you're going to risk destroying his relationship with his son, you need to be certain. You need to believe that it will work out. Because your relationship is going to be put to the test."

I didn't appreciate Emmy's tactic, but I knew she was right. Telling Jude was going to be a major test. But it wasn't going to get any easier the longer we waited. In fact, the opposite was true.

CHAPTER NINETEEN

Knox

I rubbed Kendall's shoulders, mostly to stop her from fussing over the table again. Any minute, Jude was supposed to arrive at the house to meet my girlfriend. After much discussion, Kendall and I had decided this was the best way to handle the situation. We didn't want to have this conversation in a public place or make him feel ambushed on the yacht. Nor did we want to wait any longer to tell him.

I'd been counting down to this evening with equal parts excitement and dread. Kendall and I would no longer have to sneak around, but that meant telling Jude the truth about our relationship. I was anxious about how it would go, but I didn't want to make Kendall more nervous.

I peered down at her. "You ready for this?"

"I don't think I'll ever be ready to tell my ex that I'm dating his father." The words were said in a teasing tone, but I could hear the concern and fear that lurked beneath it.

I felt it too.

But I also knew we couldn't continue as we were. It wasn't fair to Jude, and it wasn't fair to us.

But it was a big step, and I couldn't help but worry. Not

just about Jude's reaction but that Kendall would come to regret this. Regret us.

She'd already given up her dream job to take care of her mother. And I struggled with the idea of her giving up something she might truly want—children—to be with me. She might not want to be a mom now, but someday she might.

I worried that despite everything I'd given her, it wouldn't be enough. That *I* wouldn't be enough.

"It's going to be okay," I said, hoping my voice conveyed more confidence than I felt. "Jude is happy to have you back in his life."

She gave me a look full of doubt. "Sure. As a friend. As a coworker. Not..." She gestured between the two of us.

"Hey," I said, grabbing her hand and squeezing it reassuringly. "He's the one who pushed for you to work with me. Maybe he'll be more accepting than we think. I mean, look at how he reacted when he found out you were house-sitting for me."

"I wish I shared your optimism," Kendall said.

"We need to tell him," I said, determination marking my tone. Though part of my desire to tell Jude was out of selfishness.

I was tired of pretending that Kendall was merely my employee. I was sick of hiding how I felt around her. I wanted the world—and Jude—to know that she was mine. That she belonged with me.

"I know," she sighed. "I do. But I don't want to hurt him." The fact that she cared so much about my son's feelings only made me love her more.

"Neither do I. But the longer we keep this secret, the more upset he'll be when he finds out."

Her shoulders sagged. While we both knew telling my son was the right thing to do, that didn't make it any easier.

"Try not to worry." I rubbed her shoulders, wanting to put

her at ease. "He's been dating Chrissy for a while now, and they seem really happy together."

She nodded. "True. It definitely helps that he's moved on."

We were quiet for a moment then I asked, "What are you most concerned about?"

"Once we tell him," she said, staring up at me with a serious expression, "there's no going back."

"I know," I said in a solemn tone. "But it's time. Past time." I cupped her cheek, and she leaned into my touch. "Who knows? Maybe he'll be happy for us. You saw how excited he was about the fact that I was dating someone."

"Ha!" She barked out a laugh. "Were you always this happy-go-lucky?"

I laughed. "No. It's you, Kendall." I kissed her, savoring the taste of her on my tongue. "You make me feel alive. Hopeful. You make me believe anything is possible."

She smiled, but it was tinged with sadness. "I love that about you."

My phone rang, and I frowned when I saw Jude's name on the screen.

"Jude, hey," I answered. "Are you almost here?"

Kendall rubbed her hands together, and I smoothed a hand down her back. I was nervous as hell, but I wasn't going to show it. I needed to be calm, collected. For her and Jude. For all of us.

"Hey, Dad. I'm not going to be able to make it."

"What?" I asked. "Why not?"

"I forgot that Chrissy and I already had plans. And she's pissed."

"Oh, um—"

I glanced at Kendall, who mouthed, "What?"

"I understand, but we were really looking forward to tonight."

Kendall's face fell, and I hated disappointing her.

"I know. I'm sorry. Fuck." I could just imagine him dragging a hand through his hair. "I feel like I'm letting everyone down."

I could certainly empathize with that. But I just listened. That was what he really needed—someone to listen.

"You're not letting anyone down," I said. "Least of all me." In fact, the opposite was true.

"Thanks, Dad."

"Go take care of what you need to. I'm always here for you."

"Thanks." He sighed. "Sorry to ditch last minute. I guess I'll be meeting your mystery lady at the yacht party after all."

"Why do you say that?" I asked, trying to hide the panic from my tone.

"Because I'm out of town until then, remember? I have that trip to court the sponsors."

"Oh. Right." I gnashed my teeth. "Okay. Well, we'll figure something out. Have a good trip."

"Bye, Dad. Love you."

"Love you too," I said, disconnecting the call.

"He's not coming," Kendall said, sinking down onto the couch. We'd been building up to this. Preparing for it. And now...

I let out a heavy sigh. "No. He's not."

She squeezed her eyes shut. "What are we going to do?"

I sat next to her, pulling her into my arms. "We're going to eat a nice dinner and enjoy our evening alone."

"About Jude," she said flatly.

"We'll tell him soon." I kissed the top of her head.

"Not on the yacht, though, right?"

I scoffed. "Fuck no. But you should still come."

"I don't know if it's a good idea."

"We don't have to decide anything tonight. How about some dinner? Or a swim?"

"Mm." Her eyes darkened, probably thinking back to our first night together. "Definitely. But dinner first. Javier prepared an incredible meal for us, and I'd hate for his efforts to go to waste."

I pulled her into me, rasping into her ear, "And I'll have you for dessert."

She gave␣out a sexy little squeal when my beard grazed her neck. "Yes, please."

"Oh my god. How many people did he invite?" Kendall asked, peering into the distance where a large group was talking and laughing at the entrance to the yacht club.

Sea gulls swooped in the distance, hunting for scraps of food. The surface of the water was calm. The sky clear. It was the perfect weekend for going out on the yacht.

Everyone was still far enough away that they wouldn't be able to make us out. So I joined Kendall at the railing, wrapping my arms around her. If the crew members remembered that she'd dated Jude, they didn't remark on it. There were no raised eyebrows. Though I expected nothing less than complete discretion from my employees.

"You know Jude," I said. "He loves a good party."

Kendall spun to face me, her hands braced on the railing behind her. It had the effect of pushing her chest out, and my mouth watered at the sight. Now was not the time to be thinking about all the things I'd imagined doing to her on this boat, but it was a good distraction.

"You're beautiful, you know that?"

She smiled, placing her hands on my chest above my heart.

My heart that belonged to her. There was no way I'd jeopardize my relationship with my son if I weren't crazy about her. If I weren't absolutely certain that she was *it* for me.

"Do you want some champagne?" I asked.

"That sounds nice."

I grabbed the bottle from inside and poured two glasses. When I returned to the deck, she was waving at someone in the distance.

"Showtime," she murmured as I handed her a champagne flute.

Jude boarded first. He was smiling and laughing, but his steps were clipped, and his jaw tight.

"Where's Chrissy?" Kendall whispered, scanning the group like I was.

"I don't know. Maybe she had to ride separately."

One of the crew members went down to meet Jude and the rest of our guests. Soon after, my son joined us on the top deck. His sunglasses shaded his eyes, but I could tell the moment I saw him that something was off.

"What's wrong?" I asked when he immediately took a champagne flute offered to him by one of the crew. "Is Chrissy okay?"

"She isn't coming." He gulped down his glass. "We broke up."

I watched Kendall out of the corner of my eye and tried not to let my panic show. "I'm sorry to hear that."

He held his glass out to the crew member for a refill. "Don't be. I'm not."

I arched a brow but tried to otherwise remain expressionless. I could remember when he and Kendall had broken up. He'd been...upset. Down. Not angry.

"Where's your lady love?" he asked, using the nickname he'd taken to calling her.

"Lady love? Ooh," Jasper crooned, giving me a hug. "Who's that?"

"Dad's girlfriend."

Jasper tilted his head to the side. "You have a girlfriend?"

Before I could even respond, Jude said, "Yeah. It's pretty serious too."

"What's serious?" Nate asked, joining our group. *Fuck me.* "Hey, Knox."

"Dad and his girlfriend." I really wished Jude would stop making such a big deal of this.

"Well, damn." Jasper clapped a hand on my back. "Can't wait to meet the woman who's captured your heart." His gaze turned to Kendall, and I wanted so badly to tell Jasper he was looking at her. And that he better keep his eyes—and his dick—to himself because she was mine.

"You guys remember Kendall," Jude said. "My ex." He downed the rest of his champagne. "Ex-ex. Ex before my current ex? Whatever."

When he wandered over to the bar and poured himself a glass of whiskey, Kendall flashed me a look of concern. I followed Jude, careful to keep my voice low. "Would you rather take the yacht out another weekend?"

"What?" He jerked his head back. "No. I'm sure we'll have more fun without Chrissy." His attention was directed at Kendall when he said it, and a knot formed in my stomach.

"Are you sure?"

"Yeah, I'm sure." He glanced around. "So…where is she?"

"Oh. Uh—" I cleared my throat. "Something came up last minute."

He draped his arm over my shoulder. "Then I guess we're both flying solo this weekend. Let's cast off."

Despite my unease, I told the crew we were ready to leave, and then we were off. We enjoyed a charcuterie board and champagne. It was nice to catch up with Nate, Jasper, and Graham. Emerson couldn't come because she was watching Nate's daughter, Brooklyn. But several of Jude's other friends had joined us. Cade and a handful of women whose names I didn't remember.

Jude's mood seemed to improve the more the evening wore on, probably thanks to all the alcohol. It was nice. Pleasant. At least when Jude wasn't taking Kendall on another walk down memory lane.

I wondered if this would be possible in the future. I wondered if Jude would ever look at me the same once he knew the truth.

"You okay?" Kendall mouthed when Jude's back was turned. It felt as if we hadn't had a moment alone. Or maybe I was just sick of sharing her.

I nodded, smiling as if everything was fine.

"Sir," the steward said. "Dinner will be ready in an hour."

"I should go freshen up and change," Kendall said.

I nodded. "I think I'll do the same."

Everyone went below deck, splitting off to our various rooms. Kendall closed her door first. We'd agreed to spend the weekend in separate cabins, even though I wanted nothing more than to be close to her.

Jude lingered in the hall, his eyes on her door after it had closed. He straightened and then disappeared into his room. And then I finally went into mine.

I closed the door behind me and let out a heavy sigh. This weekend wasn't going at all to plan. I just hoped we'd be able to turn it around soon.

I took a shower and changed into jeans and a dinner jacket before heading back upstairs. Jude was alone, swaying to the music.

"Perhaps you should slow down a little," I said, eyeing the drink in his hand.

He arched an eyebrow. "Worried you can't keep up, old man?"

I narrowed my eyes at him, but I knew better than to let him goad me into getting drunk.

At the sound of footsteps, we both turned to see Kendall enter the room. Her satin dress flowed over her skin like water, the grayish-blue material the same color as the clouds that floated past. She looked phenomenal, but I wasn't the only one who noticed.

I didn't like the way Jude looked at her. Watching her with the same hunger I knew I wore. Wanting her.

"Shall we?" I asked, gesturing toward the table as the rest of our party joined us.

After dinner, Kendall was drawn into a conversation with Nate. I followed Jude out to the deck. "Are you okay?"

He lifted a shoulder. "I'm great."

I couldn't get a read on his tone. I didn't detect any sarcasm, yet he'd just broken up with his girlfriend.

"What happened with Chrissy?"

He rested his elbows on the railing and blew out a breath. "She said she didn't want to spend the weekend watching me flirt with my ex. She thinks I'm still hung up on Kendall."

I took a slow, measured sip of my champagne as I considered my response. Finally, I asked, "Are you?"

He glanced back to the dining room, where Kendall was talking with the other guests. "Honestly, yeah. I'm not sure I ever got over her."

Fuck. Me.

He was still in love with her. We were in love with the same woman.

"It's just—" He leaned back, glass dangling from his hand. "Seeing her these past few months, spending time with her... It all came back to me. How much I cared about her. How good we were together."

"But you broke up," I said, hating the defensive tone to my voice.

"Yeah. Because she moved." He lifted his glass, the liquid sloshing against the sides. "Or I thought she'd moved. Whatever."

He took a step forward but then stumbled. I placed my hand on his shoulder and said, "Perhaps it's time we get you to bed."

"No." He reached for his glass, but I tugged him forward.

"Come on, Jude," I said in a more forceful tone. "Time for bed."

He grumbled but allowed me to escort him below deck to his room. Once he was safely in bed, I let out a sigh of relief. "Good night. Sleep well."

He grabbed my neck and pulled me back down to him for a hug. "I love you, Dad."

I smirked. "I love you too."

"No, really. You're the best. You're always there for me. And you brought Kendall and me back together."

I stilled. *Wait. What?*

"You brought her back into my life, and now I get to have a second chance."

Fuuuck. I sure as hell hoped that was the alcohol talking.

I gave his shoulder a gentle squeeze. "I'm sure things will look different in the morning."

CHAPTER TWENTY

Kendall

I stared at the clock on my phone. It was early, but I'd given up on falling back to sleep. I'd tossed and turned all night. I'd been so consumed with thoughts about Jude's potential reaction. And I missed the comfort of sleeping with Knox's arms wrapped around me.

I wanted to go home. I wanted to go back to our bubble where Knox and I could be together. Where we were happy.

I didn't know what to make of last night. Jude had been flirtatious. Complimentary.

I wanted to blame it on the alcohol and nostalgia, but his eyes had watched me, tracked me wherever I'd gone. I knew that look. I knew what he was thinking. And it scared me. Because I knew he wanted me.

I took a shower, my mind on the two men. After I finished getting ready, I headed upstairs to the deck where Santa Catalina Island was in view. We'd anchored near Catalina overnight, and I was looking forward to exploring the island. Or at least, I had been before.

Knox was sitting at the table, breakfast laid out before

him. "Good morning." His voice was deep and smooth, sending chills down my mostly bare body.

Even from behind his sunglasses I could feel his eyes appraising me. Blazing a trail of heat over my skin. I'd purposely chosen my neon-green bikini, and I knew we were both thinking of the night when he'd told me all the things he'd longed to do to me. All the times he'd imagined me on the yacht.

And now, here we were. I might be wearing the bikini and a white mesh cover-up from the night we'd met, but I felt as if I were naked. As if he could see right through me.

Before I headed for the buffet, he circled my wrist with his hand. "*Mi cielo,* are you trying to kill me?"

I smirked at him over my shoulder. "Just helping fulfill all your fantasies." I sank my teeth into my lip.

He groaned, pressing on his cock. "I'm going to be hard all fucking day."

He pulled me closer and smoothed his other hand down my side, over my hip, his expression one of longing.

"Knox." I glanced toward the stairs. We were the first ones up, but I didn't expect the quiet to last long.

He huffed and removed his hand. "I hate not being able to touch you."

I leaned down so my lips hovered next to his ear. "Later, when we're alone at home, you can touch me all you want."

"I fully intend to," he practically growled.

I helped myself to some food from the buffet. As soon as I took my seat, he rubbed his legs against mine. I smiled, grateful for his touch. For this man. Our relationship might be a secret, but I'd never felt more cherished or adored.

Knox and I ate our breakfast in companionable silence, and I could envision many mornings spent like this. It wasn't about the yacht or the lifestyle; it was about him. About the way he made me feel.

"Morning," Jasper said, and I snapped my attention to him. I immediately pulled my legs back from Knox.

"Morning," Knox said, completely unruffled, even as Jude and the rest of the guests joined us. "Captain says we can Jet Ski today."

"Awesome," Jasper said, popping a piece of pineapple into his mouth. He helped himself to a plate of food then joined us at the table.

When I stood to add some more fruit to my plate, Jude said, "Mm. You wore my favorite bikini." And he gave me a long, blatant perusal.

I shivered. It felt *wrong* and not just because Knox was watching. When Jude looked at me, I felt as if he were appraising something he wanted to acquire. But when Knox looked at me, I felt valued, cherished.

I glanced at Knox, and his jaw was tight. I had a feeling it was going to be a long day.

After breakfast, the steward asked if anyone wanted to Jet Ski.

"Pass," Graham said.

"You're so boring." Jasper rolled his eyes then stood. "I'm in."

"Me too," Jude said, and a group of us proceeded down to the back deck where the Jet Skis were docked and waiting.

Everyone else paired off—two per Jet Ski. Then Jude climbed on one and held out his hand for me. "Come on, gorgeous."

"I, um—" I got the odd sense that he was trying to recreate our time together.

"You can ride with me if you'd prefer," Knox said.

Jude furrowed his brow. "Why would she ride with you? You're her boss. And my dad. That's just..." He shuddered. "Weird."

If you think that's weird, just wait, I thought. Because I was doing a hell of a lot more than riding with his dad on a Jet Ski. I was riding *him*.

"You know what?" Knox asked. "I'll stay here. Kendall, you can have this Jet Ski. You guys have fun."

"There," I said, smiling. "Thanks, Knox."

"What?" Jude barked out a laugh. "You hate driving the Jet Ski."

It was a fact. But I also didn't want to ride with Jude, my legs pressed against his. My heat against his back.

"Let's *go!*" Jasper called, his tone bleeding with impatience.

"Kendall?" Jude said, expectant. "Come on."

"I, uh—" I rocked on my feet, glancing at Knox.

What the heck was I supposed to do? Everyone knew I hated driving the Jet Ski. But for all the times Knox had encouraged me to use my voice, I seemed to have lost it in that moment.

"Maybe I'll just, uh—" I hooked my thumb toward the boat, even though I'd been looking forward to it.

"Nah. Come on." Jude grabbed my wrist, tugging me toward him and nearly into the water. "It'll be fun. Promise."

I wasn't so sure about that, but I forced a smile and climbed on behind him.

"Just like old times." He grinned at me over his shoulder.

I pretended not to hear him over the motor. He sped off from the yacht, the wind whipping through my hair as the Jet Ski flew through the water. I wanted to look back to see if Knox was watching, but I didn't dare.

Instead, I tried to relax. I tried to focus on the warmth of the sunshine and the shoreline.

"Race you!" Jasper called.

"You're on!" Jude yelled back before I could protest. Then he called over his shoulder to me, "Hold on!"

They took off. Jude whooped and cheered, pushing the Jet

Ski—and my patience—to the limit. It was almost as if he kept taking tight turns and fast curves to force my body against his. Between the adrenaline rush and trying to avoid touching him any more than was necessary, I was exhausted.

As soon as Jude won, the others sped away. Chasing one another around.

When Jude finally slowed and then stopped, I wondered if something was wrong. But then he pointed in the distance. "Dolphins."

I smiled, loving the sight of a pod of Pacific bottlenose dolphins. They were a big reason why I loved going out on the Jet Skis, even if I didn't like driving them. "They're beautiful."

He squeezed my hand that was resting on his stomach. "So are you."

"Jude…" I said, sensing we were veering into dangerous territory.

"What?" he asked.

"You just got out of a relationship."

"So?" he asked. "If you remember, *we—*" he gestured between us "—used to be in a relationship."

"I remember," I said. How could I forget?

I wanted to believe there was a reason for everything, but if the purpose of my relationship with Jude was to connect me with his dad, well…I wished the universe could've found another way to have made that happen. Because the longer we spent on the yacht, the more awkward and untenable this situation was becoming.

Jude clearly had the wrong idea about us. Or maybe he was just looking for a rebound. But a rebound with an ex? That sounded messy.

Was it really any messier than the situation I currently found myself in?

"Maybe we could be again," Jude said. "Maybe there's a reason you stayed in LA and that our paths crossed again."

"Yeah, my mom had cancer."

I hadn't meant for the words to come out as sharp as they had. I hadn't meant to say them at all. But I was cranky from bouncing on top of the waves and nearly being thrown off. And I didn't like where this conversation was headed.

"I know," he sighed. "I'm sorry. I…"

I smoothed my hands down my thighs. "Jude, it's fine. It's no one's fault that she got cancer."

"I'm sorry she did, but I'm not sorry about seeing you again. Spending time together this weekend, these past few months, has reminded me of how good we were together. I mean…didn't we have fun?"

What was I supposed to say? We were in the middle of the freaking ocean, and he'd effectively trapped me in this conversation.

"We did." And I'd been naïve to think it wouldn't get to this point again. But he'd moved on. He was happy with Chrissy—at least until a few days ago. "But—"

"But nothing," he said, taking my hand in his. "Please, Kendall. Let's give this another chance."

"I-I—" Suddenly, the sun was scorching, and I scrambled for a response. Any response that didn't involve telling him about Knox. "I'm actually seeing someone."

And now I understood why Knox had told Jude he had a girlfriend.

He jerked his head back. "You are? Since when?"

I cleared my throat, sliding my hand out of his. "It's still sort of new."

He let out a heavy sigh and stared toward the sky. "Does he make you happy?"

I smiled at the thought of Knox. "He really does."

Jude nodded, glancing out over the water, the sunlight sparkling off the surface. "Then I'm happy for you."

When we arrived back at the yacht, Jude docked the Jet Ski and helped me on to the boat. Knox and Graham were nowhere in sight. Jude and the others headed up to grab lunch. Tonight, we were going ashore to drink and dance at the Descanso Club.

I needed a moment to collect myself, so I made my way to my cabin to freshen up. The captain announced that we were making our way toward shore and would be docking in about an hour. Before I reached my cabin, a large presence loomed behind me in the narrow hallway. His body brushing up against mine. His scent wafting over me like a warm, summer hug. *Knox.*

I sagged with relief, even as I worried Jude or someone else would see us. And now that I knew Jude had feelings for me—or at least thought he did—the situation had gotten a lot more complicated. I'd told Jude I wasn't interested in rekindling our relationship, but the idea of breaking the news about Knox's and my relationship seemed almost cruel.

"Come with me." Knox opened the door to his cabin, and I followed him inside.

I headed for the balcony, the fresh air beckoning to me. I needed to calm down and center myself before I said something that would make this situation even worse.

"What's wrong?" Knox asked. "Did something happen out there?"

I watched a boat as it sped past in the distance, frustrated and filled with pent-up energy. For once, I almost wished we'd told Jude about us sooner.

I didn't even know how to tell Knox what Jude had said or if I even should. There was only one thing that could help me relax right now.

"I need…" I sighed, melting into his touch. "I need you."

"You have me," he said, caging me in with his arms. He pulled my hair over my shoulder to kiss my neck. "You'll always have me."

I dropped my head back, resting it against his chest. Taking a moment to ground myself.

"We should've told Jude." I inhaled slowly and let it out even slower. "We should've found a way to tell him sooner."

"I agree," he said. "But we can't tell him now. At least not while we're on the yacht, and he's fresh off his breakup."

I squeezed my eyes shut. "I know. But..." I hesitated, not wanting to drive an even bigger wedge between Knox and Jude. "He told me earlier that he wants a second chance."

"Mm." He held me to him.

"You don't sound surprised," I said.

"He said as much last night, but I'd hoped it was the alcohol talking."

I turned to glance at him over my shoulder, my eyes wide. "He did?"

"Yes." He gripped my chin lightly, pressing a kiss to my lips. "And I feel bad for him, but he's not thinking clearly."

"I agree. But this only makes it even harder to tell him about us."

"Kendall, *mi cielo*, we will tell him when the time is right. It doesn't matter who does or doesn't know about us—" Knox pressed against me, his hard-on digging into my ass as one arm came around my front, banding me to him "—you're mine."

I nodded, leaning into his touch. Into him. *This.*

"Say it," he commanded, perhaps sensing what I needed without my even verbalizing it. He brushed his fingers over the swell of my chest. "Who does this heart belong to?"

"You," I whispered, melting into him.

He kissed my neck before pulling my bikini bottoms

aside and cupping my mound. "Who does this pussy belong to?"

I moaned, loving the way he'd taken control.

"Kendall," he growled, his voice low, dangerous in my ear. His body bracketing mine above the ocean.

"You," I moaned again as he began rubbing my clit with the lightest of touches. "Only you."

"That's fucking right." He circled my clit faster, making my legs quake. "You like taking my cock, don't you?"

"God, yes." I leaned my head back, loving the possessive way he held me to him. Like I was precious. Irreplaceable.

He yanked my swimsuit down, his movements a whisper of a rustle behind me as he lowered his shorts and slid his cock between my legs.

"Yes, Knox," I cried out as he entered me.

His movements were decisive, quick, the tension rolling off him in waves as he pumped into me. I leaned back into his chest, trusting that he had me. That he'd always have me, even when everything else felt out of control.

I grabbed the railing, and Knox placed the flat of his palm on my back. His touch was possessive yet loving.

I savored the taste of salty air on my tongue. The feel of his body rocking in motion with mine. The sound of the ocean as the waves lapped against the side of the boat.

I was so lost in Knox that I barely registered a knock at the door. A moment later, Jude called, "Dad?"

CHAPTER TWENTY-ONE

Knox

"Dad?" Jude called again.

I stilled, my hands gripping Kendall's hips. My cock still buried deep inside her. Meanwhile, Kendall curled into herself, as if she could somehow magically disappear if she concentrated hard enough.

"What is it?" I asked through gritted teeth.

"Are you okay?" he called. "You sound…weird."

I tried to relax, though I'd been on the verge of coming just a moment ago. "I'm fine."

"Okay. Well, some of us are going to head over to Descanso."

"I'll come when I can."

I thought that was the end of it, but then Jude said, "Kendall didn't answer. So I'm guessing she's still in the shower. She can come with you when you're both ready."

We'd been on the verge of doing just that when my son had interrupted.

Fuck. I squeezed my eyes shut.

Someone else joined him—it sounded like Jasper. And then their voices faded away.

"We can't keep doing this," Kendall said, righting her bikini as I pulled up my shorts.

"Just a few more days," I said, knowing she was right.

I loved her, and I loved my son. And I didn't know how to reconcile the two.

I was tired of the lies. The guilt. The deep sense of betrayal I felt, especially now knowing Jude still had feelings for Kendall.

I kissed her. "Take your time getting ready. I'll meet you upstairs."

"Okay." She moved toward the door, but not before I grabbed her wrist and pulled her back to me for another kiss.

After everything with Jude, I wanted to make sure she didn't have any doubts about my feelings. About us.

"I love you." I smashed my mouth to hers.

Her lips formed the most beautiful smile. "I love you, Knox." She kissed me again, a kiss filled with passion and promise.

Guilt weighed on me, but Kendall's smile made me feel as if everything would be okay. At least, so long as I had her.

When she placed her hand on the doorknob, I said, "Wait."

I opened the door and stepped into the hallway to make sure the coast was clear. Then I turned back to her and said, "Okay. Go."

I showered and changed. When I climbed the stairs to the deck, I ran into the steward. "Would you like me to call for a ride to the Descanso Club?"

"Not yet, but thank you," I said, knowing Kendall was still getting ready.

I poured myself a drink and tried to steady my nerves, still on edge from the close call. We were playing a dangerous game.

Kendall joined me on deck, her hair pulled back in a loose

bun. Her coral dress fluttered around with the wind, tantalizing me with glimpses of her thighs.

My mouth went dry at the sight of her. "You're wearing *that* to the club?"

"Yes." She peered down at herself. "Why? Is something wrong with this?"

"It's too sexy," I said. "Everyone's going to be looking at you. And I'm not going to be able to touch you." *Fuck me.*

She wrapped her arms around my waist. "Do we have to go?" she asked, pouting those full lips in a way she knew I couldn't resist.

"Would you rather stay here?" I rubbed her shoulders.

She nodded. "After the day we've had, a quiet evening alone sounds like heaven."

"That it does, *mi cielo*." I kissed her without restraint, getting lost in the moment. In her.

"Dad?" Jude's voice seemed magnified even over the sound of a passing speedboat.

Kendall scrambled out of my arms, and I snapped my head to where my son was standing. Watching. And judging from the look on his face, he'd seen everything.

My heart slowed, and it felt as if time stopped.

"What the fuck?" he asked, dragging a hand through his hair. "Wait..." His expression was pinched. Pained. "Were you two...? Did I...?" He seemed to be struggling to breathe. To form complete sentences.

"Jude," I said in a calm tone, needing to get control of the situation. "Take a breath."

"Take a breath," he scoffed, taking a step forward. "Take a fucking *breath*?" The words came out sharp. "I came back to get my cell phone. And I find...you...*this*?"

He started pacing the deck, muttering to himself. I chanced a glance at Kendall. She twisted her hands in front of her, a worried expression on her face.

"I thought your girlfriend couldn't come. You told me..." Understanding dawned on his face as everything clicked into place.

"I know," I said. "But it didn't seem like the time or place to announce that Kendall and I are together."

There. I'd done it. Ripped off the Band-Aid.

"So that's why she..." I couldn't make out everything he said after that, but there was a lot of cursing involved.

Jude took a deep breath and faced Kendall. "So, *he's* who you're seeing?" The words were hurled from his lips like I imagined he wanted to toss me over the side of the boat.

Kendall nodded, but otherwise, neither of us spoke. I was trying to give him a moment to process everything. I was trying to let him work through his emotions.

"Was there ever actually a job in New York?" Jude finally asked her.

She jerked her head back. "Yes. Of course there was. I wouldn't lie to you about that."

"But you'd lie to me about leaving. About where you were living. About—" He pointed at me, his cheeks turning red even as he refused to meet my eyes. *"Him?"*

I hung my head. I didn't want to enrage Jude more, nor did I want him to feel outnumbered. Ambushed. But it stung that he was acting like I didn't even exist. Not that it was undeserved. It just...it fucking sucked.

"First of all," Kendall said, taking a calming breath. "I didn't lie about leaving. As I told you before, I'd taken the job and planned to leave, but then my circumstances changed."

"I'll say." He shook his head slowly, his expression one of disbelief. "Does your mom even have cancer?"

Kendall gasped as I stepped forward to shield her. "That's enough."

"Wait," Kendall said from behind me. Her hand on my

back. Giving me strength. "You think I stayed in LA for Knox?"

He lifted a shoulder. "I don't know what to think at this point. I don't believe a word either of you has to say. For all I know, you were together before we broke up. And maybe you made up the 'move' so you could be together in secret all this time."

"Listen to yourself, Jude," Kendall said. "That's insane."

He leaned forward, his cheeks growing redder by the moment. "Any more insane than the fact that my ex is *fucking* my father?"

I flinched at his crude description and the harsh tone of his voice. "It's not—"

"Like that. Right." He kicked at the deck.

"*Jude*," I said in a warning tone.

Jude shook his head. "Don't 'Jude' me. Actually, better yet, don't talk to me."

"Now, son—"

"No." He sliced a hand through the air. "You lost the right to call yourself my father."

I flinched. I hadn't expected this conversation to go well, but I'd also hoped it wouldn't be quite the disaster it was turning into.

"I'm sorry. Okay?" I dragged a hand through my hair.

Jude ignored me and turned, jogging down the stairs. I gripped Kendall's shoulders, asking her to stay put. Her expression haunted me, even as I chased after my son.

"Please, Jude. Let's just talk about this."

"Talk about what?" He spun to face me. "The fact that you slept with my ex—a woman who's young enough to be your *daughter*. Or that the two of you were lying to me about it. Sneaking around behind my back."

"I'm sorry," I said again, pleading. "I never meant for this to happen. I never meant to hurt you."

I'd always known that telling him would be painful, but I'd never imagined it would feel like this. As if someone had reached inside my chest and ripped my heart in two.

"You *knew* how I felt about her." The agony on Jude's face was heartbreaking.

I tried to choose my words carefully. I needed to handle this situation delicately. Even more so, considering how he'd found out. I worried that if I said the wrong thing—if I made it worse—I'd lose any chance of being part of his life.

"In the past," I said. "Yes. But I thought you'd moved on. If I'd realized there was any chance…"

"Oh yeah?" He scoffed. "So, you just expect me to believe that you'll, what? Step aside if I ask you to?"

"I—"

Jude lurched forward, his index finger inches from my nose. "Ha! You hesitated. Because you're lying."

"No." I inhaled slowly, trying to calm myself. How did you comfort your child when you'd been the one to hurt them? "I just—"

"What?" he yelled. "You just what?"

My shoulders slumped. "I didn't realize it was ever that serious between the two of you."

Kendall had never let on that her feelings for Jude had been that deep. Not that I was going to tell him that. In fact, I was thankful she'd stayed on the upper deck.

Jude's nostrils flared. "I was in love with her."

I tried to put myself in his shoes. I imagined what it would be like to want a second chance with Kendall, only to find out she was with someone else. To find out she was with him.

Even so, it all boiled down to one thing for me. "If you'd loved her," I said gently, "the distance wouldn't have mattered."

"She was *mine*." He jabbed his chest with his finger.

And if he were any other man, I would've reminded him that he'd let her go. Jude had let Kendall go. He'd moved on. Maybe she'd been his once, but she wasn't anymore.

He clenched his fists, and I'd never seen him look so menacing. Certainly not toward me. "You just couldn't stand that I'd have something so…"

"Stop." I held up my hand, trying to remain calm. For all of us. "Kendall is a person. Do not talk about her as if she is a possession."

His eyes darted to the bottom of the stairs where Kendall was now standing, hand to her mouth. Her bun had come loose, and tears streamed down her cheeks as the wind whipped her hair around her face. He scoffed and shook his head. "Fuck you," he spat. "Fuck both of you."

He stormed off, and I took a step to follow him before Kendall placed a hand on my arm. "Let him go."

My eyes were glued to his retreating form. "I don't want to leave it like this."

"Neither do I," she said, running her hand down my arm, soothing me in the way only she could. "But he needs to cool down. If you keep pushing, you're only going to push him further away."

I'd always put my relationship with Jude first. I'd always prided myself on being the kind of dad who was there for him. Who loved him unconditionally.

And yet…I'd done the unthinkable.

What kind of man was so selfish that he was willing to hurt his own child? What did it say about me that I'd been willing to take what I wanted, while foolishly hoping Jude would be okay with it?

I scrubbed a hand down my face. "Fuck."

I knew Kendall was right, but that didn't make it any easier. I hated hurting Jude. I hated disappointing him. I wanted to fix this, but I needed to give him space. Even when that was the last thing I wanted to do.

I cupped her cheek, scanning her eyes to make sure she was okay. She was my center even in the midst of a storm. And I'd been so focused on Jude that I'd neglected to check in with her. "I'm sorry for the hurtful things he said to you."

She rolled her lips between her teeth, leaning into my touch. "You have nothing to apologize for."

I rubbed my thumb along her jaw. "He was upset, but he shouldn't have spoken to you like that."

Her eyes fluttered closed. "Hopefully he'll calm down with time."

I pressed my lips to her cheek. Her nose. Her forehead. Inhaling her scent as I reminded myself that this was what I wanted. That Kendall was what I wanted.

"I'm worried about him," I finally admitted.

I'd never seen Jude so upset. I knew he was still processing the breakup with Chrissy. Then Kendall had rebuffed his advances. And now this... I squeezed my eyes shut.

I could only imagine how he was feeling.

Betrayed. Angry. Hurt. Rejected.

And that was on me.

I'd done this.

I'd broken my son's trust, and yet I couldn't fathom my life without Kendall. I had to find a way to fix this. I *would* find a way.

"I'm worried about him too," Kendall admitted, her expression solemn, her big heart allowing her to overlook his spiteful words. "Why don't you text Nate or Jasper?"

"And say what?" I asked, my mind stuck on fixing things with Jude. Not...involving anyone else. I didn't want to make things worse by wounding his pride even more. For now, the fewer people who knew, the better.

"Just ask them to keep him company. Keep an eye on him."

"Good idea," I said, pulling out my phone to do just that. I was glad one of us was able to think clearly.

I sent a message in the group chat with Jasper, Nate, and Graham.

> Can you guys watch out for Jude?

After a few minutes had passed and no one texted back, I added.

> Please.

> Nate: Don't worry. We'll take care of your boy.

Your boy.

I breathed out a sigh of relief. Jude might hate me at the moment, but at least he had family looking out for him. He wasn't alone.

CHAPTER TWENTY-TWO

Kendall

I stared out at the water, though I couldn't see much. The lights from a few boats. The homes and businesses dotting the coast of Catalina in the distance.

Jude had made it to shore; he had several people who loved him and were looking out for him. Based on how angry he'd been, I had a feeling he wouldn't be coming back tonight, or maybe ever.

"You hungry?" Knox asked, rubbing my shoulders.

I frowned. "Not really."

I was too busy replaying the fight with Jude. The shock on his face, the confusion. And then the anger and pain.

When had I become this person? A woman who would cause such destruction? A woman who put her needs and wants above everyone else's?

"Me either," Knox said but steered me inside toward the dining table anyway.

As always, the table was laid beautifully. It felt as if we were on a floating five-star restaurant. But even the sight of a delicious, dairy-free meal couldn't tempt me.

"Come," Knox said, pulling out a chair for me. "Sit."

I did as he asked, but I didn't know how I could possibly eat. My stomach was in knots after our blowup with Jude. I kept sneaking glances at Knox, wondering how he was coping. Wondering if he regretted it. Regretted us.

"Drink?" he asked, going over to the wet bar.

I nodded. "Definitely."

He poured us each a whiskey and returned to the table, setting the glass before me as one of the staff arrived with food. There was no toast. No clink of the glasses in celebration. There was silence, and it was glaring.

Knox kept staring at Catalina, as if he could somehow see what Jude was doing if he concentrated hard enough. I hated seeing him like this.

They'd always been close. I knew how much Jude respected his dad. I knew how much Knox loved his son. This was tearing them apart, and it was all my fault.

I pushed the food around my plate, my mind trying to catch up with everything that had happened. Spinning with ideas of what would happen next.

"I'm sorry," I finally said, trying not to cry again.

"What?" Knox peered up at me with tenderness and confusion, taking my hand in his. "Kendall, you have nothing to be sorry for."

"Yes. I do." I squeezed my eyes shut briefly, willing the tears not to fall. "I'm sorry, Knox. I, this—" I gestured between us. "This is all my fault."

"What?" He jerked his head back and beckoned me to him. "Come on." He tugged on my hand.

I stood and climbed in his lap, feeling safe in his arms. He took my face in his hands and used his thumbs to dry my tears. "Kendall, *mi cielo*. We fell in love. It's no one's fault."

I shook my head with a defeated sigh. "I know, but maybe we should've fought it harder. Maybe I should've…"

"We tried," he said. "You know we did. What's done is done."

"Yes, but..." I let out a shaky breath. "Where do we go from here?"

"I don't know, but I will make this right," he vowed.

"How?" My voice cracked.

"I don't know, but I will." He kissed my lips, the salt from my tears mingling with the taste of whiskey. Of him. "Because I can't imagine my life without you."

I leaned into his touch, wishing those words—this relationship—hadn't come at such a high price. And as I thought about the fact that Knox's son might never speak to him again, I couldn't help but worry. But when I tried to picture the alternative—never being with Knox—the tears fell more freely.

"Neither can I." I sniffled, and he pulled me to his chest, holding me close.

I clung to him, as if somehow that would tether us together permanently.

I'd always wanted someone who'd put me first. Who'd make me their priority. And now that I had that, now that Knox had done that, even at the cost of his relationship with his son, I realized how mistaken I'd been.

"Did you hear anything back?" I asked Emmy, trying not to get my hopes up.

It had been nearly two weeks since Jude had found out about Knox and me, and nothing had changed. Jude was ignoring us. *No.* Not just ignoring us—he'd shut us out completely. It was as if we didn't exist.

Emmy shook her head. I returned my gaze to the pool, staring out at the water from behind my sunglasses. As soon as we'd gotten home from the yacht, I'd called Emmy and told her everything. She'd been sympathetic but not surprised.

Since then, Knox had flown to New York for a Huxley family event, along with Nate and Brooklyn. Nate hadn't asked Emmy to attend, so she had the week off. And Knox had insisted I take a vacation as well, suggesting I invite Emmy to stay with me.

But even with Emmy here, the house felt empty. Lonely. My thoughts too loud and the silence too harsh.

While I was grateful not to have to face anyone at work—even though they were still in the dark about my relationship with Knox, it had given me too much time to think. For once, no one needed me.

Not my job.

Not the man I loved.

Not even my mom.

Mom was in remission, and she was finally feeling more like herself. She'd started working again—part time. She was still dating Joe, and they were happy. I was happy for her. She deserved to enjoy life.

But it was almost as if I didn't know what to do with myself now that nothing was expected of me. It had made me realize that I didn't know who I was anymore. Because for so long, I'd defined myself based on my relationships.

"It's like the whole group shut us out," Emmy said. "I mean, Cade even blocked me on social media. That's harsh."

Emmy had been trying to check on Jude through mutual friends, but they'd clearly chosen his side. I didn't want anyone to choose sides. I didn't want there to *be* sides.

"I could set up a fake profile…" she offered, kicking her feet, splashing water from her perch on the side of the pool.

I scrunched up my face. "No. We'll figure out something."

"What about Knox? Has he heard *anything* from Jude?" she asked.

"No," I said flatly, watching a hummingbird as it flitted between some flowers. "Well, apart from Jude texting back to fuck off."

"Right. But that was nearly two weeks ago." She lifted her sunglasses so they were resting on top of her head. "So, what do the Leatherbacks think is going on?"

"Jude has been responding to emails, but he hasn't come into the office. Knox told everyone Jude was working remotely."

She shook her head. "He's lucky he has a job that will allow him to do that."

"I know." I gnawed on my bottom lip. "But how long can it continue like this? I'm worried about Jude, and Knox has been beside himself. What if Jude never speaks to him again?" I asked, finally voicing my biggest fear aloud.

"I know you feel bad about what happened, but—" Emmy came to sit next to me, leaning against the chaise lounge and taking my hand in hers. "You can't keep doing this to yourself. I've never seen you so miserable."

"I know," I sighed. "I know, but I can't help feeling like it's all my fault." I let my head drop back against the chair, overcome by a sense of defeat.

"Knox wanted this," she said. "Maybe not the complications, but he knew there would be consequences to getting involved with you."

"So did I," I sighed. "Maybe I should've tried harder."

"To avoid him?" She laughed. "Kendall, we both know that was never going to happen for either of you. It was always there, simmering under the surface."

"But I could've...I don't know. Quit my job. Put some

distance between us." There were a million decisions I could've made that wouldn't have led us here.

"And if you really could choose differently, if it meant that Jude wouldn't be hurt but you would never be with Knox—"

I shook my head. As much as I wanted to pretend this could've been avoided, I knew I'd do it all again just for a chance to be with Knox. He'd become my everything.

"That's what I thought," Emmy said, giving me a squeeze.

I nodded. "Thanks, Emmy."

"When are you going to tell your mom?" she asked.

I chewed on my lip. "I don't know. Everything's such a mess right now, you know?"

"It might help," she said. "She would never judge you, and —as a parent, as someone who knows Jude—maybe she could provide some insight into how to handle the situation."

Emmy seemed to dance around the words. As if she knew they needed to be said, but she was hesitant to voice them aloud.

"What are you really trying to say?" I asked.

She stared up at the sky then back at me. "You're barely eating. You're sleeping all the time. I'm worried about you. Knox is worried about you."

"Everything sounds disgusting. And even when I try to eat, I end up dry heaving over the toilet afterward."

She frowned. "Do you think…" She shook her head. "No."

"What?" I asked.

"No. It couldn't be. Could it?" she mused.

"What?" I asked again, irritation marking my voice.

"Never mind." She smiled with a wave of her hand. "You're probably extra emotional since you're about to get your period."

My period? I stilled. Oh shit.

I'd been so busy, so upset about everything, that I hadn't

paid as much attention to anything else. But now that she'd mentioned my period, I couldn't stop thinking about it.

I swiped my phone off the coffee table and navigated to my calendar app. "I'm late."

"It could still come," Emmy said, but the cheer in her voice sounded a bit too forced. "And you guys use protection, right?"

"I'm on birth control, but we stopped using condoms a while ago."

"So…it's possible," she said in a gentle tone.

"Yes," I sighed, my world in a downward tailspin. "I suppose it's possible."

"Why don't I go grab some tests, and then you'll know."

I gripped the edges of the chair. "No. I can't."

"Kendall," she said. "What are you going to do? Just pretend this might not be happening?"

Knox had made it very clear that he didn't want to have any more children.

"Yes," I said firmly. Wishing it could be true. "I mean no… I want to give it a few days."

I felt sick to my stomach. Heartsick. And just…so out of control.

Hadn't I had to deal with enough between my mom's cancer and everything with Jude? I didn't know how much more I could take.

CHAPTER TWENTY-THREE

Knox

"Where's Jude?" Graham asked.

It had been nearly two weeks since I'd heard from my son. He wouldn't talk to me. He wouldn't let me explain. He'd completely shut me out.

I was trying to give Jude space, but I wondered if he'd ever forgive me for what I'd done. I wondered if this was how it would be for the rest of our lives. I wondered if I'd been naïve to think that I could have a relationship with Kendall *and* my son.

"He's not coming." I sipped my whiskey. I was attending the annual charity gala for the Huxley Family Foundation, but all I wanted was to be at home with Kendall.

"Everything okay?" Jasper asked, joining us.

"I fucked up with Jude."

Jasper raised an eyebrow, and Graham grunted. "How bad?"

"Pretty sure if he ever speaks to me again, it will be a miracle."

"What will be a miracle?" Nate asked, joining our group.

"Jude's not speaking to Knox," Jasper said. "Know anything about that?"

Judging from the way they were looking at one another, Nate did, in fact, know something. Nate huffed, and Jasper smirked.

Nate turned his attention to me, lifting his shoulder. "Jude asked if he could hide out at my cabin in Bear Creek for a while. I figured it had something to do with Chrissy and their breakup."

"Have you heard anything from him?" I asked my brother.

Nate shook his head. "No. Why?" He furrowed his brow. "Did something happen?"

I hesitated, wondering if I should say anything, considering it was still a sensitive topic with my son. But if anyone might be able to help, it was Nate.

"I made a mistake. I hurt him," I said, unable to admit the truth.

"So apologize. Buy him a new watch or something," Jasper said, as if it were that simple. As if it could be fixed that easily.

"It's not that kind of mistake," I grumbled. "And he's not five."

Nate frowned. "Even if he were, that's a terrible way to parent."

"Daddy!" Brooklyn called, running up to us with Sloan in tow. Their dresses swished behind them. "Auntie Sloan and I are going to check out the view."

"Okay, sweetie. Have fun." Nate dropped a kiss on her head, and then Brooklyn was gone, dragging Sloan along. "I swear she gets bigger every day." He watched her go with a wistful smile.

"I remember those years," I said. "They'll be over before you know it. And she'll be an adult and—"

He placed his hand over my mouth. "Nope. Don't even

say it. I'm not thinking about it. She's still my little girl. She'll always be my little girl."

We laughed, and Nate released me. But I knew how he felt.

Jasper and Graham were pulled into other conversations, but Nate stayed with me. "So, what's really going on with Jude?"

"Did he tell you anything?"

Nate shook his head. "No. Just that he needed some time alone. I would've told you he was at the cabin if I'd realized..."

"It's fine. You didn't know."

"I take it this is about more than just his breakup with Chrissy," he said.

I nodded. "Do you swear to keep this between us?"

"Of course."

I looked around, making sure there was no one nearby. "I slept with someone. Someone who was important to Jude." Even more so than I'd realized.

Nate arched his brow. "Interesting. I presume you're not going to tell me who she is."

"What matters is that I hurt Jude, and now he's not talking to me."

"Mm." Nate sipped his scotch. "Is it serious? With the person you slept with."

I nodded. "We wouldn't have planned to tell Jude if it weren't. But then..." I shook my head. "He found out before we could tell him."

Nate winced. "Yikes."

"Yeah. It was—" I smoothed down my beard. "Bad."

"How bad?"

I stared at the floor briefly. "He told me he never wants to speak to me again."

Nate winced, and it took me back to that night on the

yacht. I kept reliving it over and over. Jude's expression of hurt and betrayal. The pain that continued to lance my heart.

Jude and I had never gone this long without talking. I'd never hurt or disappointed him so deeply.

I sighed. "I don't know what to do. I want to fix it, but I don't know how or if I even can."

Nate considered it a moment then asked, "Could you stop seeing her?"

The mere suggestion made my chest ache. "No. That's not an option."

I loved Kendall, and I couldn't imagine my life without her. But it was destroying my relationship with my son.

"Wow." Nate's eyes widened. "It *is* serious, then."

I nodded. "I love her. But it's more than that. Even if I stopped seeing her, it wouldn't undo the damage I already caused. I still don't think Jude would forgive me."

"Damn." He rubbed a hand over his chin. "Who the hell is she?"

When I didn't answer, he decided to try to guess.

"I can't imagine you getting back together with Tori," he said.

I shook my head. Tori and I had always been good friends. Friends who had gotten pregnant after one drunken night together in college. I'd proposed because it had felt like the right thing to do at the time. But I hadn't loved her. Not the bone-deep, earth-shattering way I did Kendall.

"Jude's former teacher or something?"

Or something.

"Look, Nate. It doesn't really matter."

"Yeah, except for the fact that now I'm fucking curious. And the more you keep quiet about her, the more I want to know who she is. A celebrity crush," he blurted, reminding me of Jude when he'd found out I was seeing someone.

"No. Fuck." I dragged my hand down my face. "Can you please focus? I need solutions."

"And you've tried talking to Jude?"

"Of course I have. He keeps shutting me out. And I'm worried—" I gnashed my teeth, grabbing his arm and pulling him into a quiet corner for privacy. "I'm worried this rift," I said, for lack of a better word, "will have serious ramifications for the team."

Jude hadn't stepped foot in the office in nearly two weeks. Even though he was still responding to emails, his absence was already impacting the Leatherbacks.

I'd heard the whispers around the office. From the team. Everyone was worried about Jude, and I didn't have a clue what to tell them because it was clear they weren't buying my story about him researching a new project.

"Maybe he just needs some space. It sounds like this came as a big shock."

I nodded. "He definitely didn't see it coming."

"So, give him time," Nate said with a sympathetic smile.

"How much time?" I asked, exasperation bleeding into my tone. "I've never gone this long without talking to him. I'm about to go out of my damn mind. And it's hurting her too."

"Interesting," he said. "Because of *her* relationship with Jude?"

Nate was clearly fishing for clues, but it was a valid question. I'd opened the door to this conversation, and I was desperate for a solution. This wasn't just hurting my son or me; it was hurting Kendall.

"Yes," I huffed. "Look, I thought I could handle the situation with Jude. I thought he'd come around eventually, but I'm beginning to worry he never will. I mean, he was the one who told me to get out more. To start dating. And I didn't mean to fall for her. I tried to stop it…stop myself."

"Okay, now you really have to tell me," Nate said.

I groaned and stared at the ceiling. "Not until I fix things with Jude."

"Seems like I could be waiting a long time, then."

I blew out a breath. *You and me both.*

Later that night, back in my hotel room, I tried calling Jude. I wasn't surprised when it went straight to voice mail again. Nor by the fact that my texts continued to go unanswered. But I was still disappointed.

I took a few deep breaths and decided to call the one person who could cheer me up. The one person who would understand.

"Hey," Kendall answered, and just hearing her voice put me at ease. "How was the event?"

"Fine." I rubbed my forehead. "Good."

The Huxley Family Foundation had donated a ton of money to a number of important causes, but it all felt so hollow. Because all it did was remind me of my own broken legacy. My own shortcomings and how badly I needed to fix things with Jude.

"I'm ready to come home," I said. "And I talked to Nate. He's spoken to Jude recently."

"Oh, I'm so glad," she said on a rush of air.

"Me too." It was a relief to know where Jude was.

And in a few days, I'd be heading home—to Kendall. The thought of climbing into bed with her, of holding her in my arms, was the only thing helping me keep it together when it felt as if everything else was falling apart.

I pressed the button to connect to video, and Kendall finally accepted.

"Hey." I smiled at her beautiful face on the screen. But then I immediately frowned. "You look tired, *mi cielo*. Are you sleeping okay?"

She shook her head, and my heart plummeted.

"Are you worried about your mom?" I asked, knowing

she had a scan coming up. Kendall hadn't talked about it much, but I knew it weighed on her. As did the situation with Jude.

"Yeah," she said, but I sensed there was more to it. Still, I didn't push. I knew Kendall would tell me when she was ready.

"I wish you were here." I sighed, knowing everything was better with Kendall. "I miss you."

"I miss you too." She smiled, but it was tinged with sadness. "But we both know I couldn't go with you."

I nodded, but I hated it all the same. We'd agreed that until we sorted things out with Jude, we'd continue to keep our relationship a secret. He deserved some time to come to terms with the news before we went public with it.

"Are you and Emerson having fun?" I asked.

"Yeah." She yawned. She told me about their day. But before too long, she said, "It's getting late. I think I'm going to head to bed."

Late? I frowned at the screen, noting that it was one in the morning for me, which meant it was barely ten o'clock for her.

Something was wrong. She never ended the call this quickly.

"*Mi cielo,*" I said in a gentle tone. "Talk to me."

"I..." She glanced away briefly, and then I watched as a tear streaked down her cheek. She wiped it away quickly. "I'm late."

It took a second for her words to process, but when they did, I stilled. "Late. As in, your period's late?"

I concentrated on the screen, feeling as if I were staring into a black tunnel. A black tunnel that had started spinning.

"Yeah," she croaked.

My muscles tightened, and I rubbed my brow in an effort to stay calm. "Have you taken a test?"

She shook her head, tears in her eyes. "No," she whispered. "I'm too scared."

I stood and started throwing things into my bag, carrying my phone with me as I went. "I'll be there in a few hours."

"No. Knox." She shook her head. "The event. You can't come home early."

"Of course, I'm coming home early," I said. "I'll be there before morning."

"Knox—"

I cut off her protest. "I'll see you tomorrow."

"See you tomorrow." She smiled, but it was weak.

"It's going to be okay, *mi cielo*," I said, trying to reassure her as much as myself. "I love you."

"I love you," she whispered then disconnected the call.

I frowned at the blank screen, my mind spinning. Was Kendall pregnant? Because if she was, it would change everything.

CHAPTER TWENTY-FOUR

Kendall

I opened the door to the backyard and walked outside, needing some fresh air. Emmy had gone to get us some ice cream and pregnancy tests. I hadn't intended to tell Knox that my period was late, but I also knew I couldn't face this without him.

I wound through the backyard, trying not to let myself go down the black hole of what-ifs. I didn't want to add to Knox's stress, but I needed him. I needed to know it would be okay.

I was so absorbed in my thoughts that I stopped short when I spotted a figure standing by the pool. His back was to me, but I knew instantly who it was.

"Jude?" I asked.

"Hey." He turned, and I tried to get a read on his expression.

I glanced around, wondering if he was alone. Wondering why he was here. Did Knox know Jude was here?

"Your dad isn't here," I said, wishing he were.

"I know. And he's not my dad. Not anymore."

I cringed but tried to hide it. Jude was clearly upset, and I was to blame. So I nodded slowly, calmly, even though my heart was racing. "Are you…okay?"

"No." He shook his head, coming closer. "I'm not okay. I haven't been okay since that night."

I backed away slowly. Jude had never been aggressive or physical. Then again, finding out your ex was sleeping with your father would push anyone to the limit.

"Do you—" I debated whether I should even broach the topic, but I found myself asking, "Do you want to talk about it?"

He looked me over, taking his time. Finally, he said, "You were the best thing that ever happened to me."

My heart softened, and I felt bad for hurting him. Not just for moving on, but knowing I'd moved on with his dad made it even worse.

"Jude…"

"No." He shook his head. "You were. You're kind and beautiful. You really care about people, Ken."

Ironic words coming from Jude, considering what I'd done to him. How I'd broken his heart and destroyed his relationship with his father. I didn't feel as if I deserved any of his praise.

"How did we get here?" he mused. I wondered if he was asking that of himself. Me. Maybe the universe.

It was something I'd often asked myself. How we'd gotten ourselves in this situation. Why I'd ever allowed myself to come between these two men. And how I'd ever thought it would turn out okay.

This was the furthest thing from okay.

My ex was close to tears. He wasn't speaking to his dad. I might be pregnant. And everyone was miserable.

I led Jude over to a chair, guiding him to sit before joining him. Jude cradled his head in his hands. "What does he have that I don't?"

His words twisted at my heart, playing on my guilt.

"What is it?" Jude asked, pushing for an answer.

"*Nothing*," I said.

"Clearly, it's not nothing. And I know it's not about the money, so what is it?"

I lifted a shoulder. What could I say? Nothing would make it better. So, I settled for, "You're a great guy, Jude. You're just not the guy for me."

"But *he* is?" he seethed.

The fact that Jude couldn't even say his dad's name didn't bode well for the future of their relationship. I hated that it had come to this. I hated myself for tearing their family apart.

I didn't want to hurt Jude—well, not any more than I already had. But I couldn't lie either. "I'm sorry," I whispered through my tears.

"Kendall." He took my hand in his, his expression surprisingly serene. Almost...pitying. "I don't blame you."

"You don't?" I asked, taken aback by his abrupt change in demeanor.

But it quickly shifted from forgiveness to anger once more. "No. *He* should've known better. He's older. And he *clearly* took advantage of you and the situation."

I frowned, not liking Jude's tone or the language he used. It all felt all...wrong.

Still, I tried to remain calm. I was determined to defuse the situation and repair the harm I'd done to the extent I could.

But that didn't mean I could stay silent. Knox had helped me find my voice, and I'd always use it—especially to defend him. So I took a deep breath. "I'm sure you don't want to hear this, but we are both adults. And this was a consensual relationship."

"He's a powerful man." Jude lifted a shoulder, a sympathetic expression on his face. "A rich man. No one would fault you for feeling pressure when the power balance was so firmly tipped in his favor."

"Jude," I said, shaking my head and standing. "That's not what happened."

He closed the distance between us. "I'm worried about you, Kendall. That's why I came here. To help you."

He placed his hand on my shoulder, his expression one of concern. Yet something felt...off.

"Help me how?" I asked.

"Help you get away from him, of course. He's manipulated you and the situation. And I won't stand for it."

"Stop." I held up my hand. "Just stop," I said more firmly. "I know you don't want to believe it, but I love your dad."

Jude's expression morphed into one of disgust. He backed away slowly and shook his head. "Fine, then. Have it your way." He sauntered toward the gate.

Maybe it was the ominous tone to his voice or the unexpected visit, but my chat with Jude left me feeling unsettled.

I returned inside, but when the alarm chimed and the front door opened moments later, I jumped.

"Kendall?" Emmy called.

"In here," I said, trying to steady my breathing.

My mind kept playing over my conversation with Jude. Wondering what he intended to do.

Emmy took one look at me and asked, "What's wrong?"

"Jude was here."

Her jaw dropped. "What?"

I nodded, still trying to piece it all together. "He was here. In the backyard."

She dropped the shopping bag on the sofa and wrapped her arm around my shoulder. She ushered me to the couch. "What happened?"

"He—" I blinked a few times, still trying to process what

had happened. "H-he kept talking about how he wanted to help me. How Knox had taken advantage of the situation."

She jerked her head back. "Jude said that?"

I nodded.

"Shit. Have you told Knox?"

"No." I dropped my head into my hands. I told her about my earlier conversation with Knox. "He's flying home tonight, even though I asked him not to."

"Oh, Kendall." Emmy rubbed circles on my back, and I started crying again. "What a mess."

We sat there for a while until I'd calmed down some. Then she asked, "What do you want to do now?"

"I don't know." I stared ahead, numb.

"Do you want to take the test?"

"No," I answered immediately.

"Kendall, you might feel better if you know."

I shook my head. "I want to wait for Knox. I want to do it with him."

"Okay," she said. "Are you going to tell him about what happened with Jude?"

"I-I—" I blew out a breath. "I don't know. I have to deal with one thing at a time. And I don't want to make things even worse, you know?"

"I'm not sure it can get much worse at this point."

"You're wrong." I laughed, but it was humorless. "I might be pregnant with my ex's half brother."

The mattress dipped behind me, and I froze. *"Mi cielo,"* Knox exhaled my name like a prayer, pulling me into his arms.

I softened, grateful he was home. Surprised I'd actually fallen asleep.

"Knox," I said, turning to face him in the darkness. "I missed you."

"I missed you too." He dotted my skin with kisses, and my body relaxed. *He was home.* "How are you feeling?"

"Tired," I said. I was *so* very tired.

"Then rest," he said in a soothing tone while rubbing my back. "I'm here."

When I woke again, I had to squint against the bright morning sun. I turned to grab my phone from the nightstand, smiling at the sight of a huge bouquet of fresh peonies. I wondered when Knox had even had the time to pick them up.

I pulled on my robe and padded downstairs to the kitchen. Knox was sitting on one of the barstools, working on his laptop. He looked delicious, and I wrapped my arms around him, trying to ignore the box of pregnancy tests Emmy had left for me.

"Hey," he said, placing his hands over mine. "You're up."

I nodded against his back, letting his warmth seep into me. "Where's Emmy?"

"She left earlier. But she said to call if you need anything."

"Thank you for the flowers," I said, resting my cheek against him.

He turned to face me. "My pleasure." He grasped my chin, bringing my lips to his mouth for a kiss. It was languid and sensual, making me feel centered once more.

"Mm." I hummed, getting lost in his kiss.

"How about some breakfast?" he asked. "Javier left some pancakes in the fridge. Or I'm happy to whip up anything your heart desires."

When my eyes landed on the pregnancy tests, my good mood vanished. "Thanks, but I'm not hungry."

"Did you take the test yet?" He tucked my hair behind my ear.

"No." I shook my head. "I couldn't."

"Look—" He placed his hands on my hips. "I want you to know that no matter what happens, we're in this together."

"Yeah, but..." I lowered my voice, my throat strangled with emotion. "What if I'm pregnant?" We both knew he didn't want any more kids.

"We'll cross that bridge *if* we get there, *mi cielo*. For now, we just need to know. Right?"

I took a steadying breath, knowing he was right. Knowing I couldn't put this off any longer. "Right."

I swiped the box of tests off the counter and carried them upstairs to the bathroom. Knox followed but waited in the bedroom. I peed on the stick, set a timer, and then washed my hands, all in a daze.

I left the test sitting there and went out to him. In a few minutes, my whole world might be completely different. But until then, I wanted Knox to hold me and pretend that everything was fine.

Knox rubbed my back and held me close, whispering words of love. But when the timer sounded, my stomach plummeted.

"Do you want me to look?" Knox asked when I didn't move to check it.

I shook my head and stood. "I'll do it."

He wrapped his arm around me. "We're in this together, remember?"

I nodded, but I wasn't sure I believed it. I wasn't sure what that meant if the test was positive. I supposed I was about to find out.

I picked up the test, and my stomach immediately sank when I read the result. "Not pregnant."

It wasn't until I saw the words on the screen that I realized how much I wanted the opposite to be true. It was like flipping a coin but realizing you knew the answer you wanted before it landed. And in my heart of hearts, I wanted a baby. I wanted *Knox's* baby. I just hadn't admitted it to myself until that moment.

Until I'd felt such devastating disappointment.

"Why are you crying?" he asked, wiping away my tears. "It says you're not pregnant. That's good news, right?"

I nodded slowly. The rational part of my brain knew this would've been the worst possible time to be pregnant. As much as I might want a baby—someday—Knox didn't. And I'd never want him to feel forced into something he didn't want.

He held me to him, smoothing his hand down my hair over and over and over as my heart shattered. I clung to him like a lifeline, his scent grounding me. His touch making me feel more at home than I had in a week. I'd missed him. God, how I'd missed him.

I didn't know how long we stayed like that. His arms wrapped around me. My head against his chest. And I let him believe that they were tears of relief. Because they were. But they were also tears of disappointment and sadness.

CHAPTER TWENTY-FIVE

Knox

Someone knocked at the door, and Kendall jumped. I watched her out of the corner of my eye. I'd been watching her the past few days, trying to figure out what was going on. She was barely eating. She seemed to struggle with sleeping, when she never had before. And I was worried about her.

"You okay?" I asked, smoothing a hand down her back.

"Yeah." She smiled, but it was forced. "Yeah. I'm good."

"It's just…" I tilted my head, trying to phrase this so as not to make her defensive. "You seem really restless lately."

"I, um—" She glanced out toward the pool then back at me. "I'm fine."

"Mm." I pulled her close to me. "Maybe you should go for a swim. That always helps you feel more centered."

"I'm not sure it will help," she said, mostly to herself.

I frowned. Something more was definitely going on.

"Would talking about it help?" I asked, pulling back so I could see her face.

She gnawed on her bottom lip, and I wanted to suck it between my teeth. I wanted to soothe her and make her forget her worries. But I sensed this went deeper. That this wasn't something that could be fixed with sex.

"Come on, Kendall. Talk to me."

She peered up at me. "Promise you won't get mad?"

I furrowed my brow. "Why would I be mad?"

"Just…" She huffed. "Please, Knox. Promise."

"Okay." I smoothed my hands over her shoulders. "I promise."

"The last night you were in New York, Jude stopped by."

I jerked my head back. "What? Jude was here?"

She nodded.

"What did he say?" I rushed out. "What did he want?"

As she told me what had happened, I held her hand, growing madder and madder. I knew he was upset, but for him to come here and make her feel anxious. For him to…

I stood, ready to storm over to his condo and demand he talk to me. I'd had it. "This has gone on long enough. I'm going over there."

My footsteps pounded the floor, determination and anger swirling through me. I'd gotten us into this mess, and I was going to get us out of it. It was my responsibility.

Kendall chased after me. "Knox, please." She hung on my arm. "Think this through."

"I've had enough thinking," I said, resolved. "It's time for action."

"Are you sure that's a good idea?"

"Yes."

She sighed. "I'd offer to go with you, but I think that will only make things worse. Please," she said, pressing up on her toes. "Please just…be careful."

I kissed her hard. "I love you."

I sped across town. As soon as I arrived at Jude's condo, I banged on the door. He opened it, only to shout, "Go away!" and slam the door in my face.

"Jude." I pounded on the door again. "Open up."

When he didn't answer, didn't say anything, I called, "I'm not going anywhere, so the sooner you open the door and face this, the sooner we can move forward."

I waited a few minutes, slumped against the wall. Debating my options. We were all at our breaking point, and I couldn't allow this to continue.

"Jude." I banged my fist against the door.

Then finally, the door opened just a little. "What do you want?"

"We need to talk." My tone was sharp.

Jude said nothing. Nor did he offer to let me in. He merely leaned against the doorframe, ready to step inside at any minute. And slam the door in my face forever.

I didn't know where else to start, so I said, "I'm sorry. I'm sorry that we hurt you—"

"*We?*" he asked, stepping forward with malice in his eyes. "No. *You* hurt me." He jabbed at my chest. "You. Not Kendall. If anything, I feel bad for Kendall. She clearly felt pressured by the situation. You're older than her. Wealthy. Powerful. *Her boss.*"

The way he'd said "boss," coupled with everything Kendall had told me, gave me pause. And then it all clicked. Jude was going to try to use the woman I loved to punish me.

"What do you want?" I asked, pushing forward, into his space.

All along, I'd been so focused on how this would impact Jude that I'd failed to consider the larger ramifications. This wasn't just about falling for my son's ex. It was about the team. About Kendall's job. About the rumors that would be printed about us—some of them true, most of them not.

"This is about Kendall." He jutted his chin forward, but it was his placid expression that put me on edge. "*Not* me. I'm concerned about her," he said in a sympathetic tone. "As her friend, I worry that she was taken advantage of. That she was coerced into an inappropriate situation by a superior."

Looking from the outside in, I could see how someone might draw that conclusion. Even if it was wrong.

"I appreciate your concern. But as Kendall told you, it's unwarranted."

He seemed surprised that I knew about their conversation. But then his expression hardened. "Consensual or not, it's against the rules."

Fuck me. The nonfraternization clause.

I was beginning to think this wasn't an idle threat. And if word of my relationship with Kendall got out, there was so much more at stake than my place in the world of major league soccer. There was Kendall's future. Her privacy. If this story leaked, it would... Everything would change. How would I protect her then?

"What have you done?" I seethed.

Jude crossed his arms over his chest. "It sucks to feel like someone you loved, someone you trusted, betrayed you, doesn't it?"

"Jude." I gnashed my teeth. "I'm sorry. I don't know how many times I can apologize for what I did. Please just..." I felt desperate. *Sounded* desperate. "Don't do this. Don't ruin everything we've worked so hard to build."

"You're the one who ruined everything," he spat. "I could go to the commissioner and have you removed."

He was right. About everything. And while part of me couldn't believe he'd do something like that, I also wouldn't blame him.

All along, I'd been so focused on my legacy. On the team. But legacy was more all-encompassing than my limited vision. It was how I treated the people I loved. And if I couldn't do the right thing by them, then I had no business leading the Leatherbacks.

In that moment, I realized what needed to be done.

"No need," I said, taking a deep breath, putting my wishes aside and focusing on what Jude needed. What was best for the team. Best for Kendall. "I'll resign."

Jude jerked his head back. "What?"

I nodded. For so long, I'd clung to the team and its success as a measure of my own. As a marker for the impact I'd had. But I was so much more than that. Kendall had made me realize that.

He narrowed his eyes at me. "You're bluffing."

I didn't flinch. Didn't look away. "I'm not."

In fact, the more I thought about it, the more it made sense. Maybe Jude would finally realize what Kendall meant to me.

"I'll call the commissioner today to let him know that I'm resigning and handing the team over to you," I said, feeling an incredible sense of lightness.

"Fine." He strode over to his phone. "Let's call him now. Together."

"Okay," I said, waiting for Jude.

He lifted his brow as if challenging me to stop him. When I made no move to do so, he pressed the contact to dial the MLS commissioner. It rang twice, and I mentally prepared my speech. But just before the third ring, Jude let out a heavy sigh and ended the call.

I met his eyes. "What are you doing? Why'd you hang up?"

"I can't..." He shook his head, drawing in deep breaths. "I'm so pissed at you, but this is not what I wanted to happen. This isn't what I want for the team." He started pacing. "I can't believe this is what you'd want. I can't believe you'd do this for *her*?"

He turned away, but I still heard the words he spoke next. "You'd never do that for me."

I moved closer as if to hug Jude then stopped myself.

Judging by his clenched fists, a hug from me was the last thing he wanted. I was still surprised he was even talking to me. Surprised but incredibly grateful, even as painful as this conversation was.

"Is that what you really think?" I asked. "Jude?" I placed a hand on his shoulder, grateful when he didn't flinch or try to push me away.

Jude hung his head, and in that moment, I hated myself for failing him as a father.

"I don't want this," I said. "But if you think it's what will make this right, if this will help make things right between us, I'll do it. Gladly."

"You'd really give up the team?" he asked, head still bowed.

"Yes." I turned him to face me. "Of course I would. I'd do anything for you."

He curled his lip. "Except give her up."

"I..." Spots danced before my eyes. His words stung, but they weren't undeserved. "I can't. I love her."

He had to understand that. He might not accept it, but we couldn't move forward unless he at least acknowledged it.

His shoulders slumped, and I caught him before he sagged to the floor. "I can't do this anymore."

"Do what?" I asked, getting us settled on the floor.

"I can't live with all this anger." He scrunched up his face. "It's eating me up inside."

I nodded. "I'm sorry I did this to you. To us. I've been worried sick about you these past few weeks."

He curled into a ball, wrapping his arms around his knees. "I don't want to continue like this."

Neither did I. But until Jude accepted my relationship with Kendall, I was afraid we were at an impasse.

"Then what do you suggest?" I asked.

"That's the problem." He seemed to curl even tighter into himself. "I don't know."

"Do you want me to step down from the team?"

"No." He relaxed some.

"Do you want to continue to work remotely?" I asked, even though I hoped the answer was no.

He shook his head. "I love my job. I love the team. And I —" He hesitated then said, "Loved working with you."

I noticed it was in the past tense. I tried not to worry about what that meant for the future.

"What if we take baby steps?" I offered. "You could come back to the office when you're ready. Ease back into things."

"I'd still have to see her every day. And I was an ass."

"Kendall has a big heart, and I hope the two of you will smooth things over. In the meantime, Kendall can work remotely. That's not a problem." In fact, she preferred telework.

"Right, but I can't avoid her forever. Especially not if you're going to continue seeing her." This was good. Progress.

"True, but we can give you time and space to get used to the idea of us."

"Not sure I'll ever get used to the idea," he muttered. "But I want to try."

"I have to ask," I said, not wanting to break the fragile trust we'd rebuilt but needing to know. "What changed your mind?"

"Honestly?" he asked, and I nodded. "When you said you'd give up the team, I knew…" He blew out a breath. "I finally understood how serious you were about her. And it made me realize that I've never felt that way about anyone. Not truly."

I kept listening, grateful we were talking again. Relieved to have my son back in my life.

"I thought I loved Kendall, but if you'd asked me to give

up the Leatherbacks..." He chuckled. "I wouldn't have done it. Not even for her."

"I'm sorry," I said again. "Truly."

He met my eyes, and for the first time since that night on the yacht, I felt as if I could breathe fully again. "I know, Dad. I do."

I smiled in relief and gratitude. He'd called me "Dad." That was sweeter than any victory on the field.

I wrapped my arms around him and held him close. "I love you, son."

And in that moment, I was confident we'd get through this. Though our relationship might not be the same as before, we could build something new and different.

We talked for a while longer. About the team, about everything and nothing.

When I left his condo, I felt lighter. I called Kendall immediately, but it went straight to voice mail. I frowned. I knew she'd been nervous about my visit with Jude. And I couldn't wait to tell her about our conversation. But as my calls and texts continued to go unanswered, my concern grew.

I headed back to the house, trying to convince myself that she could be swimming laps or taking a shower. Hell, maybe she was asleep. Whatever she was doing, I needed to see her. I knew she'd be just as relieved as I was about everything with Jude.

But when I pulled into the garage, the Range Rover was gone.

I frowned at the empty bay. She usually texted if she was going to be out late. And I didn't think she'd had plans with Emerson. Normally, I'd give it time, but I'd been so worried about her lately. Worried enough to call Nate to see if Emerson was there.

"Hey," Nate said, answering on the second ring.

"Is Emerson there?"

"Hello to you too," he joked.

"Sorry." I unlocked the house and disabled the alarm, searching for any clues. "I'm worried about Kendall. I wondered if she'd gone out with Emerson."

"Kendall?" Nate's tone was full of confusion. "Why would you be..." There was silence and then, "Ohhhh. Oh shit. Kendall's your mystery woman? That's why Jude was so upset, isn't it?"

I placed my palms flat to the counter and dropped my head. I'd been so focused on Kendall I'd forgotten that Nate didn't know about us. But I was done keeping secrets.

"Yes."

Nate let out a low whistle. When he started to say something, I asked, "Can you please just tell me if Emerson's there?"

"She's here," he said. "She and Brooklyn are making pizzas."

"Can I talk to her?" I asked.

"Sure. Just a sec." His tone was more serious, perhaps picking up on the note of panic in my own.

"Knox?" Emerson asked.

"Yeah. Hey. Do you know where Kendall is? She's not answering my texts, and my calls keep going straight to voice mail." I didn't want to seem like an overbearing asshole, but Kendall hadn't been herself for weeks.

"Oh, um..." I could hear Brooklyn in the background, then Emerson said, "Let me text her."

I waited on the phone, silence filling the space between us. Until she said, "No response. But my app shows that she's at her mom's."

"Oh. Okay." I furrowed my brow. "Thanks, Emerson."

I debated going over there but talked myself out of it.

Kendall had given me time and space to talk to Jude. She deserved the same with her mom.

"Knox, is everything okay?" Emerson asked.

"I hope so," I said, but deep down, I was worried. "How do you think Kendall's doing lately?"

Emerson blew out a weighted breath, which only made my blood pressure spike even more. "I think she's struggling."

I nodded slowly. I only hoped Kendall would feel better after hearing about my conversation with Jude. I hoped that would reassure her about our future. Because there was nothing standing in the way of our happiness—not anymore.

CHAPTER TWENTY-SIX

Kendall

When Knox left to talk to Jude, I'd debated following him. But I didn't want to make the situation worse. I sighed and wandered upstairs to get dressed. But when I pulled down my pajamas, there was a spot of blood. *My period.*

Knox and I weren't trying for a baby. He didn't *want* a baby. But the sight of my period reminded me that *I* wanted a child. I didn't know what to do.

I cleaned up and went down to the garage. I couldn't just sit here, waiting for Knox. Worrying about what was happening with Jude. And I was too upset about everything to be alone.

I drove across town in a daze, not realizing where I was headed until I pulled up to my mom's condo. Her car wasn't in her spot, so I took the elevator up to her floor and took a seat at the kitchen table, waiting. Thinking. Crying.

I didn't realize how late it had gotten until the front door opened. Mom and Joe entered the condo, their laughter so light and joyful compared to how I felt.

"Kendall?" she asked, coming to my side. "Honey, are you okay?"

"I-I—" I gazed down at my lap, wondering if I'd made a mistake. And not just in coming here.

She furrowed her brow. "I'll start some coffee."

"I, uh—" I let out a heavy sigh. "No thanks to the coffee."

"What?" She jerked her head back, her expression one of alarm. "Now I'm really worried." She said it in a teasing tone, but I knew she was serious.

"I'm going to run to the store and grab us some ice cream," Joe said. "I'm craving something sweet."

"Thanks." Mom kissed his cheek, and then we were alone.

As soon as the door closed, I started crying again.

"Sweetheart, what's wrong?" She took the seat next to mine, wrapping her arm around my shoulder. "Whatever it is, you can tell me. I will always be here for you. And I will *always* love you."

"I've been lying to you." The words were garbled, but she understood them all the same.

"About what?" she asked. Her tone was filled with nothing but love.

"Jude." I took a deep breath then said, "I'm sorry, Mom. Jude and I never got back together."

"You mean you had sex without a relationship?" she said it in a faux British accent that mocked the idea. "So what?" She lifted a shoulder. "You wouldn't be the first person in history to fall back into bed with an ex."

"No. Jude and I weren't together in any sense. At least, not as more than friends, and even that…"

"But all this time… All these months, I thought you two…" She furrowed her brow. "I don't understand. Jude came to visit at the hospital. He paid my medical expenses. He's been there for you."

I took a deep breath and braced myself for her reaction. I

prepared myself for shock. Disappointment. Confusion. "Jude didn't pay them. Knox did."

She furrowed her brow. "Jude's dad?"

I nodded, trying to gauge her reaction.

"Why would he do that?"

"Because he loves me." I started crying.

Her eyes widened. "What?"

"And I love him. I'm in love with Jude's dad."

"Holy…" She promptly closed her mouth.

Mom's earlier words only made me feel worse for not telling her. "I'm sorry. For keeping this secret from you. For lying, but…"

"Kendall, sweetheart—" She stopped and turned to face me. "Were you worried about how I'd react?"

I focused on my hands as if they were the most interesting thing in the world. "Maybe. Yeah."

"I would never judge you, sweetheart." She cupped my face. "You know that."

"I know, but we've been through so much. And you were so happy when you thought Jude and I were back together. And I…I didn't know how to tell you."

She smiled, though it was tinged with sadness. "I'm sorry you felt that way, but I'm glad you told me now."

Now that I'd confessed, the words came spilling out of me, along with a never-ending stream of tears. I gave her an overview of what had happened, including how everything had blown up with Jude. "And then I thought I might be pregnant—"

"Wait." She held a hand to her chest, blinking rapidly. "Hold on. Wait a minute. You thought you were pregnant?"

"My period was a little late, but I think it was stress."

"So you *aren't* pregnant," she said.

"Right. No. I'm not pregnant, but it made me realize that I want to be a mom. Except Knox doesn't want more children…" My breath came in short bursts, my chest tightening.

"Deep breaths, Kendall." Mom smoothed her hand down my back. "Take your time."

When I'd finally calmed down enough to speak again, I wiped my tears with my sleeve.

"He told you that?" she asked.

I nodded. "In the past. Well, before I thought I might be pregnant."

"Knox knows the joy of being a father. And though a pregnancy would've been unexpected, I'm sure he would've loved that baby so much."

"How do you know that?" I asked, though I knew she was right.

Knox might not want more children, but he'd always been a committed and involved father. Even just imagining him holding our child filled me with such longing…

She dried my tears. "From everything you told me, it's clear he loves you very much."

"I love him, Mom. I love him so much it aches. But I'm scared that we don't want the same things."

She hugged me to her. "I hate that you've been keeping all this in. That's a lot to deal with alone."

"I wasn't alone," I said. "Emmy has supported me every step of the way."

"I'm glad she could be there for you. She's always been such a good friend. And I'm not surprised she supported you through this."

"I'm lucky to have her."

"How did Knox react to the test result? Or did you even tell him?"

"He was with me when I took it. The moment he realized it was negative…" The tears started falling again as I relived that moment. "He seemed so relieved."

"How did that make you feel?" she asked in a gentle tone.

"Relieved for him. For us. I know it's not the right time. But also—" I rubbed my hands, my arms. "Incredibly sad and disappointed."

She nodded slowly. "That's understandable. And it sounds like you've been on quite the emotional roller coaster lately."

We fell silent a moment, then she asked, "Do you think Knox would ever change his mind?"

My shoulders slumped. "He says that he's too old. That he's already raised a child."

She nodded slowly. "He's not *old*, but his age is definitely something to consider. Not just in raising the child. Advanced paternal age has been linked to an increased chance of miscarriage or birth defects."

I dropped my head to my chest. "Maybe this is too hard. Maybe I'm..." My chest tightened. "Too much. I already ruined his relationship with his son. At some point, he's going to realize that I'm not worth all this."

"Sweetheart." She pulled me into her side. "*You* didn't ruin anything. Knox was fully aware of the consequences."

"But Jude won't speak to him, and..."

She placed her hand on my thigh. "I'm going to stop you right there. And say that maybe Knox and Jude can use this to build a stronger, more authentic relationship."

I was skeptical. They'd had a good relationship. Or at least, it had always seemed that way to me.

"Look at us," Mom said, giving my shoulder a squeeze.

"What about us?"

"Who knew that something so awful—my cancer diagnosis—would lead to so many wonderful things. It gave us time together. I found Joe. And you found Knox. All I'm saying..." She smiled. "Is that something that seems horrible or terrifying at first can end up being a blessing in disguise."

"I see your point, but this is different." I slumped. "What am I going to do?"

"I think you know the answer," she said. "You need to talk to him."

I squeezed my eyes shut. "I don't know if I can. Not about this. I'm scared it's a deal-breaker for him."

"Is it for you?"

I considered it a moment then finally nodded. "Yeah. I think it is."

And then I started crying all over again.

"Hey," Mom cooed, holding me closer. "It's okay. It will all be okay."

I shook my head because I wasn't sure I believed that anymore.

It was late by the time I pulled into the garage. Knox's car was parked in its spot, and I felt bad that I hadn't called or texted him. But I just…couldn't.

The alarm chimed when I opened the door, and Knox padded out from the office in a pair of gray sweatpants, his hair deliciously mussed.

"I'm glad you're home," he said, sounding relieved. The way he said the word "home" hit me in the gut. I had a feeling this wouldn't be my home much longer.

He pulled me in for a hug and pressed a kiss to my cheek. "Mm." He held me closer. "I'm so glad you're here."

I nodded into his chest, listening to his heartbeat. "How did it go with Jude?" Part of me was scared to ask, but I needed to know the truth.

"Better than I could've hoped," he said, taking a step back but keeping his hands on my shoulders. "Have you eaten?"

I nodded. "Yeah. Earlier. I'm sorry I didn't text. I was with my mom."

He dipped his head and met my eyes. It felt as if he could see right through me. "Everything okay?"

"I, um..." I chewed on the inside of my cheek. "I told her about us."

His brow rose. "How'd that go?"

"Good. Now, I want to hear more about what happened with Jude."

Knox guided me over to the couch. "Good? That's it?"

"Yep. She's cool like that." I smiled, grateful I had such an amazing mom, one who loved me unconditionally. "And Jude?"

"I finally got through to him." Knox toyed with the ends of my hair, my thighs resting on his lap. "He realized how important you are to me."

"How did you make him understand that?" I asked.

"It doesn't matter," Knox said, pulling my shirt aside to kiss my collarbone. "What matters is that he wants to come back to the office. And he's talking to me again."

I moaned, even as I tried to stay focused on the conversation. "I still don't understand..."

Knox pressed a finger to my lips. "*Mi cielo*, it's taken care of."

I shook my head. It didn't make sense. "He was so angry. And now he's not? Just like that?" I snapped my fingers.

Knox let out a heavy sigh. "I didn't want to tell you this, but he threatened to oust me from the Leatherbacks."

"What?" I jerked my head back. "How? Why?" I paused, and then the answer dawned on me as I connected the dots between Jude's questions that night by the pool. My eyes went wide. "Oh my god. The nonfraternization clause."

Knox nodded. "But it's not going to happen. And I would've never let him go through with his threat."

"We broke the rules. How would you have stopped him?"

"I wouldn't have," he said simply.

I narrowed my eyes at him. "What do you mean, you *wouldn't* have stopped him?"

He smoothed my hair over my shoulder. "I would've given up the team willingly, if that's what it took for us to be together."

"I can't…" I shook my head, my chest tightening. "You've already given up so much to be with me. Too much," I added in a quieter voice.

"Don't you get it?" Knox cupped my cheek, bringing my gaze to his. "None of it matters without you."

He slanted his mouth over mine, his kiss deep and passionate. It felt like coming home, and I moaned, needing that connection. Needing him.

He rolled so his body was on top, covering mine. I roamed his back with my hands, memorizing every inch of him. Committing it to memory.

How could I ever think of asking Knox for more? Of asking him for a child?

I couldn't. Not after everything he'd been willing to sacrifice to be with me. His relationship with his son. The team… *No.*

Over and over again, Knox had put me first. He'd prioritized my needs.

For now, this was enough. Or at least, I wanted it to be.

CHAPTER TWENTY-SEVEN

Knox

Kendall burrowed deeper into my side just as she had my heart. I smoothed my hand over her skin from the top of her underwear, up to her ribs, then back down again. It had been a few weeks since my talk with Jude, and life had settled into an easy routine once more.

Kendall worked from home most days. Jude was back at the office, but he'd apologized to Kendall. And I fell more in love with her every day.

I made the same circuit again, rubbing slowly. But this time, she arched her back slightly, moaning when I teased the bottoms of her breasts, practically thrusting them into my hand.

"Morning." She hummed, sliding her hand over my sweatpants and stroking me through the material.

I groaned. "You're going to make me late."

"Is that a problem?" she teased, shifting her hips to give me a tantalizing view of her body. "I thought you were the boss."

"Kendall," I ground out, rolling us so I was on top. I grabbed her wrists and held them above her head.

"Knox," she said, arching her hips so our pelvises were crushed together. We started rocking in unison. "I need you. Please."

I pressed my lips to hers. "You know I can never say no to you."

Her expression darkened, but then it passed. But when we resumed kissing, it felt as if her mind was somewhere else, as it often was lately. I pushed up on my elbows and brushed her hair away from her face.

"Mi cielo?" I kissed her forehead. Her cheek. Her chin. "Is something wrong?"

"No, it's—"

"Don't say it's nothing. Something's clearly bothering you." And I had a feeling it had been for a while. I just couldn't figure out what it was. Especially when life was so good.

The team was winning. Jude was speaking to me again. And I got to wake up every morning with the woman I loved.

"Talk to me," I said, rolling onto my side and propping up on one elbow so she'd have more space. "You know you can always tell me what you're feeling."

She shook her head. "I'm not sure I can this time."

"What?" I furrowed my brow, not liking that answer. "Why?"

She was silent a moment, the pressure building in my chest. And then she whispered, "Because I'm afraid it will break us."

My heart stuttered as I took her hand in mine. "Whatever it is—" I brought her hand to my lips for a kiss "—we'll get through it together. Please just tell me," I pleaded. I tried to remain calm, but she was really starting to scare me.

Considering everything we'd been through together, I couldn't imagine what would possibly be so terrible that we couldn't move past it.

"I don't know how to tell you this..." She hesitated, and my anxiety only continued to increase. Still, I lay there. Silent. Patiently waiting for her to tell me what she needed to.

"You know how I thought I might be pregnant," she said, and I stilled. Was her period late? It was about that time of the month.

All I could do was nod.

Last month had been such a roller coaster. Thinking that she might be pregnant. Realizing she wasn't. Imagining a future where she could've been carrying my child, even if it seemed as farfetched as buying that time machine I used to wish for.

"Well," she said, distracting me from my thoughts. "Seeing the negative test made me realize how badly I want to be a mom."

It felt as if the floor dropped out from beneath me. "I see."

"And I know that's not what you want. And I would never ask you for something you weren't willing to give. Which is why I can't figure out where we go from here."

Wow. That was a lot to process. I dragged a hand down my face, trying to compose a response.

"Say something," she finally whispered. "Please?"

I clenched my jaw, but instead of remaining calm, I asked, "Why can't this be enough? Why isn't what we have enough?" *Why am I not enough?*

"It is. I love what we have." She kissed me, and I could feel the sincerity in her words. The passion and connection in our kiss. "And it feels almost selfish to even mention it, but..." She wiped away a tear.

"But you want to be a mom," I said, finishing the sentence for her.

She nodded, and I smoothed my hand over her back. I was at a loss for words. I'd been afraid this would happen all along. And now that Kendall had admitted what she wanted…

"I'm not asking you to change your mind. I'm just—" She sighed. "I've been carrying this with me, and I tried to give it time. I tried to convince myself otherwise. But I can't."

My chest was so tight, it was difficult to breathe. Yet I found myself asking, "What are you saying?"

Her eyes were rimmed with red, and yet she was still the most gorgeous woman I'd ever seen. She placed her hand over my heart. "Knox, I would never want you to change what you want for me. Just as I know you'd never want me to compromise what I want for you."

"You're right. But you have such a tight grip on my heart, on my very soul, that…" I took a shaky breath, unable to fill my lungs completely. "*Mi cielo*, the idea of living without you…it kills me."

I placed my hand on her waist, hoping I could get through to her with my touch. Hoping she'd let me in. Let me love her. Hoping it would be enough.

She choked on a sob, her hands still pressed to my chest. "I don't want to live without you either. But we want different things. And it's not like having a child is something you can compromise on. You either have one or you don't."

It was clear she was hurting. I wanted to soothe her pain, but I had a feeling nothing I could say would make any difference. Kendall had made up her mind. And she wanted something more. She deserved more.

She deserved everything. Even if I couldn't be the one to give it to her.

"I'm sorry," she whispered, tears cascading down her cheeks. "I'm so sorry."

"So am I," I said, knowing I had to let her go.

"Come on," Jude said, entering my office. "It's time."

"I'm busy," I grumbled, my eyes focused on my laptop.

It had been nearly two months since Kendall had ended things, and I'd practically lived at the office since then. I couldn't go home. I couldn't stand being there alone—without her.

Soon after that morning when everything had fallen apart, she'd resigned from the Leatherbacks. Moved out. It was as if she was trying to erase every part of herself from my life. Which was impossible because she was permanently embedded in my heart.

But it didn't matter how much I loved her. Or how hard I tried. She wanted the one thing I couldn't give her.

Despite knowing that, part of me still couldn't believe it was over. That she really wasn't coming back.

"It's Brooklyn's birthday party," Jude said, interrupting my thoughts.

The one good thing about the past month had been that Jude and I had had time to repair our relationship. It wasn't healed. It wasn't like it had been before. But different wasn't necessarily a bad thing. And I had faith that our comeback would be stronger than our setback.

Every day, I was grateful that we got to work together. Build something so incredible together. It was part of what drove me, what kept me going.

"I have work," I grumbled.

"It's a bye week." Jude rolled his eyes. "Besides, Nate picked this date specifically so *we* could come to Brooklyn's party."

"Well, I'm not going. I already sent a kick-ass gift."

I wasn't sure I could suffer through another function, pretending I was fine. I wasn't fine. I missed Kendall, and I wondered if I'd made a mistake.

I appreciated that she hadn't tried to persuade me to change my mind. I loved her even more for that. But also... why wasn't I enough? Why wasn't what we had—which had been wonderful—enough?

"Dad," Jude chided, crossing his arms over his chest.

"What?" I asked, my mind still stuck on Kendall. Like always.

"You're going." He shut my laptop.

"Hey!" I scowled.

"Come on." He tugged on my arm. "I know you're upset about Kendall, but this isn't healthy."

"Who's the parent here?" I teased.

"I'm serious." He glared at me. "I don't know what happened between you two, but you've been a mess ever since she left."

"Wow." I scoffed. "Don't hold back, son."

"I won't." He kicked my foot. "Now get your ass up. Get a smile on your face. And let's go celebrate the birthday girl."

"Fine." I marched over to the door. I was only doing this for my niece.

Once we were in the car, I switched on the radio. But the song reminded me of Kendall, so I quickly turned it off again. I loved her, and if I were younger, if I didn't think it would jeopardize my relationship with my son further...well, maybe having children would've been an option for us. But it just wasn't anymore. And that was the most painful thing of all.

It wasn't that we didn't love each other enough. Or that we weren't happy together. It all came down to timing.

"Do you want to talk about it?" Jude asked.

"With you?" I barked out a laugh. "I can't even believe you'd offer."

"You've got to talk to someone. Hell, I might understand what you're going through better than anyone."

I twisted my hands on the wheel. "I wouldn't be too sure about that."

"Try me," he said. I scrutinized him quickly then returned my attention to the road. "I'll just pretend we're talking about someone else. Not...you know."

"The fact that you didn't even say her name speaks volumes." I couldn't imagine my son would want to hear the postmortem of my relationship with his ex, even if he and Chrissy had gotten back together.

"I don't get it. You guys were willing to risk..." He peered out the window. "So much. And then one day, you just wake up and decide it's over?"

"We didn't just *decide* to break up." I gripped the wheel, annoyed by his flippant tone. "We realized we wanted different things."

"What? Like she wanted to move to New York, and you want to stay here? Or you can't agree on how to spend money?"

"You really want to know?" I asked.

"Yeah. I do. I've never seen you as happy as you were with her. Or as miserable as you are now."

"I was miserable when you weren't talking to me," I said. "And I don't want to go back to that place. I'm afraid that discussing this will put us there."

"I wouldn't have asked if I weren't willing to listen," he said.

"Fine," I huffed. "But don't say I didn't warn you." I glanced over at him, double-checking that he was sincere. That he didn't want to back out. And then said, "She wants a baby."

Out of the corner of my eye, I saw his jaw drop. He closed it slowly. "A baby? Kendall?"

I nodded. "She wants to be a mom. But she knows I don't intend to have any more children."

"Why not?"

My laugh sounded hysterical to my ears. "You're kidding, right?"

"You love kids," he said. "And you're a great dad."

"Well, thank you." My chest warmed. "That means a lot, especially after what we've been through."

"If you weren't such a great dad, I wouldn't have cared so much about having you in my life."

I placed my hand on his shoulder. "I don't deserve you, Jude."

"Yeah. You're probably right about that," he teased. But then his tone grew more serious. "I was always kind of surprised you and Mom didn't have more kids."

I huffed out a laugh, thinking of all the times Tori and I had discussed it. But she'd always been opposed. And while I'd understood, it hadn't taken away that desire.

"What's funny?" he asked.

"Your mom didn't want more kids. She loved you, and she said one was enough." And I knew firsthand how difficult the pregnancy had been for her mental health. Tori had made her wishes clear long ago, and then we'd gotten divorced.

"So, you would've had more if she'd agreed?"

"Oh yeah." I smiled. "I loved growing up as part of a big family. I always saw myself as having that too."

Could I really have that now? With Kendall?

I wanted it more than anything, but I was scared. Scared to get my hopes up. Scared to think it could still be possible.

For so long, I'd convinced myself that part of my life was over. A dream unrealized.

"It sounds like you still could—with Kendall," Jude said.

I got the distinct impression he was encouraging me. And I didn't know what to make of this unexpected support.

"But wouldn't that be weird for you?" I asked.

A dry laugh escaped him. "Oh yeah. It would be weird as fuck."

"Because she's your ex," I said, trying to understand.

"There's that. But I was thinking more of the fact that I'm at the age that I could have a kid the same age as yours."

I laughed, running a hand over my beard. "Yeah. Now that would definitely be weird."

"Right?" He chuckled. "But maybe it could be cool too."

Wow. I hadn't seen that coming.

I pulled onto Nate's street and put the car in park. I turned to Jude and frowned. "Really?"

"Yeah." He rubbed the back of his neck. "Look, I appreciate you taking my feelings into consideration. But you've always told me that it's my life and I should do what's right for me. I'm sorry I didn't see that before with you and Kendall. But I do now. So, if having more kids feels right to you…"

I swallowed back my emotion. "Wow. I'm…" I was shocked. "Thank you."

He opened the car door. "Just don't expect me to babysit," he teased.

I stayed in the car, staring straight ahead. Still trying to make sense of my conversation with Jude. Had he really just given me his blessing?

I felt lighter than I had in weeks.

If it was my life, and I should do what was right for me, I knew what the answer was. Kendall. Always Kendall.

CHAPTER TWENTY-EIGHT

Kendall

"Uh." Emmy flopped down on Mom's couch. I'd already deflated the air mattress and put it in the storage closet. "Why do you always get the best placements?"

Emmy was right. When the Hartwell Agency had called to offer me my new position, I'd thought it was a joke at first. House-sit a luxury apartment in Paris? Yes, please!

It was a dream come true.

I'd get to practice my French daily. I'd get to live in the most amazing home. And even though their winter was much colder than ours, there were so many things I was looking forward to. The museums. The culture. The food.

"I thought you loved Brooklyn," I said as I held up two sweaters, debating which one to pack.

"I do." She smiled. "She really is the sweetest kid." She pointed to the black sweater. The dressier one. "This one. And take that silver metallic accordion skirt."

I furrowed my brow. "I doubt I'll be going out much."

She lifted a shoulder. "Always good to be prepared. Besides, it's Paris freaking France. You don't want to look like a tourist, right?"

"Right." I laughed and added both the sweater and the skirt to my suitcase. "I wish you could go with me."

She crossed her legs. "Me too, girl."

"Can't you come for even a week?" I pleaded. "I mean, it's a seven-room luxury apartment overlooking the Eiffel Tower."

She groaned. "I know, Kendall. I know. And if I could, I would. But I already have to skip Christmas with my family in Aspen because Nate's about to start filming on location."

"I know," I smiled. "I'll miss you."

"I'll miss you too." She pulled me in for a hug. "But this is going to be good for you."

I knew she was right. I'd been stuck in a rut.

After I'd ended things with Knox and quit my job with the Leatherbacks, I'd moved back in with my mom. I'd told the Hartwell Agency I was interested in live-in assignments, and I'd started taking on jobs as a caption writer.

I loved getting to see movies in advance, and it was a good way to practice my listening and typing skills. Always racing to ensure accuracy for the English, French, and then Spanish subtitles. But I was ready for something more. Different.

Or at least a change of scenery.

It had been months since we'd broken up. And everywhere I went, I thought of Knox. It didn't help that the Leatherbacks had just won the MLS Cup. I was so happy for him, and I wasn't the only one. Everyone in LA had been rooting for the team, and the buzz was palpable. From billboards to bus clings, it seemed as if the Leatherbacks—and, in my mind, Knox—were everywhere I looked.

I'd tried to stay busy. Keep my mind off him, but it was impossible. And not just because of the Leatherbacks' win.

I kept remembering how happy we were together. How

things had finally been going well with Jude again. And then I'd had to go and ruin it.

"Hey, now," Emmy said. "It's only for a month. We can video chat whenever you want."

I smiled. "Thanks, Emmy. I was…" I waved a hand through the air. "Never mind."

"Thinking about Knox?" she asked.

I blew out a breath and sank back on my heels on the floor. "Yeah."

For the most part, I'd tried not to talk about him. It was too painful. I missed him too much.

"It's understandable that you miss him. What you guys had was…" She shook her head. "Intense."

I nodded. "It was.

"But you wanted something different, and that's okay."

"Is it?" I asked. Because lately, I wasn't so sure.

"Yes!" She joined me on the floor, crossing her legs and sitting next to me. "Kendall, you followed your heart. You told him what *you* needed. What you did wasn't easy. And I'm really proud of you."

I rested my head on her shoulder. "Thanks, Em."

"So what's got you so down?" she asked. "Because, girl, you are about to take a private jet to Paris. And live it up in an apartment worth twelve million euros."

"It's a dream come true," I said, but then I faltered. "And yet, I can't help wishing I were experiencing this with Knox."

"Because you know he'd take you on an epic shopping spree?" she teased.

"Oh, I'm sure it would be epic. But no." I didn't miss the gifts, though they'd certainly been nice. I missed him. "I just…" I groaned, rubbing my face. "I can't help feeling like I made a mistake."

"Accepting the placement?"

"No." I shook my head. "With Knox. I mean, I was so emotional. And exhausted. And stressed."

Time had given me some perspective. But I kept going back to that morning, to when it had all unraveled. Knox's words continued to haunt me.

Why can't this be enough?

Why isn't what we have enough?

"Yes, but you *knew* you wanted to be a mom. And that hasn't changed, has it?"

"No." I swallowed past the lump in my throat. "But... He's so incredible. And my heart is breaking because I love him. And I know he loves me. And yet we can't agree on this."

"Maybe he was a stepping-stone. Someone who came into your life for a short time to help guide you to your future."

My chest seized, a sob bursting from my lips. I didn't want to think of Knox like that. I couldn't. "I can't ever imagine loving anyone else as much as I do Knox."

"Oh, Kendall." Emmy pulled me to her, holding me tight.

"What am I going to do?" I sniffled.

She pulled back and smiled. "Go to Paris. Experience *all* the things. Then see how you feel."

"Okay." I nodded, knowing this was the trip of a lifetime. "I'll go."

I finished packing then zipped my bag. Double-checked that I had my passport. Everything was in order, even if I felt unsettled.

When the town car arrived that afternoon to take me to the airport, I was ready. Excited, even. This was an adventure. An all-expenses-paid trip to Paris, where I'd be living the first-class life.

I hugged Emmy and Joe goodbye, and then Mom walked me outside. While the driver loaded my bags in the trunk, she pulled me into a big hug.

"You're going to have the best time," she enthused. "I know it."

I nodded, trying to absorb some of her optimism. "You sure you're okay with me missing Christmas?"

"Are you kidding? If I'd been given this opportunity, I would've jumped on it. And I'm glad you did. You deserve this, Kendall. You do so much for everyone else, especially for me. It's time to do something for you."

"Thanks, Mom."

"Of course, sweetheart. I love you, and I can't wait to hear all about it." She gave me one more quick hug, and then I climbed into the car and waved goodbye.

When we arrived at the airport, we were waved through the gate and taken to the plane. The driver took care of my bags, and a flight attendant met me on the tarmac.

"Right this way, Miss Kendall." She smiled.

"Thank you…"

"Tabitha." She grinned, and I realized she couldn't be much older than me. "I'm with the Hartwell Agency too."

"Nice to meet you." I followed her up the stairs and stepped inside the plane but then stopped short.

Knox stood from his seat, as handsome as ever. His beard was cropped shorter than before, and his blue eyes sparkled as they scanned me head to toe. My breath caught in my chest, even as my heart pounded a mile a minute.

Was he…was this for real? Surely there'd been some mistake. Why would Knox be here? On the private flight I was taking to start my new placement in Paris? Nothing about this made sense.

"Is something wrong?" Tabitha asked, glancing between us.

"I, um—" I shifted from one foot to the other, twisting my purse strap in my hands. "I think there must have been some mistake. I'm going to Paris."

"Nope." Knox shook his head, stepping closer. "No mistake."

Tabitha excused herself, leaving me alone with Knox. I couldn't believe it. After all this time…it was him. God, how I'd missed him. Seeing him again made me realize just how much.

"Are you…" My blood whooshed through my ears, making it difficult to think. "What are you doing here?"

"I could ask you the same thing," he said, taking me back to that first night in his kitchen. The night when I'd thought he was a burglar and he'd comforted me after I'd nearly attacked him with a hockey stick.

I furrowed my brow. "I'm traveling to my new placement for the Hartwell Agency."

"About that…" He looked chagrined, and my stomach sank.

"There is no placement?" I asked. He shook his head, but I was still stuck on it. "But the apartment overlooking the Eiffel Tower…" I trailed off.

"There's no placement, but I did rent the apartment the Hartwell Agency showed you for the next month. For us. Or at least, that's what I was hoping." He closed the distance between us, taking my hands in his. "I want you to go to Paris. With me." He stroked the back of my hand with his thumb. "I've been miserable without you, *mi cielo*."

He cupped my cheek, and I leaned into his touch, aching for him. "I've missed you too. So much. And I'm sorry."

"You are?" He frowned. "Why?"

"For ever making you feel like what we had wasn't enough." I took a shaky breath. "I want to be with you, whatever that looks like. You are more important to me than anything."

He smiled then, sliding his hand down my back. "That's funny."

I tilted my head. "What's funny?"

"I've had a similar realization. And I want to be with *you*—whatever that looks like. Kids, no kids. Marriage or not. I want it all, Kendall. With you."

Had he really just said he wanted kids? Or that he was at least open to the possibility?

"But...what's different now? What changed?"

"It wasn't that I didn't want more children. I guess..." He blew out a breath. "For so long, I'd given up on that dream. And then you offered it to me, and I was scared. So I put up roadblocks. I was too old. I told myself that Jude would never support it and it would put a strain on our relationship. And so on."

"And now?" I asked, practically holding my breath.

"I realized they were just that—excuses."

"But what about...?"

"Jude?" He chuckled. "A lot's changed since you left. He told me to do what's best for me. And if that meant growing a family with you, then he supported it."

I gaped at him. *What?*

Knox smirked. "Better close that mouth or I'll put it to good use."

Even as my mind worked to process his words, my blood simmered with lust. I licked my lips as I reached out to wrap my arms around his waist. "Mm."

"Kendall," he groaned. "There's so much more I want to tell you, but you're distracting me."

I smirked, loving the effect I had on him even after all this time apart. Because I felt it too. I'd always felt it. And I was done denying what I wanted.

He slid his fingers into my hair, leaning his forehead down to mine. "Tell me it's not too late."

I smiled, reaching up to place my hands on his forearms.

"It's not too late. But there's also no rush. I'm happy just as we are."

"I love you." His voice was clogged with emotion.

"I love you, Knox," I said through my tears. "Only ever you."

He claimed my lips with his, and it was a homecoming. A promise for the future. I lost myself in his touch, flattening my body to his. Needing to be closer to him still.

Someone cleared their throat, and we broke apart, breathing heavily. My cheeks heated at being caught, and I buried my face in Knox's chest.

"We've been cleared for takeoff," Tabitha said. "That is, if you're ready."

Knox pulled back, glancing down at me with a smile of contentment unlike any I'd ever seen on his handsome face. "Are you ready, *mi cielo?*"

My answering grin was huge. "Definitely."

I didn't care where we were going, so long as we were together.

CHAPTER TWENTY-NINE

Knox

The plane's engine hummed pleasantly as we cruised over the Atlantic. Though it had been hours since we'd boarded the plane, I kept staring at Kendall, touching her. I was never taking my eyes—or my hands—off her again.

"Knox." She turned to me with a lazy smile on her face and a glass of champagne in hand.

We'd finished dinner and spent a long time talking. It was as if no time had passed at all. As if we'd been apart a few days, not several long, agonizing months.

"Yes, *mi cielo*?"

"Are you just going to sit there and watch me?" she teased.

I leaned in, brushing my thumb across her bottom lip. "I don't know. Are you ready for bed?"

Her lips parted slightly, and I slid my thumb between them. She nodded slowly, her eyes darkening as I pressed my finger flat against her tongue.

"Good," I said, withdrawing my thumb and standing.

"Can I get you anything else, Mr. Crawford?" Tabitha asked.

I shook my head, my attention solely on Kendall. "We're good. Thank you."

Kendall linked our hands, and I led her to the bedroom at the back of the plane. The covers had already been turned down, and the lighting was soft. I closed the door and locked it, cocooning us in the soundproof space.

"This is incredible," she said.

"*You're* incredible," I said, backing her toward the bed as I dotted her skin with kisses. "I've missed you."

She angled her head, granting me more access. "I've missed you too, Knox. If I'd known..."

"If you'd known what?" I asked.

She combed her fingers through her hair as if to smooth it then dropped her hands and smiled. "If I'd known you were waiting for me on the plane, I would've worn something different. Maybe put on some makeup or something."

I grasped her chin, forcing her gaze to mine. Wanting her to see the truth of my words. "I like you just the way you are."

She smiled, stroking her hands down my back. "I know, but..."

"But nothing," I said, kissing her. "There will be plenty of time to dress up in Paris. Trust me. We're going to all the best stores. You're getting a new wardrobe—shoes, purses, clothes, lingerie." I kissed her neck. "Especially lingerie."

"Mm. Is that so?" Judging from her lazy hum, I had a feeling she'd agree to whatever I wanted.

"Yes." I was glad she was so pliant. So relaxed and finally ready to let me give her everything. "I plan to spoil you, *mi cielo*. And I won't take no for an answer."

But then she gazed up at me with fire in her eyes. "You won't, huh?"

"Nope." I pushed her shoulders gently so she fell back on the bed.

She laughed and propped herself up on her elbows. "So bossy."

"You love it." I smirked, removing my tie and unbuttoning my shirt.

"I love *you*," she said, and I could feel the sincerity in her words. The intensity.

"I love you," I whispered against her lips before kissing her. "And I like you even better naked." I started removing her clothes. Pulling her sweatshirt over her head. Sliding her pants down her legs until she was bared to me.

I ran my hand over my beard. "So fucking gorgeous." I knelt to the floor between her legs. "So fucking mine."

"Yes, I am." She dug her fingers into my hair. "Now prove it."

I grinned, loving how assertive she was. So unlike the woman I'd first encountered. The woman who was reticent in expressing her wishes and desires. Who was scared to speak her mind.

"Gladly." I licked her slit, loving the way she moaned my name.

I sucked on her clit until she was panting, sliding one finger inside her tight channel then another. "That's it, *mi cielo*," I said as she writhed on the bed, clutching the sheets in her hands. "Let go. I've got you."

"I know." She grabbed my hand, our fingers intertwined. Our connection stronger than ever. "Oh god." Her eyes rolled to the back of her head. "I know, Knox."

And then she came in a burst of pleasure, her body contracting and then releasing. Letting go.

When she didn't move, I kissed my way up her stomach. I was already imagining what it would be like to see her belly full with my child. And it made me even harder.

"What are you thinking about?" she asked, peering down at me.

"How sexy you're going to look pregnant with my child."

Her smile was full of contentment. She looped her arm around my neck and pulled me toward her.

"What?" I asked, hovering over her, my cock digging into her thigh.

She wiped away a tear. "I'm so happy. And I love you. *So* much."

I brushed my lips against hers, coaxing a kiss from them as I continued to caress every inch of her. "Me too, *mi cielo*."

She arched her back as I ran my hands over her breasts, teasing her nipples. "I need you."

"You have me," I said, sliding into her. Sliding home. "Always."

IN PARIS, TIME SEEMED TO PASS BOTH SLOWLY AND QUICKLY. Kendall and I would spend lazy mornings in bed then eat breakfast overlooking the Eiffel Tower. Then we'd go out for the day, shopping or seeing the sights. We'd visited the Louvre, Versailles, Sacré Cœur. We'd even had our caricatures drawn by a street artist. I didn't care what we were doing so long as I was with her.

"I still can't believe we get to stay here for another week," Kendall said, marveling at the parquet floors, the high ceilings, the view. Her enthusiasm was adorable.

"I'm glad you like it." I sipped my coffee, the sun setting on the Eiffel Tower in the distance. We had dinner reservations later, and she was wearing one of her new dresses. I was dressed in her favorite three-piece navy suit.

"Like it?" she scoffed. "I love it."

"Should I buy it?"

She choked on her macaron. "What?"

"Maybe we need a vacation home."

She placed her macaron on the plate and went over to stand by the window. "You're absurd."

"But you like the apartment," I said, trying to understand.

"Yes. It's even better than the pictures." She shook her head. "I still can't believe you tricked me."

I joined her at the window, standing behind her and wrapping my arms around her. "I'm sorry for the deception, but I hope you think it was worth it."

"Of course I do." She leaned against me. "Did Emmy know?"

"No. I couldn't risk you figuring it out."

"Does the Hartwell Agency know?"

When I remained silent, she smiled back at me over her shoulder. "You're trying to get me fired, aren't you?" she joked, though we both knew she had no plans of returning.

We'd talked about the future some, but for now, we were content to just be. To enjoy each other and our time together in Paris. And Jude was doing such a good job with the team in the off-season I was tempted to extend our trip.

I slid my hands up her waist, over her ribs. "I have other plans for you, *mi cielo.*"

"Mm. Is that so?" She swayed in my arms. "And were you planning to consult me about these 'other plans'?"

"Of course. But I have a feeling you'll like them."

"You want me to take back my job with the Leatherbacks?" she asked.

"I never filled the position, but no. I had a different title in mind." I released her and stepped back, my heart pounding.

"What's that?" she asked, her eyes still on the Eiffel Tower as the lights started to flash.

I knelt to the floor, knowing it was time. Then I said, "Wife."

Her eyes snapped to me. I was waiting on bended knee, and I opened the red velvet box to reveal a large oval-cut diamond set on a band of smaller pavé stones.

She held her hand to her mouth, her eyes wide. "What? What are you doing?"

I smiled. "Kendall, you are my everything. Say you'll marry me."

She blinked a few times. "Knox. I—" She shook her head. "I... *Really?*" It was almost a squeal.

"Yes." I chuckled. "I want to spend the rest of my life with you. Say yes."

Her answering smile was so fucking beautiful, just like her. And then she said, "Yes. Yes, of course I'll marry you. I'm sorry, I'm just..." Her breath hitched. "I wasn't expecting this. I figured when you mentioned marriage, you meant in the future."

"You are my future," I said, sliding the ring on her finger. "And I'm done waiting. Hell, if you wanted to elope right now, get married while we're here, I would."

She draped her arms around my neck, pressing up on her toes to kiss me. "I can't wait to be your wife. But I want to celebrate with our family and friends. I mean...Emmy would be a little upset if I came home married."

"Not your mom?" I teased.

"Nah." She kissed me again. "She'd probably be happy."

"Are you happy?" I asked.

She slid her hand down my chest, covering my heart. Her ring sparkled, and her smile was just as dazzling.

"So incredibly happy," she said.

I covered her hand then held it out so we could admire the ring together.

"This ring is...incredible," she said, her eyes wide as she studied the setting.

"I had it custom designed for you. I hope it's not too much."

She shook her head. "It's perfect."

"Good." I pecked her cheek. "Champagne?"

"Yes, please."

I headed for the kitchen, grabbing two glasses and a bottle of champagne. When I returned, she was lying on the bed, naked except for my ring. She crooked her finger, beckoning me closer.

I smirked and loosened the wire cage from the champagne before removing the cork with a pop. I took a swig and then carried it over to the bed, deciding to forgo the glasses. Now that I'd seen her, I had other plans.

"Open for me," I rasped, my cock already hard.

She tilted her head back and parted her lips. I watched in fascination as she swallowed the champagne down. When some dribbled out of her mouth and down her cheek, I licked it clean.

"Mm. Delicious." I licked my lips and then took another drink from the bottle.

"More," she pleaded, opening her mouth again.

I held the bottle to her lips, watching again as she drank. Forget all my previous fantasies, nothing could compare to this. To seeing my ring on her finger, watching it sparkle every time she slid her hand through her hair. Every time she smoothed her hand down my shirt.

"Touch yourself," I said in a gravelly voice. "And make sure I can see your ring while you're touching what's mine."

She slid her hand down her stomach, parting her folds with hooded eyes. I poured champagne on her tits, and she gasped. I watched in awe as her nipples puckered, goose bumps rising on her skin.

"Fucking sexy," I said, kneeling to lick her clean.

She grasped my tie, wrapping it around her hand and

tugging. Bringing my lips to hers for a kiss. "Mm. Hello, fiancé."

I grinned. "Hello, my future wife."

She bit back a smile. "I can't believe I'm going to be your wife!"

I chuckled and slanted my mouth over hers, the champagne mixing with her, a potent elixir. The bottle was heavy in my hand, but when I tried to set it down, she stopped me.

"More." She arched her back.

"Yeah?" I asked, tilting the bottle.

"Yes," she sighed.

I poured some on her stomach, drinking it from her belly. Lower still. This woman was intoxicating, and I wasn't sure I'd ever have my fill.

I knelt to the floor, busying myself between her legs. Bringing her to the brink of pleasure then backing off before taking her to the edge once more. All the while, we drank champagne. Laughed. And made love, while the Eiffel Tower sparkled in the distance.

I'd never been happier, and it was all because of her. The woman with the kind heart and the soulful eyes. A woman who had once seemed completely off-limits but had shown me that anything was possible.

Acknowledgements

This story was so much freaking fun to write. I'm honestly not sure I've ever had as much fun as I did with Kendall and Knox (and yes, even Jude LOL).

I kept trying to explain the joy I had in writing this story to my husband. And the best comparison I could come up with was that it felt like getting to eat all your favorite foods every day and yet feeling awesome. If you're wondering, for me that would be homemade pizza, chocolate, and Topo Chico everyday all day.

I hope this story was as delicious and satisfying for you as it was for me. ;)

Thank you for going on this journey with me. I've been blown away by the response to *Temptation* from the moment I revealed the tropes to the release. And I am so so happy that so many of you love these characters as much as I do!

A HUGE thank you to all the readers, bloggers, bookstagrammers, booktokers who share your love for my stories. I could not do this without you.

Nor could I do this without my incredible team. Thank you to Angela for always being encouraging and supportive. For helping me with all the details, so I can focus on the big picture.

A huge thank you to my beta readers. Thank you for making me a stronger writer, for offering your unique insight and advice. You each bring something different to the table, and I'm always amazed and impressed by your suggestions. I'm so incredibly honored to have you on my team!

Thank you, Jade. You make me a stronger writer, and you challenge me on pacing. You are so clever and always provide great insight. I'm so grateful for your friendship, and our long chats! This story wouldn't be the same without you.

A huge thank you to Kristen for being such an amazing friend. I value your judgment and honesty, and I so appreciate your support. We've been through so much together, and I treasure your friendship and advice. Seriously, I cannot thank you enough for all that you do. You're always willing to read "just one more time," and I so appreciate it. You always pump me up and make me feel fabulous.

JudyAnnLovesBooks, you are so freaking awesome. I appreciate your honesty and your opinion. Your details always make the story sparkle. And I love that you loved this story as much as I did. Thank you for being my hype woman and for gushing over these characters.

Thank you to Ellen, as always. Thank you for being so supportive and positive, for being a friend. And thank you for sharing your incredible eye for detail. Your comments are always priceless, and this book was no exception! I couldn't do it without you.

Thank you to Brit! I love writing strong, badass female main characters, and you help ensure that they live up to their potential. And that the men who dare to love them do too. I love our two-author support group. LOL I love our voice mail chats, and I can't wait to meet in person.

To my editor, Lisa with Silently Correcting Your Grammar. I so appreciate your attention to detail, and your patience with my questions. You always go above and beyond and this time was no exception. I value your insight and your friendship. Thank you for being honest and kind in your comments and for helping me see what was missing at the very end.

A huge shout out to all my fellow authors. Sometimes this

job can feel so solitary, but I know you're all out there. And we're all cheering each other on.

A big thank you to the Hartley's Hustlers and my Girl Gang (not just for girls!). You rock! I cannot possibly tell you how much your support means to me! I appreciate everything you do to promote my books and to encourage me throughout my writing journey.

Thank you to @caropalmier and @TakeALookAtMyBookshelf for coming up with the name for the hockey team —Hollywood Hawks. Definitely much better than Hollywood Hummingbirds. LOL

Thank you to my husband for always encouraging me. For always supporting my dreams and believing in me. You are better than any book boyfriend I could ever imagine. You constantly build me up, and I couldn't ask for a better partner.

And to my daughter, for always putting a smile on my face. You are spirited and independent, and I wouldn't have it any other way. Dream big, my darling.

Thank you to my parents for always being so encouraging. For reading my books. For being my biggest fans!

Dear reader, if this list of people shows you anything, it's that dreams are often the effort of many. I'm grateful to have such an awesome team. And I'm honored that you've taken the time to read my words.

About the Author

Jenna Hartley is *USA Today* bestselling author who writes feel-good forbidden romance, much like her own real-life love story. She's known for writing strong women and swoon-worthy men, as well as blending panty-melting and heart-warming moments.

When she's not reading or writing romance, Jenna can be found tending to her growing indoor plant collection (pun intended), organizing, and hiking. She lives in Texas with her family and loves nothing more than a good book and good chocolate, except a dance party with her daughter.

www.authorjennahartley.com

Also by Jenna Hartley

Love in LA Series
Inevitable
Unexpected
Irresistible
Undeniable
Unpredictable
Irreplaceable

Alondra Valley Series
Feels Like Love
Love Like No Other
A Love Like That

Tempt Series
Temptation
Reputation (coming 2024)

For the most current list of Jenna's titles, please visit her website www.authorjennahartley.com.

Or scan the QR code on the following page to be taken to her author page on Amazon.com

ALSO BY JENNA HARTLEY

Printed in Great Britain
by Amazon